Captivating Captains

THE CAPTAIN
AND THE
CAVALRY TROOPER

CATHERINE CURZON &
ELEANOR HARKSTEAD

The Captain and the Cavalry Trooper
ISBN # 978-1-913186-10-4
©Copyright Catherine Curzon & Eleanor Harkstead 2018
Cover Art by Posh Gosh ©Copyright April 2018
Interior text design by Claire Siemaszkiewicz
Pride Publishing

THE CAPTAIN
AND THE
CAVALRY
TROOPER

Dedication

CC — To the Rakish Colonial, Nelly and Pippa.
Thanks for the snuggles!
EH — For Vivian. Never forgotten.

Chapter One

Northern France
1917

The wagon carrying Jack Woodvine bumped and jerked along the poplar-lined lanes, a fine spray of mud rising up each time the huge wooden wheels splashed through a puddle.

He had given up checking the time and, even though the journey was far from comfortable, tried to doze as he passed along under the iron-gray sky. A chateau, they'd said. Different from the barracks he'd been in when he was first deployed. Doubtless it would be a dismal old fortress, but was it silly of him to hope for bright pennants fluttering from a turret?

Finally, the wagon drew up at a gatehouse of pale stone. As Jack climbed out, dragging his kitbag behind him, sunlight nudged back the clouds and turned the gray slate of the roofs to blue.

"You the new groom?" A soldier appeared from the gatehouse. His cap was so low over his eyes that Jack couldn't make out his expression.

"Yes—Trooper Woodvine. Jack Woodvine." He took a letter from his pocket and held it out to the man. "I've been transferred from another battalion. This is the Chateau de Desgravier?"

"Yes, Trooper! Turn left at the bottom of the drive for the stables. Quick march!"

The last thing Jack wanted to do was march, quickly or otherwise, but he shouldered his kitbag, jammed his cap onto his head and marched down the tree-lined avenue.

It was thickly leaved, but through the branches he could see the white stone of the chateau ahead. He rounded a bend in the driveway and he saw it— Chateau de Desgravier.

An enormous tower rose up in front of him, its roof reaching into a delicate point. Jack sighed, the spots of mud on his face cracking as he smiled. It might not have had pennants floating from it, but it was exactly like something from a fairytale. Beside the tower were the stone and brick and filigreed windows of what looked to Jack like a palace. Who would ever think that the front was only a few miles to the east?

Quick march!

Jack continued on his way, turning to his left just as he'd been ordered. The path here bore evidence of horses—straw, manure, the marks of horseshoes. Ahead, an archway, figures at work. A lad of Jack's age maneuvering a wheelbarrow, another leading a horse out to the paddock.

This wouldn't be so bad. It seemed to be a peaceful place, and easy work for a lad like Jack. He raised his hand and grinned at the grooms as he headed under the archway and into the vast stable yard.

Then he heard singing. In French.

Jack dropped his kitbag and looked round. The voice was that of a man, yet heightened slightly, giving it a teasing, effeminate edge, and Jack couldn't help but follow it like a sailor lured by a siren, pulled along the row of open stables toward that lilting chanson. Inside those stables young men labored and sweated, brooms swept and spades shoveled, yet one of the boxes at the far corner of the yard seemed to have been transformed into an impromptu theater.

Jack hardly dared glance through that open door, yet he couldn't help himself, blinking at the hazy darkness of the interior where half a dozen grooms lounged in the straw, watching the *chanteur* in rapt silence.

Right in front of Jack, his back to the door, was the figure of a young man, clad in jodhpurs, polished riding boots and nothing else. No, that wasn't quite true, because he *was* wearing something, the sort of something Jack didn't really see much of in Shropshire. It was some sort of silken scarf, a shawl, perhaps, that was looped around his neck twice, the wide, dazzling red fabric decorated with intricate yellow flowers. They were bright against the pale skin of his naked back, as bright as the tip of the cigarette that glowed in the end of a long ebony cigarette holder that the singer held in his elegant right hand. He gestured with it like a painter with his brush, making intricate movements with his wrist as he sang, his voice a low purr, then a high, tuneful trill, then a comically deep bass that drew laughter from his audience.

He moved with the confidence of a dancer, hips swinging seductively, head cocked to one side, free hand resting on his narrow hip and here, in this strange fairytale place, he was bewitching.

The singer executed a near-perfect pirouette yet quite suddenly, when he was facing Jack, stopped. He put the cigarette holder to his pink lips, drew in a long, deep breath and blew out a smoke ring, his full lips forming a perfect *O*.

"Well, now." He sucked in his pale cheeks and asked, "Who on earth have we here?"

Jack blinked as the smoke ring drifted into his face.

"Tr-trooper Woodvine, reporting for Captain Thorne. I've been transferred—I'm his new groom. I don't suppose—"

The words dried in Jack's throat. As enthralling as this otherworldly figure was, with his slim face and high cheekbones, there was an unsettling glint of mockery in his narrow blue eyes.

"Sorry." Jack took a half-step backward. "I interrupted your song. I should…"

The singer moved a little, just enough that he could dart his head forward on its slender neck and draw his nose from Jack's shoulder to his ear, breathing deeply all the way. They didn't touch but the invasion, the *authority*, was clear. However lowly their station, Jack had wandered innocently into someone else's domain.

When the young man's nose reached Jack's ear he threw his head back and let out a loud sigh through his parted lips, arms extended to either side. Then he finally spoke again, declaring to the heavens, "I smell new blood!"

Behind him, his small audience tittered nervously and his head dropped once more, those glittering blue eyes focused on Jack.

"Trooper Charles, *sir!*" He executed a courtly bow, the hand that held the cigarette twirling elaborately. "But you're so darling and green that *you* may address me as Queenie. Aren't you the lucky one?"

Jack reached for the doorframe to casually prop himself against it and essay the appearance of calm. *Queenie?*

"You may call me Jack."

He extended his free hand to shake. A handshake showed the mettle of a man, his father was always telling him so. A good, firm hand at the market and a fellow would never have his prices beaten down.

Queenie's narrow gaze slid down Jack like a snake and settled on his hand. He didn't take it, didn't move at all for a few seconds as the silence between them grew thicker. Then, in one quick movement, he placed his cigarette holder between Jack's fingers and said, "Have a treat on me. Welcome to Cinderella's doss house!"

Jack brought it hesitantly to his lips, smiling gamely at the grooms who made up Queenie's audience. He pouted his lips against the carved ebony and inhaled.

The cough was so violent that Jack nearly dropped the holder, but an instinct in him born of a lifetime on a farm of tinder-dry hay meant he clamped it between his fingers. As he heaved for breath, he stamped on the nearby straw, suffocating any sparks that might have fallen.

The other grooms laughed and Queenie's head tipped back to emit a bray of hilarity as a strong hand walloped Jack's back.

A friendly Cockney burr chirruped, "Cough up, chicken — there's a good lad!"

"We have a new little chicky in our nest," Queenie told his audience, turning to address them. "I want you all to make him terribly welcome, or he might burn down our stables and then where would your Queenie sing?"

The stocky lad who had rescued Jack from his coughing fit was a head shorter than him. He pulled a face that could have been a smile or a sneer and took the cigarette holder from his fingers. He passed it to Queenie, all the while fixing his stare on the new arrival.

"Trooper Cole. Wilfred, that's me. You're Captain Thorne's new boy, aren't you?"

He laughed, then turned his head to spit on the floor, pulling a skinny roll-up from behind his ear.

"I'm Jack Woodvine. I mean…Trooper Woodvine."

"I s'pose me and Queenie better take you to your quarters?"

"That would— But…oughtn't I to introduce myself to Captain Thorne?"

"I'd say that's a bit difficult, seeing as he's not here at the moment." Wilfred picked up Jack's kitbag as easily as if it were spun from a feather. "Come on, soldier. Your palace awaits!"

"Captain T is an *angel*." Queenie draped one arm sinuously around Jack's shoulders and walked him back across the stable yard, his naked torso pressed to Jack's rough tunic. "You're going to have a bloody easy war, he's soft as my mother's newborn kitten."

He glanced back at Wilfred and asked, "Wouldn't you say so, Wilf?"

"Not half!" Wilfred laughed, striking a match to light his cigarette. "You couldn't find a nicer bloke in the entire regiment."

Jack grinned as they headed up the creaking wooden stairs above the stables. New quarters and new friends, and he wouldn't have to rough it in a tent. Maybe there'd even be warm water for a bath.

"Well, that's good to know. The officers were a bit...brusque at my last place."

"Brusque?" Wilfred raised an amused eyebrow. "That's a fancy word for a groom!"

"Ignore our lovely Wilf. Strong as an ox, bright as a coal shed." At the top of the stairs Queenie turned to address Wilfred and Jack, his pale hand resting on the crooked handrail. "Thorny is adorable, not *brusque* at all. Welcome to our little slice of heaven!"

With that he lifted the latch and threw the door open, directing Jack to enter with another low bow.

The loft's low, sloping ceiling made it difficult to stand anywhere other than in the middle of the floor. Dormer windows with murky, cracked glazing made no attempt to lift the gloom. The beds were lined up with military precision, as was to be expected, but they were a mixture of sturdy metal bedsteads and low camp beds. Above each, the soldier-grooms had left their imprint of personality, albeit their personalities were almost all the same. Images culled from the pages of gung-ho magazines, of tanks and explosions and enormous guns and heroic men leaping through barbed wire. Shapely stars of music hall and burlesque in enormous hats, elaborate costumes cut to show the boys a lot of leg. The occasional postcard from home had been tucked beside a poster of a woman wearing rather little.

At the far end of that simple loft, someone appeared to have opened a door to an exotic land, a place far removed from the simple rustic pleasures of the grooms. From floor to ceiling hung richly embroidered tapestries depicting scenes of battle from another time, long since lost. Knights jousted on a field of emerald green, a sapphire sky above, dotted with pristine white clouds. Innumerable jabs of the needle had gone to create the sun that blazed down on the curiously bloodless battle, each thread of tapestry teasing out a story from another century.

Between the two tapestries stood a tall screen of black lacquer that served as a door to the mysterious realm beyond, the sort of screen behind which a gentleman's mistress might tantalizingly undress. A rainbow of butterflies fluttered over its polished surface but only one of its panels was folded back, affording no glimpse of the treasures within.

Was it Queenie's place behind those tapestries? Was that the peacock's nest? The only thing Jack knew was that this wasn't *his* chamber.

"Now, little Jack, where shall we plant your magic bean?" Queenie strolled along and pointed to one of the metal beds, addressing his followers in a drawl. "Our lovely young Trooper Miles pissed all over this mattress on the night before he got shipped out. He was terrified, poor thing."

He took a draw on his cigarette and gestured with it toward the bed, its single scratchy blanket concealing that same soiled mattress.

"Mardy Miles was gassed last weekend, so I'm sure it must be dry by now. Your home from home, little Jack!"

The smile was fading from Jack's face. *Sleeping in the piss of a dead man — they never mentioned that in* Boy's Own Paper.

"Thank you." Jack forced a grin. "You've made me feel very…welcome."

Wilfred threw Jack's kitbag onto the bed.

"The crapper's through that door at the other end. You want to get on it early in the morning—it's been known to flood."

"Smashing. Thanks for the tip, Trooper Cole."

All three of them turned at the sound of feet hammering across the floorboards. A breathless groom ran into the attic.

"Just heard—the officers are nearly back! They rang in from the village."

"Don't forget, Jacky," Queenie twirled the end of his scarf, whirling it before Jack's eyes, "Thorny is sweet as cherries, and Apollo is a donkey at heart!"

Jack followed Wilfred back down the stairs and into the yard. Hoofbeats were approaching, drumming down the avenue like a distant storm drawing nearer. Jack fidgeted with his buttons, his cuffs, straightening his collar to look smart for his captain.

A voice could be heard in the distance, raised in a furious bark. It was the voice of an officer, a voice that could never belong to a trooper.

"Get out of the bloody way!" Those plummy vowels sang of Sandhurst and swagger sticks, of punting down the river on a balmy afternoon while other men toiled in the fields. It was the voice of rank.

"Next time, Trooper, next time!" The owner of the voice clattered into the yard at a canter, mounted on a perfect gray stallion, its snow-white mane flying with each movement of its muscular neck. The captain sat tall in his saddle, still looking back over one shoulder at whoever had come close to falling beneath those pounding, powerful hooves. His whip was raised in a warning to the unfortunate soldier, brandished high in the air, dark against a clear blue sky.

The horse pulled itself back with the barest twitch of the rider's gloved hand on its reins. It was something that Jack had rarely seen, a suggestion of a man and animal in perfect harmony.

"You're a damned fool!" The officer gave one last bellow then, with a creak of the leather saddle on which he sat, he turned to survey the yard.

None of the grooms approached. Jack was still listening for other hooves on the avenue, because this couldn't be Captain Thorne. The officer's dark eyes blazed their way around the grooms in the yard and finally alighted on Jack.

"Oh, Lord." The captain heaved a theatrical sigh at the sight of him. He leaned forward to tuck his whip down the side of one highly polished boot. "Are you the chap they've sent Apollo for supper? Woodvine, is it?"

Could this really be Captain Thorne, after what Queenie and Wilfred had just told him? Jack felt the eyes of the other grooms on him as he tentatively crossed toward the officer and his horse. He saluted and dropped his arm to his side.

"Yes, sir, Trooper Woodvine, sir… Captain…? You have a very fine horse, sir."

"Thorne!" Captain Thorne snapped his gloved hand to his brow in a sharp salute. "I hope you've a firm hand, Trooper, you're going to need it."

Brusque. That described his new captain after all.

Jack approached the horse. Its round black eye twitched at him as he came nearer. Jack made a soft clicking sound in his throat as he lightly stroked the back of his hand to the side of Apollo's face.

"Handsome fellow, aren't you?" he whispered.

The horse flinched back a step, eyes growing wide then it bowed its head to accept the touch. From his place in the saddle Thorne murmured, the words indistinguishable, his fingers working softly at the nape of Apollo's neck.

"A firm hand, Captain? But a gentle touch will do as well, sir."

Jack looked up at the man in the saddle. He struggled to see his face with the sky so bright behind him, his face thrown into shadow. Jack had an impression of those blazing dark eyes, a strong jaw and a mouth set into a straight line. Which, as Jack continued to smile up at him, showed the slightest sign of an amused quirk at its corners.

"Forgive me, Trooper, because I *may* have misheard." The captain shifted in his saddle and asked, "Did you just presume to tell me how best to handle my mount?"

"Gosh, sir…no, I would never… I only… It's my way, sir. See? I think Apollo likes me."

Jack looked away from the captain, conscious of his *faux pas*, and continued to stroke the horse, running his hand along its nose but careful to avoid Apollo's impressive teeth.

"Fear not, soldier!" Thorne dropped his feet from the stirrups and, in one fluid movement, swung his leg round and hopped down to stand beside Jack. "I'd sooner thrash you than thrash Apollo, he's *far* less trouble!"

Jack's glance fell to the whip that poked over the top of the captain's boot. He bit his lip and met the captain's eye, then returned his attention to the horse.

"I'll…I'll gladly take him off you now, sir."

"Apollo has his routine, Trooper, you're on *his* watch now." Thorne drew the whip from his boot and gestured as he spoke. "Saddle off first—he *won't* like you fumbling his girth, so I hope you're sure-fingered. Then brush, water, down to the paddock, bridle off and let my boy have his pasture."

He swept the whip down, cracking it against his boot, and commanded, "Jump to it!"

Jack shuddered at the snap of the whip then took the reins. As his eyes met the captain's glittering gaze, his heart began to beat just a little faster.

"You must excuse me, sir, I have only just arrived. Would you show me where Apollo's stable is?"

Thorne, however, was preoccupied with lifting the horse's hooves. He held out one hand and clicked his fingers without looking to Jack. He commanded, "Pick!"

"Sir, I haven't one to hand."

The fingers clicked again.

"Captain Thorne, sir… I'm—I'm new."

Something in those words or perhaps what Jack knew was a gently imploring tone appeared to reach through the officer's concentration and Thorne set Apollo's hoof on the ground once more. He returned the whip to his boot and straightened, cocking his head to one side as he peered at Jack through brown eyes so dark that they were almost black.

"Of course you are, yet you've survived two minutes with Apollo, so the signs are good." He nodded once and moved to roll up one stirrup, calling to Jack, "Deal with the other stirrup, Trooper, and Apollo and I will show you the lie of the land!"

Jack went around to the other side of the horse, nimbly working the leather straps. He secured it and patted Apollo's flank.

"Good boy."

There was so much power in the creature. It was in perfect condition, its muscles firm. The captain seemed to have ridden it hard — or at least, the last couple of hundred yards as he knocked grooms flying — and yet Apollo didn't seem tired at all. Thorne was watching him all the time and when Jack's hand touched the horse's flank, the captain visibly tensed, as though he thought he might need to leap forward and intervene. Apollo, however, gave a snort of approval and lowered his head a little farther, glowering from beneath long eyelashes at the grooms who moved this way and that across the yard.

With a soft murmur to comfort his steed's dark expression, Thorne swept his cap off and tucked it beneath his arm. He smoothed his hand over his already immaculate black hair and told Jack, "Come along then, soldier!"

They walked on either side of Apollo as Thorne led the horse across the yard to the stable which had earlier played host to Trooper Charles' command performance. It really wouldn't do for Jack to say anything to the captain about Queenie smoking in Apollo's stable. But there was a pang in Jack's belly. What if a spark had fallen from the cigarette? What if there had been a fire and Apollo —

Jack dismissed the thoughts, because he knew his face would betray him. In fact, he was worried that it already had.

Jack's breath hitched as he looked over at the captain and remembered his words.

'I'd sooner thrash you than thrash Apollo.'

It had been in jest, of course.

Thorne twitched his nostrils and grimaced, setting his cap firmly back on his head. "You've been smoking again, Apollo." Then he snatched up a bucket crammed with brushes and combs abandoned by one of the grooms who had been enjoying Queenie's show and told Jack, "Your fellow grooms are a slovenly bunch, soldier. I hope you'll prove to be stronger meat!"

He pulled a currycomb from the bucket and tossed it across to Jack. "Saddle off, give him a good rub-down and I'll see to the hooves!"

"Yes, sir."

If Thorne heard, he didn't acknowledge, already occupied with scraping at the bottom of Apollo's hooves. All the time Jack could hear him murmuring to the horse in a soft coo, a world away from the furious character who had ridden into the yard as though charging up from hell itself.

Jack reached under Apollo to unfasten the girth then lifted the supple, well-cared-for saddle. He strode past the captain, almost brushing his knee against his bowed head as he passed in the cramped space, and hung the saddle over the stable door.

He unbuttoned his jacket, threw it onto a hook on the wall and rolled up his sleeves to comb the horse. He was aware of the amused quirk of the captain's mouth again but went on with his work, picking loose hair and bits of mud out of the comb as he went.

"That's it, Apollo, aren't you a good boy... You're enjoying this, aren't you? Yes, you are!"

"You're our third chap in the last twelve months," Thorne told Jack, his voice growing more stern with every word. "First one got his foot smashed by this cheeky lad. Second couldn't get anywhere near him to begin with. I don't know what magic you're working, Trooper, but do it with your jacket on, or ask an officer's permission to remove it."

Jack's cheeks flamed and he tugged awkwardly at his shirt.

"Sorry, Captain. May I ask your permission now, please?"

"You may, soldier." Thorne fell silent at a soft whinny from Apollo. He furrowed his brow as though listening and said, "Apollo has his doubts, Trooper. He's finding the baby-talk disconcerting."

Jack met the captain's eye. There was a flash of humor there, he was sure. But he wasn't going to laugh, even if he started to grin.

"*What a big, brave, handsome chap you are, Apollo!* There, is that better, Captain?"

"Are you patronizing my horse, Woodvine?" Thorne returned to his task, his head bowed. "He'll have your guts if you don't watch out."

After a pause, Jack said, "He's a very fine horse, sir. Have you had him long?"

"From his first months." The captain straightened and threw the hoof pick into the bucket with a clatter. "Gather up the reins, Trooper. I'll show you the tack and feed, we can pick up some water and get him into the grass."

Jack shrugged himself back into his jacket but didn't button it up. He had to draw near to the captain in order to take the reins, but he found himself distracted by an extraordinary smell — the spicy scent of expensive pomade, blended with warm leather and saddle soap. He tightened his grip on the reins, aware of a slight tremble in his hands. What a contrast that masculine scent was to Jack, who used only carbolic soap and cheap peppermint shaving cream.

"Right you are, Captain."

Jack smiled at his officer, but when the captain's gaze swept over him, Jack avoided his eyes and closely examined the reins instead. He was relieved when they stepped back into the sunlight, then there was no time to think of anything as Thorne toured him around the yard, pointing out tack rooms and feed stores, and listing the names of horses and their riders that Jack couldn't hope to remember. All the time he was issuing those barked orders and criticisms to the grooms who were laden with saddles and sacks and they jumped at the officer's say-so. This was clearly not a man to be trifled with.

A bark of the word *bucket* to one slight red-haired lad resulted in the sudden appearance of the requested item and Thorne drew the whip. He flourished it and Jack interpreted the gesture as a command to take the bucket from his fellow groom. Then they were off again, Captain Thorne striding out ahead like a king surveying his court.

Jack followed obediently behind. He couldn't help but be impressed by the captain. He knew he really shouldn't, but he stole glances at him, at the breadth of his shoulders in his tailored tunic, at the suggestion of his firm thighs inside his spotless breeches, at his thick sweep of dark hair tapering down to the nape of his neck.

He had to stop. He couldn't afford to moon after officers. Last time it had been one touch, a stray hand on a knee as he passed a captain a whip. Just a brush of his fingertips, but it had been enough, because the look in his eyes had given him away.

And now he had been sent here, to work for this man. The universe was taunting him for his unnatural desires.

As they moved through the yard and its bustle Apollo grew more fractious, a little less willing to go along with his new groom and a little more agitated with each passing second. Eventually they passed through a narrow avenue between two stable blocks and there, in the shade of the structures, was a water pump. The ground around it was saturated and Thorne reached to take the reins from Jack. He placed the tip of his right ring finger between his teeth and plucked off his brown leather glove before placing his bare palm against the horse's muzzle in a gesture of calm.

"Fill the bucket, soldier, then put it down for Apollo." Thorne tucked the glove into his pocket and removed the other, slipping that into his pocket too. "You and I need a quick parley."

Jack swallowed and stepped into the mud to reach the pump. Water spilled out as Jack worked the handle. He kept his back to the captain, drawing out the moment until the captain told him what he had to say. *I saw how you looked at me, you ought to be court martialed.* That would be it. He'd barely been at Chateau de Desgravier an hour and his card would already be marked.

"The bucket, sir." Jack paused, running his wet hand through his too-long chestnut locks.

"I'm not going to drink out of it, Trooper." He sighed deeply. "Put it down for Apollo, he's parched!"

"Yes, sir."

Apollo tried to push his muzzle into the bucket before it was on the ground, and Jack stroked the horse. Feeling the captain's gaze on him again, he came forward and stood to attention.

"Sir?"

"Your hair is—" The captain seemed to reconsider whatever he was going to say, instead withdrawing the whip once more. He held it out, touching the tip to Jack's face. "You're muddy, Trooper Woodvine."

Jack brought his fingertip to his cheek, the whip whispering against the slender digit.

"Golly, sir... I am sorry. The roads were very muddy. Unless you mean my freckles, sir? I-I hadn't... I'd only just got here when you arrived, sir, or I'd have scrubbed properly before I ever... You must think me a terrible slob, Captain Thorne. I'm sorry." Jack braved himself to meet the officer's eye. "I didn't want to disappoint you."

Thorne didn't speak, but reached into his pocket and produced a white handkerchief. It was pristine, and he unfolded it with a flick of his wrist then held it beneath the pump to catch a few of the drips of water that fell from it. Then, like a father with an insolent boy, Captain Thorne pressed the wet handkerchief to Jack's cheekbone and began to gently scrub at the mud.

Jack, still standing to attention, tried to distract himself by watching Apollo with the bucket, but the captain was so close to him that he was overwhelmed once more by the scent of the man. He felt the captain's warm breath on his neck and, as if in answer, a blush broke over his face again.

"At ease, soldier." It seemed like a low purr, the captain's hand on his cheek more of a caress than— Jack pushed the thought aside as soon as it occurred to him.

"Thank you, sir."

It was a whisper, and Jack glanced at the captain. He saw something, then, in the captain's eyes. Something that he—

"Thorne!"

The voice was a parade-ground bark. Jack flinched away from his captain. Whatever connection he had thought—imagined—for a moment, snapped.

Thorne pressed the handkerchief into Jack's hand and winked, whispering, "Our secret, Woodvine. One can't put a wet hanky back in one's uniform."

Then he stepped back and snatched up Apollo's reins a moment before the horse began to pull against him, its nostrils flaring and dark eyes rolling to reveal white at the edges.

The officer was fastening his flies as he approached, with a glare for Captain Thorne and an interested stare for Jack.

"This the new boy, eh? Is it?"

He leaned in toward Jack, his lips slightly parted, his breath smelling of stale tobacco and booze.

Jack wasn't sure if he was supposed to speak, and waited for his captain to say something. Still Apollo pulled, shying back from the new arrival, and Thorne's arm visibly tensed inside his uniform, one strong shoulder setting firm with the effort of holding the reins that he now wrapped around his knuckles.

"This is Trooper Woodvine. Woodvine, Captain Marsh." Thorne made a gesture with his eyebrows that was clearly intended to suggest the younger man should salute. Yet Marsh was peering ever closer at Jack, freezing him with that rheumy, pale stare, and Thorne thrust the reins toward his new groom, filling Jack's hands with the leather and saving him the awkwardness of that missed salute.

"Excuse the lack of ceremony, Marsh, you know what a two-hander Apollo can be." Thorne patted the horse's snow-white shoulder. "You'll have to excuse us, Captain, I'm just showing our new arrival the ropes."

"The ropes, eh? Yes...the ropes." Marsh cleared his throat and stood to his full height, aided, Jack noticed, by strategically stacked heels to his boots.

"Sure this isn't a girl, Thorne? Eh?" Marsh's gloved hand slid toward Jack's chin but stopped an inch away. "Ought to be a milkmaid with a face like that, what? You smell of the country, boy..."

Jack saluted at last, hammering out the words in basic training staccato.

"Captain Marsh, sir. Pleasure to meet you, sir."

"Ha! Very good. Got manners after all, boy, haven't you?"

Thorne's hand pressed into the small of Jack's back, urging him to move even as he told Marsh in those same withering public school tones, "We can but hope, Marsh. Excuse us, old man?"

Jack moved forward, guided by the captain's touch.

Marsh leaned against the pump, mud seeping around his boots, his oppressive stare not leaving Jack even after they had rounded the corner and were out of his sight. Thorne's hand, however, pulled away and he walked ahead once more as Apollo relaxed, the tugging at the end of the rein ebbing to a gentle amble.

"Captain, sir...may I tell you something?"

They were out of earshot now of the stables, following a path to the paddock.

"You're not a bloody woman, are you?" Thorne's voice was deadly serious but he glanced back and winked. "One hears such things nowadays. Tell away."

Jack allowed himself a chuckle, then looked Thorne carefully in the eye.

"One mustn't tattle on a fellow, sir, especially not when one shares quarters with them. But...I felt I really ought to say...about...that smell in Apollo's stable, sir. The cigarettes."

Jack waited for a reaction on the captain's face. Did he realize what would happen if he betrayed the other grooms? But Jack Woodvine always did the right thing. Jack Woodvine, who had broken his shoulder falling off a horse just before conscription began. Jack Woodvine, who had healed, and who had answered the call to do his bit for King, Country and Empire. Jack Woodvine, who had left his father and the farm behind him because ten boys in his year at the grammar had already been killed and he couldn't chase their faces from his dreams at night.

"Sir...I know who it was. Who was smoking. I cannot tell you who, sir, but I want you to know that, as Apollo's groom—as *your* groom, sir, I won't allow it anymore. Apollo is my concern, sir, and I...I won't have it. That shilly-shallying about—I simply won't!"

The captain looked back at him, his face set in a stern expression, those full lips a hard, tight line. When he spoke again, his voice was that of a commander once more.

"The grooms here are a shower of layabouts, rascals and hooligans. Don't let them draw you into their ways, Woodvine, I won't tolerate it."

"Don't worry, sir. I won't."

But even so, Jack didn't like the idea of lying on that mattress with its ammonia stink of fear, alone, without some fellows to talk to. Even if he had to make up some ludicrous story, as he had before—of losing his virginity to a farmhand's buxom daughter in a hayloft. When he hadn't even held a girl's hand.

And hadn't wanted to.

At the end of the narrow path was a bright green paddock where half a dozen other horses grazed contentedly, with no idea of what was happening just a few miles away. It was fenced all around and bordered with trees that provided cool shade for those that might wish it. Threaded along the fence and off through the trees was a stream, deep and wide, the sunlight glittering and dancing on the surface like stars in a night sky, and they walked alongside it to reach the gate, which was held in place by a heavy iron bolt.

As soon as Thorne pulled back the bolt and opened the gate Apollo began to surge toward the paddock, the mighty creature pulling at Jack with enough force to have him trotting to keep up. The captain darted out one hand and seized the reins, admonishing the horse with a swift, "Fall back, Apollo!"

The horse responded immediately, though not without a certain insolence as he pulled just a touch, just to make the point that the choice was his to make, not that of the captain or the trooper. When the trio stepped into the paddock, Thorne unbuckled the bridle in a few swift movements and pulled it gently over the horse's head. He patted his elegant hand against Apollo's firm shoulder and told him, "Go on then, lad."

And the horse was gone, cantering as happily as a pony across the paddock and into the shade. There he dropped his head and began to drink from the stream, leaving the captain to watch him with a soft gaze.

As he watched the gentle glee of the great stallion, Jack beamed. He looked back at the captain and tried to push aside the wavy hair that had fallen into his face.

But a breeze was stirring up from somewhere, and Jack's unruly forelock flopped back again.

"What a…a lovely paddock."

Jack shoved his hands into his pockets. He must've broken some protocol somewhere — *should one be so casual when faced with one's captain?* What did he remember from training? Being shouted at a lot, shimmying on his hips face down through mud with a lump of wood that was supposed to resemble a gun and finally, when he had been given a real gun, and had been hopeless at firing it. He'd had more luck with the bayonet, but in reality he didn't fancy his chances if he had to look a fellow in the eye and twist a sharp bit of metal into his guts.

"Loveliest paddock I think I've ever seen."

"And not even twenty miles from here…" Thorne knitted his hands behind his back, his shoulders squaring, his feet set apart in their shining leather boots. He drew in a deep breath and surveyed the horses as they grazed in peace, all except one gathered at the far end of the field. "You'll soon learn, trooper, Apollo likes his own company as a rule. Perhaps he might make an exception for you, we shall have to see."

"I…I hope so, Captain." Jack peered at him from the corner of his eye. The captain's face was set in a firm expression, as if it were hewn from stone. "I should like, sir, to please you."

He stared ahead, tugging at a loose button on his jacket.

"Work hard and show proper respect and you and I will get on." Thorne took a long, deep breath before speaking again. "And if you see anyone raise a hand to Apollo, I want his name, groom's code or no. Understand?"

Jack nodded.

"Yes, sir. And…I'm sorry, Captain Thorne, if I didn't show you respect earlier. With my muddy face and taking off my jacket without your permission. It won't happen again, sir. I promise."

"You'll find me a fair master, but I brook no nonsense." Thorne took the gloves from his pocket and slipped his hands into them, flexing his fingers a couple of times as if to test the supple leather. "Now back up to the yard and get yourself settled. Tomorrow we'll go through your duties. Really put you through your paces, eh?"

"Yes, sir."

Jack began to walk away, realizing that the captain was standing still, as if his feet had grown roots and those fine, sturdy legs had become tree trunks. He gave a salute.

"Good evening, sir."

With a strange feeling of loss that he couldn't quite account for, Jack went back to the stables.

Chapter Two

During supper, Jack tried to make conversation with the other grooms, but his new friends were just out of reach. Wilfred larked about, trying to grab other fellows' rations, a sport that Jack had no wish to join. Queenie sat at the head of the table, smoking and looking bored and slightly disgusted, picking occasionally at his lip as if trying to remove something that was stuck there.

Jack lolled on his bed for a while with Keats, but the evening seemed pleasant, and at least outside he wasn't haunted by the smell of his mattress.

He swung his jacket over his shoulder and decided to wander down to the paddock, a far more peaceful place than the grooms' quarters.

He climbed the gate rather than draw it back, his long legs carrying him over with ease. He wandered the slow, sinuous course of the stream, wondering if, should he float in it, it would eventually carry him out to the sea.

O what can ail thee, knight-at-arms,
Alone and palely loitering?

But as he rounded a bend, he spotted a figure in the water.

And he realized who it was.

Captain Thorne was swimming through the water at the widest part of the stream, the hair that had been so carefully pomaded now slicked down with the clean, cool water. As the powerful arms of that handsome man scythed through the moon-flecked surface the water splashed around him, yet he seemed untouched by it, his broad shoulders propelling him down into a dive and out of sight.

Moments later he resurfaced in the middle of the stream and tossed his head back, closing his eyes as he turned to face Jack. Jack's teeth caught his lip just for a second when Thorne reached up both hands and passed them over his hair, sweeping it back as he shook his head to clear the water from his eyes.

Jack knew he should turn away, that this was something he had no right to be watching, yet still he looked on, gazing at the sight of Captain Thorne unencumbered by authority or propriety, swimming through the deep stream with all the grace of Neptune himself. It did no harm to look, Jack told himself, and nobody would ever know that he *had*, for who else was here to see?

He would never speak of the neat pile of clothing that was folded on the bank, nor the cap that lay atop it. The boots were there too, of course, one standing, one fallen carelessly to rest in the grass and there, protruding from the lip of that boot, was the whip.

Jack's breath caught and he told himself that he would leave, that he had no right to intrude on this, because even unseen, he knew that he *was* an intruder here. Yet he seemed to be held there by some invisible shackle, his gaze fixed on Captain Thorne, who was now surging through the water toward the bank just as Apollo had surged into the stable yard like a thing possessed.

When Thorne reached the bank he hauled himself nimbly out to stand on the grass. Now a tremble ran through Jack at the sight of the captain's nakedness, at the wide shoulders, the way the water slid down his taut, dark-haired chest and over his flat, lightly muscled stomach and— Jack closed his eyes, telling himself not to look, that it was wrong, that the only thing worse than watching this was being *caught* watching this. Yet he couldn't keep them closed, couldn't know that such a vision was right there before him, bathed in the glow of the dusk that turned those steady rivulets of water into liquid gold.

When his eyelids lifted, Jack saw that Thorne had turned and now stood looking back at the stream, yet this was no less thrilling than the previous vision. Now he could watch without fear of detection, could let his gaze wander over the contoured planes of the captain's back, the muscular firmness of his buttocks, the toned sweep of his thighs. How must it be to be a man like this, to know what was concealed beneath that sharply cut uniform, the tight breeches and tailored tunic? A man who looked like this would never struggle to find the right words or be told to sleep on a stinking bed. He wouldn't arrive at a chateau with a muddied face, let alone break his shoulder so badly that he couldn't even get out to the action until it was surely almost over. A man like this would always be sure and confident. A man like this would always know how to wield a whip.

Jack, his focus entirely on the man before him, who seemed to be a Greek statue come alive, didn't notice that Keats had slipped from his hands until the canvas-bound volume landed on the ground with a quiet but definite thud. He crouched to pick it up, but it was too late.

"Trooper Woodvine!"

"Captain!"

Jack stood to attention, the book clutched in one hand. He fixed the direction of his stare just over the top of the captain's head, not daring to meet his eye.

Thorne was looking at him though, facing him once more. He stooped to retrieve his breeches even as he called to Jack, "Here. Now."

Then Thorne began to dress, the tightness of the breeches as they clung to his wet skin doing nothing to make the vision any more innocent. If anything, it made it even more tempting.

Jack came at a march, hindered by the strategic position of Keats rendered necessary by his body's traitorous reaction to the sight of his naked captain. *Unnatural desires.* But what could be unnatural about appreciating such perfect human form?

"Trooper." The captain rested his hand on his hip and spoke again, his voice full of flint. "Have you entirely given up saluting an officer?"

"Sorry, sir. Captain Thorne — sir!"

Jack made his salute, his other hand still clutched to the book.

Thorne returned it with parade-ground precision, sending a small spray of droplets showering from his sculpted arm.

"I hardly dare ask what sort of *gentleman's literature* you're reading." Thorne held out his hand, his eyes fixed on Jack's face.

What could Jack say to deter him? Perhaps he wouldn't notice. Why should the captain pay a groom any regard?

"Keats, sir."

He passed the captain the well-worn volume, only just stilling the tremble in his hand.

"Sweet, sweet is the greeting of eyes." Thorne looked down and smiled for a second, his expression nostalgic. Then his jaw set and he held the book in a grip so tight it whitened his knuckles, as though battling with the pages in their desire to be read. His voice was firm once more when he sniffed and declared, "Well, they tell me war is good for poetry."

"I've written some poems, sir." Encouraged by the captain's interest, Jack decided to share a confidence. "I sent them to *The Morning Post*, but they...they said they weren't *strident* enough."

"*The Morning Post* wouldn't take you?" Captain Thorne laughed and clapped one strong hand to Jack's shoulder. "I consider that proof that your poetry must be very good indeed, Woodvine!"

Jack grinned, touching his hand to his shoulder for a moment.

"Perhaps I might be brave enough to let you read them one day, sir."

And he realized then that the captain was looking into his eyes because it was the safest place *to* look, to avoid the obvious embarrassment that had been standing between them rather too literally.

"That would be an honor indeed, Trooper Woodvine, strident or otherwise." Thorne held out the book to him. "How're the boys treating you?"

"They're a nice bunch of lads, sir, but I don't know them well enough yet to… Troopers Cole and Charles showed me to my quarters… Cole carried my kitbag for me—he seems a good egg. The others…well, save talking about horses, I'm not sure I know what to talk to them *about*, sir. Football, perhaps, though I don't really follow it. Cricket's more my thing."

Jack was rambling, he knew, but in thinking of the other grooms, his body's reaction was waning. *Thank God.*

"A cricket man!" Thorne smiled again and Jack found himself glad that he had been able to conjure such joy with his simple admission. "What's your county?"

"Shropshire, sir." Jack blushed. His accent had only a vague Shropshire tinge, blurred out by the masters at the grammar school, but it came out rather loudly when he said the name of the county of his birth. "And…and yours?

"Surrey, for my sins. Home of Hobbs, as I needn't tell you!" Thorne stooped once more, this time to retrieve his shirt, and Jack caught a glimpse of something white peeking from beneath the jacket that still lay folded on the grass. It was the corner of a sketchpad, he realized, though in the dusk light the image that was drawn there faded into indiscernible gray.

"Do you draw, sir?"

It was, Jack knew, mildly impertinent to ask, but the question was out of his mouth before he could stop it.

"I dabble. *Drawing* is far too strong a word for my appalling efforts." Thorne sat down on the grass, focusing now on dressing, on returning to rank and role and that immaculate uniform. His skin, so lightly burnished by the sun, was fast disappearing beneath khaki and his leather boot creaked as he slid it onto his foot, an earthbound accompaniment to the chirping birds above.

"Bloody hell!" The captain's furious exclamation split the peace wide open and he cast the boot down. From it emerged an enormous wasp, buzzing furiously toward Jack before it spiraled up into the sky, leaving Thorne languishing there on the grass to spit, "What the devil —"

"Gosh, did it sting you, sir?"

Jack dropped to his knees, about to yank the captain's sock off, but Thorne waved him away, grimacing. Instead it was left for Thorne to gingerly remove his own sock, this tall, commanding captain reduced to a pale, pained figure by something so simple as a wasp. He brought his foot up to rest on the opposite knee, peering at the underside and there, in the tender skin of his instep, was the wasp's sting, embedded deep in what was already a sore-looking swelling.

"Sir, if you'd let me — I can…"

There was no nervousness — Jack Woodvine was doing the right thing once more.

He threw aside his book and took the captain's foot in his hand, bringing his face down toward it. Before Captain Thorne had time to protest, Jack had nudged the sting out with his fingernails.

"Good God, man, I thought you were —" Thorne let the sentence hang, too intent on peering at his foot and the tiny pinprick hole left by the sting. "He packed a hell of a punch for a little 'un!"

Jack got back up to his feet. It was as if the captain's delicate flesh was still there in his hands. He looked away, over to the stream, listening to the babble of the water.

"Nasty thing, sir, a wasp sting. Got one in my neck once, and I swear my head went numb!"

"Lord help me if I ever have to see battle." Thorne's laugh was pained, though, betraying his attempt at humor.

"Do you need a hand getting up, sir?" Jack wouldn't hold his hand out. It was too familiar, even though he'd just been on his knees beside the man, cradling his foot.

Thorne, abandoning his efforts to replace the boot on his stung foot, shook his head. "No, no, I can—" He was silenced by a gasp as soon as his foot touched even that soft grass, his ankle giving way beneath him.

"Come on, Captain Thorne…lean on me."

Jack picked up the discarded boot, his Keats tucked into his armpit, and, deciding that a matey gesture might reach the officer, even if protocol forbade it, reached his free arm toward the captain. Thorne tucked his whip into his boot, pulled on his jacket, placed his cap on his head and scooped up his pad. Only then did he put his free hand in Jack's and gingerly stand, putting his weight on the good foot as though he feared that one might also betray him.

"There you go, Captain."

Jack stared back across the field, deliberately avoiding the temptation to look down and see the captain's strong hand in his.

"Are we leaving the horses out tonight, sir?"

Thorne looked at Apollo, still apart from the other animals, cropping lazily at the grass. Perhaps he sensed his master's gaze, because he raised his large head and blinked at the captain and Jack, watching them in turn.

"It'll do them no harm. Tomorrow morning, bring him up to the stable and give him a brush down, then get him tacked up. I'll be riding out." Something seemed to occur to Thorne then, but he maintained that same, sensible manner. "And when you're done, give his stable walls a check, will you? He's had one or two nasty scratches overnight. I'm damned if I can find what's causing them, but your eyes are a decade younger than mine!"

"Yes, Captain. Now…do you want me to help you back to the chateau?"

Jack wondered at the sense of this, as the captain would have to lean on his bad shoulder. But it had healed enough for him to pass his Army medical — it could surely take the weight of his captain without any trouble at all.

"I'm afraid you might have to. I imagine you wish you'd stayed back at the barracks now." Captain Thorne put his arm around Jack's neck so that he could hobble more easily. "This isn't getting your poetry read."

Even though the captain had been for a dunking, his scent was little changed. Jack's nostrils flared involuntarily and it took all his effort to stop his body from showing how much the closeness to this man excited him. The captain's arm was so strong that Jack wondered at the accident that had left Thorne reliant on a puny fellow like him. And pressing, just a little, against Jack's side, the captain's firm torso.

He mustn't think of officers in this way. He mustn't think of *any* man this way.

But he couldn't help it. He always had. It was how the Good Lord had made him. Wasn't it blasphemous to protest?

"I-I could write a poem about the wasp, sir!"

"If you can think of a rhyme for wasp, I would love to see it." Thorne laughed, though the rather faraway look that overcame his face suggested that he was attempting to do just that. "Is it orange that doesn't rhyme with anything? Add wasp to that illustrious list, Trooper!"

"You don't have to rhyme things *exactly*, though, sir. Not in English. We've got too much Viking in our language, you see." Jack adopted a grand, deep tone, comically at odds with the content of his verse. "*Warrior wasp, cannot slay canny captain!* There, see?"

"Is this Dadaism, Trooper? Must I put you to the whip?" Thorne's voice was a stern tease but his eyes sparkled with humor and when he met Jack's gaze he gave the hint of a smile. "I rather suspect you will have to be the poet for both of us. I struggle enough with the sketching, let alone attempting rhymes that don't rhyme."

"I can barely hold a pencil, so we make a good pair!" There was a change in the tension of the strong arm across his neck. He felt his face burn beetroot and added, "Just...just joshing, Captain."

Was that even worse? Presumptuous, in a trooper, to dare joke with an officer. And yet, at the mention of the whip, Jack's mind had whirred.

"Sorry...sorry, Captain Thorne."

"At least you can't forget to salute since your hands are already full, Trooper Woodvine. Let's be grateful for small mercies."

"Yes, sir."

They continued on their shambling way, through the gate that Jack had earlier climbed over, and skirted past the stables.

The tower loomed up before them, almost bronze now in the gloaming of the evening. Jack paused and gazed up at it.

"It must be fantastic, to live in an actual castle, sir!"

"Here be dragons, Woodvine…"

Captain Marsh had been standing in the shadows cast by the building, the tip of his cigarette a glowing red eye.

He came at a clip across the gravel, his boots crunching toward them.

"A fine evening for a stroll with the beloved!" Phlegm rattled in his lungs as he laughed. "And still none too quick with your salutes, eh, Trooper?"

"He has one hand full of books and the other full of his captain. The War Office has yet to send us any three-armed troopers!" Thorne said with authority. "Wasp in the bloody boot, Marsh!"

"Wasp, eh? Reminds me of my time in the Raj. Bloody snake in my boot, Thorne! Bit me on the heel." His barrel chest expanded as he inhaled. A sneer crept onto his face. "Still walked unaided, though."

"Whereas the poor old serpent was stretchered off with septicemia?"

Marsh crushed out the golden tip of his cigarette under his boot.

"Ha!" There was no mirth in his laugh. He leaned into Jack, his lips moving as though tasting a flavor. "And you, Trooper, eh? Been enjoying yourself, have we? Think you'll like your time at our humble bolthole? Of course, the grooms' quarters aren't much to write home about to *Mummy*, but a nice fellow like you will soon find his way to the perks, I don't doubt!"

"It seems an all right sort of place, sir."

Jack distrusted the insinuating glint in Captain Marsh's expression.

"Trooper Woodvine has a knack with Apollo, Marsh. He's a sensible sort." Thorne's arm grew momentarily tighter on Jack's shoulders. "We need more like him."

Marsh brushed his hands together, his stare not leaving Jack.

"Oh, that we most certainly do, Thorne."

He reached toward Jack, his wedding ring glinting in the moonlight, and gave his cheek a pinch.

Jack was so affronted that he didn't know how to react, how he was *allowed* to react. Perhaps Marsh had an unfortunate manner. Perhaps there was no reason to feel uneasy. Perhaps it was just a habit in this battalion, an initiatory jape for the new grooms.

Yet it was all too obvious that Thorne really did not like Marsh.

"Get along, Woodvine, back to your quarters." Thorne withdrew his arm from Jack's shoulders and, in turning to take back his boot, insinuated himself between Marsh and Jack. With his back to the other officer, Thorne offered the barest hint of a smile and said, "Thank you, Trooper. Dismissed."

Jack took one step backward before remembering he should acknowledge the captain somehow. He nodded then turned, running across the square to the stables, not looking back because he didn't want to know if Marsh had decided to follow. He wouldn't. He was a married man, after all. How silly to even entertain such a thought.

When Jack arrived back in his quarters there was the usual racket, which he was by now quite used to, of approaching bedtime. Lads wandering about nearly naked, demanding admiring glances from their fellows, throwing things across the room to one another, cheering whether it was caught or dropped, bawdy banter and swapped cigarettes.

How, he didn't know, but Jack managed to get to his bed without attracting comment and turned his back to the room as he changed into his pajamas. He was under the thin covers before a shout of 'Lights out!' from the NCO who had arrived in the entrance to their dormitory.

"Night, night, *mes amis*!" Queenie's voice trilled out from behind the tapestries and lacquered screen where a dim light still burned, glowing pale against the ceiling. "And don't wake me until the tea has brewed!"

At the sound of Queenie's voice, Jack smiled. Had he found himself in a fairytale after all, in this strange castle populated by extraordinary people?

His ears still ringing with the splashing of the stream, Jack twined Captain Thorne's handkerchief between his fingers and began to fall asleep.

Chapter Three

How could he have slept so well in such an uncomfortable bed? Jack blinked himself awake and stretched. The other beds were full of sleeping grooms.

Quietly he picked up his clothes and headed down to the tack room to change, to avoid waking anyone. He dressed, stashed his pajamas in a corner and collected the halter and lead rein.

Trooper Jack Woodvine walked out smiling into the cool, bright morning to meet his new horse.

It was a glorious time to be about. No one else was up. He could hear whinnies and splutters from the stalls of the other horses as he walked by, and once he reached the path, Jack broke into a gleeful run. All the morning was his—all the chateau, all the sun, all the bright blue air.

Just as he was about to unbolt the paddock gate, Jack realized that something was amiss. He had left Apollo only hours earlier cropping at the sweet grass, but now the stallion appeared to be in distress. Jack paused.

Should he run for help? But he was Apollo's groom, he couldn't leave him.

Jack flung the halter and rein over the fence. Dispensing with the gate, he vaulted after them.

Apollo stood at the far end of the paddock, alone as ever. This was not the calm horse of last night, though, but a different animal entirely. His head was held high, eyes watching Jack suspiciously, ears flat down against his skull, one hoof pawing at the grass.

What the hell had happened? Was the front so close here that the horses could hear artillery bombardments that were imperceptible to humans? Or had there been a storm overnight and Jack had slept too soundly to hear it?

And yet the other horses seemed unaffected.

Jack approached slowly, holding the tack, his side facing the horse. Not face-on, which might seem aggressive, and definitely not with his back to him. He had to be able to see Apollo as he drew near.

He made the same chuckling, clicking sound in his throat as he had yesterday, interspersed with an approximation of Captain Thorne's soft coo. He tapped one finger lightly against his thigh to the rhythm of his steps, lowering his eyelids a little to avoid frightening Apollo with what he might read as an intimidating stare.

Jack stopped, coming as close as he dared for now.

Still Apollo glared at him, the hoof moving with even more pronounced agitation, scraping up divots of turf where it dragged. Yet he lowered his head just a little, a fraction of give in the muscles as those flat ears twitched.

Slowly Jack sank into a crouch, keeping himself small and unthreatening. He was careful to keep his legs tensed in case Apollo should rush at him.

"Hey, handsome fellow."

With any luck Apollo would remember his voice from yesterday, would associate him with the captain. But the horse might yet be too scared to recall anything other than whatever it was that had terrified him in the night. Jack went on, clucking and cooing as gently as he could, creeping closer, trying to befriend a horse that was determined to remain solitary.

Apollo rolled his eyes and scraped at the ground harder, shifting his weight from one hoof to the other. He snorted and peered around Jack, looking for the likeliest route of escape.

A soft breath escaped Apollo's nostrils and still he watched, as though waiting for some imagined horror.

Jack estimated the number of paces to get to Apollo from where he was crouched. If he could get the tack on him, then he might be able to control him—but he would also be far too near his hooves, even if he could get the halter on him without being stamped on or bitten.

Instead, Jack slowly turned his back on Apollo, rose enough to be able to walk and crossed toward the stream. He headed to the point along the bank where Apollo had stood yesterday, where he had leaned toward the water and drunk. Hanging on to a branch, Jack went as close to the edge as he could. The marks of Apollo's shoes were in the dust. He knelt on the bank and scooped a handful of the cold, clear water into his mouth.

He sensed movement in the paddock behind him, the gentle sound of hooves beating on grass, coming closer and growing slower and more tentative as they did.

A long shadow fell across the grass beside him yet Apollo didn't make the final approach. He stood back, twenty feet or so from where Jack was kneeling. There came another snort then an intrigued whinny.

Jack quietly clicked and cooed and brought more water to his own mouth. The sound of the water splashing from his hands made the stream sound like the most appealing, refreshing stretch of water on the planet. He waited. And as he waited, he looked into the water and remembered the sight of Captain Thorne, naked, uninhibited, muscular. A slight shudder went through him at the thought. For a hopeless moment he wondered if he would ever see that sight again. Of course not. What a fool he was, an accidental peeping Tom on an officer.

An officer who would go spare if his horse wasn't ready in time for him riding out this morning.

Jack brought a handful of water up again but this time didn't bring it to his own mouth. He turned very slightly and, without looking Apollo in the eye, showed him that his hands were full of the fresh, delicious water.

And Apollo came closer, his ears swiveling up now, intrigued by this strange new display.

Rising carefully to his feet to avoid spilling the water or spooking the horse, Jack edged toward Apollo. He clicked and he cooed, and as he looked at the horse, he saw that he no longer feared him. He probably thought that Jack was an idiot, but that was better than being thought a threat.

He held out his hands to Apollo, the morning sunlight glinting off what was left of the water that he had carried from the stream. He smiled as the horse took a step toward him.

As gentle as a babe, as gentle as Thorne's hand had been in Jack's, Apollo lowered his muzzle to the proffered water. He lapped softly, his dark eyes blinking, gaze settling on his groom.

There was a sensation of warmth in Jack's breast, the same that always came to him once he had earned an animal's trust. Even if, in the case of Apollo, it might only be temporary.

Once the water was finished, Jack moved his hands up from Apollo's muzzle, brushing across the stiff velvet of his hair with his fingertips until he was able to stroke his face. A contented chunter came from deep in Apollo's chest and Jack spent several minutes fussing him, enjoying the animal's warmth, his smell.

"Let's take you back to the stable, Apollo," Jack said.

He stepped back from the horse, fully expecting the animal to dash away from him. But instead Apollo came with him, following to where he had left the tack.

"You're on your best behavior now, aren't you? Let's get you ready for your dad."

Apollo seemed to fret slightly as Jack put the halter on him, but he maintained a steady hand and Apollo calmed again. Still clicking and cooing, Jack took the rein and led his charge across the paddock.

"Hello, sailor." Apollo froze on the spot at the sound of the still-unseen Queenie's singsong voice. Then he took a step back, stilled only by Jack's hand on the halter. "You're up bright and early. I haven't even been to bed!"

Now Apollo pulled against Jack, snorting, eyes rolling to seek out the hidden man. Again he snorted, hooves dragging at the turf.

"Shhhh, Apollo... Shhhh..."

Trying not to alarm the horse, Jack raised his voice. There was an edge to his words.

"What do you want, Queenie? Apollo's spooked and you're scaring him."

"He's such a bloody fairy!" Queenie emerged from the trees where he had been concealed. He wore only a long silk robe of bright blue, belted at the waist with the scarf he had sported for his song and dance routine. On his face, that pretty face, was a smirk, his flashing eyes directed only at the horse. "Scared of me?"

"Queenie, get back. I told you, he's spooked! Do you want him to trample you? Because you're going the right way about it."

Jack tried to stand between the horse and Queenie, while keeping Apollo moving. If he could get him into his stable, shut the door and get some quiet, then he could calm the horse before Captain Thorne demanded him.

"Fairy horse!" Queenie pouted. He looked tired, though, dark circles beneath his eyes and his hair disordered as if he had spent a night rabble-rousing with the best of them. "Who could be scared of little old me?"

He did retreat a little, though, then asked Jack, "Do you dance, little Jack?"

"Dance? Who, me? What are you — Queenie, please, I don't have time for this. I've got to get Apollo ready for Captain Thorne."

"Don't you mean Cinderella?" He grinned. "With his missing boot?"

"Has he lost his boot? I wouldn't know… Please, Queenie, I —"

"Nothing goes on here that I don't know about." Queenie swished the scarf and gave a wink. "You'd do well to remember that."

What had Queenie seen? Jack spying on the naked captain? *He couldn't have done.* Jack swallowed.

"Captain Thorne got a really bad wasp sting in his foot and I helped him to the chateau, and Captain

49

Marsh pinched my cheek like…like a weird uncle. If you can make a scandal out of that, then you have a far more vivid imagination than I do."

"He pinched your cheek, did he?" Queenie pouted and let out a huff of breath. "How very unromantic. But I think you're a good little Jack to tell me all the news." He slipped a hand into the pocket of the robe and withdrew a cigarette before looking at Jack as though he had quite forgotten he was there. "Off you go now, Jack and his fairy steed! I shall enjoy my smoke and then get off to bed… It's a tiring old life."

Jack sighed and led Apollo to the stables. Why had he thought that Queenie was so fascinating? He was a thoroughly unusual creature, but at the same time there was something dangerous about him, threatening Jack with gossip. About what? About him helping a captain with a wasp sting? There'd have been far more gossip if he'd left the man sat helpless on his arse. *Best not to think of Thorne's arse, though.*

Apollo was jittery until the paddocks were behind them, and Jack washed away the unease he had felt with Queenie, concerned that it might transmit to the horse. Finally the stables appeared before them and Apollo almost led Jack. The yard was still empty save for the sounds of horses waking from their slumbers and Jack was mindful of Thorne's expectations, of the need to make his new captain proud. He was mindful of everything about Captain Thorne, he realized, and he would need to become *less* so.

The door to Apollo's stable stood wide open once more. When Jack entered he knew straightaway where Queenie had been carousing. There were empty wine bottles strewn across the floor, the straw was banked up into what had clearly been a makeshift pillow and there, peeping out from beneath it, was a single brown leather glove.

With a calming murmur for the horse, Jack stooped to retrieve the glove. He could see that it didn't belong to Thorne. It was ill-cared-for and aged, stained with God knows what, and when he put it to his nose Jack recoiled, his stomach leaping into his throat. This wasn't the captain's smell of pomade and leather, but a dirty stench of sweat and tobacco, the smell of a man Jack couldn't imagine *wanting* to romp in the hay with.

Not that he wanted to romp with Captain Thorne, of course. Not at all.

This meant more work, for the stable would have to be tidied, the bottles thrown away and the straw searched for any that might have become hidden. He could hardly risk Apollo stepping on broken glass, Jack knew, as he tethered the horse to a post and began gathering up Queenie's empties.

Apollo watched the coming and going with his large, dark eyes, entirely at ease now. He gave an occasional snort just to remind Jack of his presence, but otherwise all was peaceful once more.

Chapter Four

By the time his fellow grooms were busying themselves with brushes and brooms, feed and tack — Queenie excepted — Jack was warm in the knowledge that he had already done his most important duties for the morning. Apollo's coat, mane and tail were immaculate, the horse well-fed, clad in his gleaming tack and ready for his rider. Just as Thorne had requested, Jack had made a fingertip search of the by-now perfectly laid stable but found nothing that might be to blame for any mysterious *scratches* that Thorne had told him about. There was no nail or splinter anywhere, nothing that might cause the horse any discomfort.

Apollo waited in the stable that seemed to be Queenie's favorite playground and the very thought of that left Jack's annoyance rising. This was the horse's home, his sanctuary, not a place for drinking and *assignations*. From now on, Jack decided, Apollo's stable would be looked after.

Jack was humming a tune, a ballad as ancient as the Shropshire Hills that Mrs. Byatt on the farm had taught him as a boy. It was about an old battle, a soldier far from home. And just as he began to sing the words, learned at Mrs. Byatt's knee as she crimped the pie crusts, he heard footsteps approach.

"Here's a lad who's not afraid to sweat!" Captain Marsh's voice boomed across the yard and Jack fell silent, praying that *he* wasn't the subject of that comment. Apollo's reaction was to scrape one hoof on the back of the stable door, ears flattening down. "And here's a horse who'd be more use as glue than as a steed, horse and rider each as strange as the other!"

Trooper Woodvine saluted and stood to attention.

"Captain Marsh, sir, good morning." He kept his tone as flat as possible, his face expressionless. "Were you looking for something, sir?"

"This thing—" He gestured vaguely in the direction of Apollo. "How do you do it?"

Marsh pushed his face toward Jack, that smell of sweat and tobacco and—

He knew without a doubt who owned that glove.

"He'll let nobody near him, lassie, nobody but Thorne. You've tamed the stallion with your wicked, winsome ways." Marsh's rheumy eyes narrowed and Jack forced himself not to look away from the broken veins and blocked pores, the bloodshot lines that webbed into his eyes. "I'm known as something of a stallion myself, lass."

There was a tremor in Marsh's lips again, as if he had something in his mouth and was considering its flavor.

"I'm a farmer's son, sir. I wouldn't be much cop if I didn't have a way with even the scariest of beasts."

Jack took the broom and swept at the straw, hoping that by robbing Marsh of his audience he'd get bored and bother someone else. The unwashed odor of the man was still there as Captain Marsh continued to linger at the door. A thread of nausea rose in Jack's throat.

He realized too late that he had cornered himself in the stable. Yet Marsh stilled on the threshold, frozen on the spot at the sound of Apollo's warning snort. The horse paced around beside Jack, tail swishing with a rapier speed, those oiled hooves scuffing at the straw.

"If you cook and screw as well as you sweep, you'll make a fine wife for some lucky soldier," Marsh told him in a voice that almost oozed from his lips.

Jack stared at him. He was either going to be sick on him, or crack the broom over Marsh's head and claim the horse had jostled him.

Jack adopted his best gung-ho Tommy voice.

"It's very nice that an important officer like you chooses to chat with a groom like me, sir, but it's not going to beat the Hun."

"You'd do well to learn how things work around here, *boy*," Marsh growled, though he remained outside the stable. "There are some people it doesn't do to cross —"

"If you're looking for a billet better suited to your table manners, Marsh, the search continues!" Thorne's voice soared over the other officer's tobacco-stained vitriol, silencing him mid-threat. "One might find a pigsty somewhere nearby but Apollo has no wish for a stablemate. Move along, Captain!"

"How's your foot?" Marsh threw the question at Thorne like an insult as he stalked away.

"Happily not in my mouth!" Thorne's reply was cheery and he strode to the open door to peer into the stable, his face lit by a bright smile. He looked from Apollo to the well-ordered straw and the full hay net then told Jack, "Bloody good job, soldier!"

Jack saluted, unable to hide his grin.

"Thank you, sir! Good morning, Captain Thorne, sir."

"Good morning, Woodvine, good morning, Apollo." The salute was returned with a swift confidence. "All ready to go. You've set a hell of an example, Trooper. The stable looks like new. Any luck on the source of those nasty scratches my boy's been turning up with?"

Jack bit his lip. The threat of Queenie and his gossip nearly stopped up his mouth, but he had to say something. Sometimes one did have to tattle on a fellow.

"I… When I brought Apollo in from the paddock, his stable was a mess. Like someone'd had a party in here. Bottles on the floor and it smelled of cigarettes. And…" Jack glanced over to the corner where he'd left the glove. "Sir, I wouldn't want to get in trouble, but I know that if I don't say anything, it's just as bad. I'm in rather a bind, sir. Will you…will you go to that corner, sir? I found something in the straw. I think…I think I know who it belongs to, but perhaps you should see it first. Before I say anything. They can't say I told tales on them then, can they, Captain?"

"What's this blather, Trooper?" Despite his words, Thorne stepped into the stable and crossed to the corner. In the dim light he scooped his cap from his head and tucked it beneath his arm then leaned down, peering at the glove.

Jack spoke in a whisper, conscious that he sounded like a conspirator.

"I think I know who he was with, sir. He went to bed not long after I'd got up. I bet he's still up there, sleeping."

Jack pointed to the ceiling, even though Captain Thorne had his back to him, still staring at the glove. Finally, however, he bent over and picked it up with a murmur of, "Sleeping, eh?"

Jack couldn't have avoided it if he'd tried – Captain Thorne's toned bottom, the breeches straining to contain the shapely, muscular curves. Jack stared, hoping that the captain wouldn't – couldn't – notice. He was such a fine figure of a man.

A small sigh escaped Jack's lips, but surely the captain was too engrossed in the glove to have heard.

"You did the right thing, soldier." Thorne stood and replaced his cap, the glove clutched in his own leather-clad hand. He sounded furious, Jack realized, but in that quiet way that was somehow worse when the teachers at the grammar had used it. Better to be bellowed at than this controlled, seething anger. "About your business, there's about to be a hell of a ruckus."

"Sir... Sir, they won't know it was me who told you, will they?"

Jack gripped the captain's arm fearfully.

"Who told me what?" He furrowed his brow, studying Jack's face. "I came into the stable to collect Apollo and found a glove in the corner and bottles strewn about, isn't that what you saw too?"

Jack nodded, his face beginning to regain its color. He let go of the captain's strong arm, realizing he'd held on for too long. But it had made him feel so safe.

"You might like to be somewhere *other* than this stable for the next ten minutes." Thorne smiled despite the warning. "Leave Apollo in here and close the door, then get his halter back to the tack room. Better not to be seen at the scene of someone else's crime."

Thorne executed a quick salute then strode out into the yard and headed for the rickety staircase up to the grooms' quarters with a shout of, "Trooper Charles! The Hun won't wait for you to catch up on your damned beauty sleep, you layabout!"

Jack went to the tack room at a calm walk, even though his heart was racing. He hid himself in the shadows, but positioned himself so that he could see outside into the yard. If anyone asked, he was familiarizing himself with the room. Of course.

And all hell seemed to break loose.

The door to the grooms' quarters was flung back and out came Captain Thorne, the rather shell-shocked figure of Queenie being marched ahead of him. Now at least mostly dressed, the barefoot trooper's shoulder was held tight by Thorne's hand as the unlikely couple descended the stairs into the yard, Queenie complaining every step of the way that the horses had kicked the wall and kept him awake, that the other grooms snored, that the light of the moon was too bright and that he, by order of Captain Marsh, should be allowed the sleep he had missed on the previous night.

It meant nothing to Thorne, of course, and as the whole world seemed to slow to a fascinated, horrified and perhaps amused halt, all was silent save the footsteps of Thorne and Queenie as the officer pushed the soldier across the straw-strewn yard toward the water pump.

"A sharp blast of cold will wash away the sleep, Trooper Charles." With a firm push, Thorne sent

Queenie sprawling. As the young man let out a howl of protest, the captain pumped the handle, sending a stream of freezing-cold water cascading over the by-now-apoplectic Queenie. He bawled a torrent of garbled abuse, his pale hands clasped over his hair as he buried his head against his narrow chest, yet still the water flowed until he was utterly drenched.

Only then did Thorne address the yard in general, his eyes blazing.

"These stables are *not* drinking dens. You're in the bloody army now, you don't sleep, eat or breathe unless an officer tells you to!" He snatched the whip from his boot and cracked it down hard, gesturing toward Queenie. "Trooper Charles will transport the manure down to the muck heap today *alone*, no one is to help him.

"Standards here have become sloppy." He cracked the whip again, then tucked it beneath his arm. "Keep in line, gentlemen, or there'll be hell to pay!"

It was only then that Jack realized that he hadn't been breathing. He inhaled, the sudden lungful of morning air rasping in his throat. Each whip-crack echoed in his ears.

God forbid that he should ever rile the Captain.

The door creaked ajar, admitting Trooper Cole. Jack tried a smile.

"Morning, Wilfred."

Wilfred slapped Jack on the shoulder.

"Morning, Jack. Cor, your Captain Thorne's got batey!"

"Yes…I saw."

"I'll wager you're wondering what you'll have to do for him to take on like that against you?"

"Lord in Heaven—no!"

The whip-crack still sounded in his ears.

Wilfred gathered up a bridle, watching Jack.

"Looking for something?"

Jack had been asked that once in some public conveniences in Shrewsbury, by a silver-haired man with lonely eyes. He shook the image of the man's pale hands from his head.

"I...I was just..."

"It'd be a shame, wouldn't it, if the new boy made a habit of running to teacher."

Wilfred's smile didn't reach his eyes. He banged the door shut behind him as he left.

"Trooper Woodvine!" The captain's voice rang out across the yard like a thunderclap at the departure of Wilfred. "Show yourself!"

Jack came outside into the sunlight and stood to attention.

"Captain Thorne, sir!"

Standing in the center of the yard, the captain clicked his fingers to indicate Jack should follow him. They set off at a brisk pace toward Apollo's stable. The horse watched all of this with interest, his head protruding from the open top of the door as he took in all the new drama.

Jack followed at a march, feeling the stares of the other grooms on him. Only when they had reached the stone stable building did Thorne stop and turn. His dark eyes moved this way and that, watching the scurry of the soldiers. They did their best not to look at Queenie as he tied his boots. They always did their duty to the letter while Thorne was in the vicinity. The pump water was cold as ice, after all. No man would risk a dunking.

"The state of this stable this morning was a bloody disgrace, soldier, consider your copybook blotted." He reached into his pocket and withdrew the glove, holding it up with a grimace as though it was a foul-smelling carcass he had found beneath a hedge. "Is this *yours*?"

Trooper Woodvine couldn't speak. An unnameable terror gripped his heart. He stood to attention but his spine wouldn't hold straight and his head drooped.

"S-sorry, Captain Thorne. It won't happen again, sir."

Thorne didn't reply, but continued to hold Jack's gaze with his own, those dark, bright eyes seemingly seeing right into him. He would know, Jack thought with dismay, know about the *thoughts*, would see right into his very heart. A muscle in the captain's smooth, strong jaw twitched and he asked again, as though addressing an imbecile, "Is. This. Yours?"

That dirty, stinking glove hung there between them like the remains of a bat, leathery and decaying, entirely at odds with the elegant man who now had it in his possession. Captain Thorne would never allow his kit to look like that, Jack knew, and he felt a new surge of horror that Thorne might for a moment imagine it belonged to *him*.

"No, sir." Jack managed not to stammer. He was telling the truth, after all. Doing the right thing, even though he had no idea what he had done for the captain to turn on him so abruptly. "It's not my glove, sir. I have mine in my pocket, sir."

"No, sir!" Thorne barked an echo. "Not my glove, sir! Then we find ourselves with a mystery, Trooper, that might never be solved."

He spun on his immaculate heel and swept his whip from where it had been resting in his boot, nestled beside one smooth calf. With a gesture to the stable door, he snapped, "Get the door unbolted, Woodvine. Let us inspect your handiwork properly!"

His hand only shaking a little, Jack unbolted the stable door and stood to attention, allowing Captain Thorne to enter before him. The whip was still in his gloved hand, and Jack's heart beat faster. He mustn't think of it, mustn't even look at it.

"In, and close the bottom door before the bloody horse escapes!" Thorne's furious tone was at odds with the gentle touch he offered Apollo when he lifted his free hand to stroke the horse's shoulder. "Now, Trooper, the war won't wait for you!"

Jack pulled the door closed with a smart bang, which surprised even himself. He stamped his foot as he turned to the captain and stood to attention again. This time his stance was perfect. He would weather this, he would endure, even if later he took himself off to hide within the willow by the stream.

"At ease, although I should bloody keep you at full stretch until the sun sets!"

Captain Thorne continued to glare at him, his voice now dropping to a low growl. Anyone passing by would not hear *what* was being said, but by its tone it would unmistakably be a hell of a telling-off. He gestured this way and that with the whip, giving a very good account of a man indicating every single fault, real or imagined, in this immaculate stable.

"Don't look so wounded, Trooper Woodvine." He turned a little, peering around the stable with a critical eye. "Better that your pals see you getting a good roasting, wouldn't you say?"

"Yes, sir."

Jack understood at last—this was all an act. Captain Thorne was only doing this to protect him. But the officer's fury had not felt fake, and the anguish in Jack's heart had been real.

"Well, you've done a fine job for a new 'un." Thorne nodded his approval and took up Apollo's reins. "The yard'll keep you busy in my absence, I have no doubt, and if you could give Apollo's second tack a polish, it'd be a job well done. The door, if you would!"

"Yes, Captain Thorne."

Jack opened it for him and followed the captain into the yard behind Apollo. He still felt dazed, as if he had received a stinging slap across the face. It was as well. If he had reappeared from the stable with a smile, then it would have been all the worse for him.

"Should I fetch a mounting block, sir?"

"Don't be a damn fool, Trooper!" At the overheard exchange, the redheaded groom who had provided Apollo's water bucket just a day earlier dared to chuckle, no doubt glad it was Jack and not him who was on the end of the tongue lashing.

Thorne's arm shot out. The whip was fully extended toward the hapless lad, who cowered, though it was still inches from him. "Get about your business, soldier, or your arse'll taste this crop!"

As the groom scurried back to his sweeping, Thorne tucked the whip into his boot and told Jack, "An officer in need of a mounting block is an officer in need of a swift trip to no man's land. It's a bloody disgraceful show for a chap of rank!"

He lifted one polished boot to rest in the stirrup and reached up to take a firm hold of the cantle. Then, in one fluid movement, he hauled himself up into the saddle with a creak of leather, leaving Jack with another impression of that unmistakable scent he carried with him. With a moment to slightly straighten his cap, Thorne took up the reins and looked down his long nose at Jack, his face hard as granite.

"About your business, Trooper. Apollo wants to see his tack gleaming!"

Jack saluted and held his hand to his forehead until Captain Thorne had gone. He kept it there some moments afterward, some essence of the captain still remaining in the air.

Jack stepped over a pile of sweepings and the red-haired groom threw him a sympathetic grin.

"Is he always like that?" Jack knew the captain wasn't, but he was willing to play along.

"That's him on a good day!" The groom's north Wales accent was at once recognizable to Jack.

"Trooper Woodvine — Jack." He held out his hand. "I'm a Shropshire lad. You're from — ?"

"Flintshire. The name's Bryn, by the way. Bryn Pritchard, but everyone here calls me Taffy."

"Taffy?" Jack rolled his eyes. "Bryn's a nice name — doesn't it mean 'hill'?"

Bryn laughed as they shook hands.

"You've bloody impressed me, you have. An Englishman who knows a word of Welsh!"

"But of course — I can almost see Wales from my front door. Our housekeeper — "

The NCO was hovering, so Jack gave Bryn a friendly nod and went into the tack room.

From the stacked shelves, Jack gathered the cloths and tins he would need to get Apollo's tack up to the captain's standard. He carefully set them down on the rickety bench that divided the room in two along its length. Standing back, he looked at the racks of saddles, each with its bridle hanging on a hook beside it. He stepped forward, examining the handwritten luggage labels that dangled from a length of string at every rack. Each bore the name of the horse and its rider and he scowled at the no-nonsense printed hand that had written *Edmund Marsh – Tsarina*. Beside it, Jack saw a label written in an elegant copperplate that read *Apollo Thorne*.

Jack laid Apollo's tack across the bench. He examined each piece. It was extremely good quality, but that hardly came as a surprise. Supple, well-cared for. Jack wondered if this was the work of the other grooms, or if the captain took it upon himself to take so much trouble over the tack.

A great weight of expectation lay heavy on Jack's shoulders. He sponged and he lathered, he soaped and he polished, he waxed and he buffed. He took a tiny brush to every crease and seam in the leather. The smell of the saddle-soap didn't remind him of the tack room at home now. He saw a pair of blazing dark eyes and a raised whip, an amused smile and a sketchbook.

As he worked on the girth, Jack noticed that Captain Thorne's name had been stamped on it in gold lettering. *Apollo Capt. R. B. Thorne.*

Jack smiled to himself. Only knowing the man as Captain Thorne, it hadn't occurred to him that his officer might actually have a first name. It was the same surprise he'd felt as a child when Mrs. Byatt had addressed his father as *John*.

But R.? What could it stand for?

Not that Jack would ever know, of course. He would never address the captain by his first name. And the captain would never address Jack by his. Even though he must know what Jack's name was, as well as every other possible detail that the Army had deemed necessary to record—his date of birth, his place of enlistment, his height, eye color, complexion, his chest dimensions when expanded and relaxed.

Robert. Captain Robert B. Thorne.

Now that was a name with gravitas.

But what about Richard, or Ralph, or Randolph, or Roland, or Roderick, or Raymond? Given that the captain was rather posh, the R might even have once been a surname. Something grand. Something that sounded like the name of a large Georgian house, with a lake and fountains and a lime tree avenue. Something that Jack could never even guess at.

Yet his mind kept coming back to the first idea that had struck him—Captain Robert B. Thorne. And he repeated the name in his head, rolling it around his tongue as he worked.

He didn't know how long passed as he worked at the tack but the day was drawing on when the latch of the tack room lifted. On the soft breeze from the opening door Jack heard the sounds of toil, of raised voices and scraping shovels. He caught the scent of manure and straw before a shadow fell over the room as Trooper Queenie Charles leaned on the doorjamb.

Gone was the playful look of yesterday, the consummate performer with the hint of rouge on his lips—this was a young man who was exhausted. His pale, delicate face was filthy, his uniform stained with sweat and muck, and he let out a long, soulful sigh and declared in a beaten whine, "I cannot go on another moment, Jacky."

"Tiring work, then?"

And you bloody deserve it.

"Poor old you," Jack added, attempting a supportive smile.

"Thorne's a miserable old bastard. I hate him!" Queenie stepped swiftly into the tack room and closed the door. Then he set his lips in a pout and cocked his head to one side, wide eyes imploring. "Not for what he did to me, but for how he spoke to you, my newest friend."

Newest friend? What sort of almighty buffoon does he take me for?

"Well, that's officers for you." Jack sighed, shrugging as he picked up a cloth. "They can't talk without bellowing their heads off."

"But he fancies himself as a sort, don't you think? Pomaded and perfumed, strutting about!" Queenie's lips curled back like a terrier showing sharp, white teeth. "He's not the king of fucking England, how dare he?"

Then the look of sad exhaustion returned and he slid down the wall to slump on the floor, every inch the picture of a Dickensian heroine. "I shall have to speak to Captain Marsh about this. He knows my people, you know, and they won't like this at all."

"You surely didn't expect this to be easy, did you?" At the mention of Captain Marsh, the unwelcome stench of the man returned to Jack's nostrils. "There's a bloody war on, Queenie. Just down that road, there's lads like us up to their eyeballs in mud, shitting with dysentery, their heads half blown off. And then there's us. Living in a bloody chateau. And yes, the officers shout at us, but that's what they're meant to do. None of us get a free pass, you know. Until you shoot your toe off and get a Blighty One. But me, I'll keep my nose clean, jump when Thorne yells *jump*, and…and…I'll pray God gives me the strength to endure whatever is thrown at me. And maybe we might even be the lucky ones who get to go home."

Queenie's face hardened beneath the grime, his eyes narrowing just a touch, just enough to say, *challenge accepted*.

"I didn't want to get into *rank*, Jacky, but I'm sort of important around here, you know?" He grinned, a cold shark's smile. "You're new, so I'm going to let that go, but perhaps I should explain. Around here, things don't work quite as they do elsewhere. We have our own ways, as they say in your rustic back of beyond." He rose to his feet and crossed to the bench, setting his palms flat against the surface. "Among all the ranks and medals and all of that nonsense, we have a structure. There are the *lads*—that's people like you, Jacky. Then there are the captains—some are useful, some will still be pomading their hair when they're tied to a stake in no man's land. Then somewhere up in the clouds, you'll find the generals. Just above them, and just below the king, is Trooper Quentin Charles. Do you understand *now*?"

"Oh, yes, Trooper Charles—the groom who stinks of horse shit."

Yesterday Jack had pretended to himself that this fabulous creature had not been looking at him in mockery. That he could be Jack's friend. But Queenie had shone with a luster that Jack had only imagined. He'd been here twenty-four hours, yet his understanding of how Chateau de Desgravier worked was fixing in his mind. Queenie let Marsh romp with him. Queenie whored himself to the most repulsive man in the regiment. And Queenie didn't like it when he couldn't get his own way.

"Have you done here, Trooper Charles? Only I must get on."

"I do hope you find whatever's catching dear old Apollo on that glorious snowy coat of his. Blood always spoils a look, don't you think?" Queenie tossed his head as he stood, a sly smile on his face. "And it'd be a shame if one of those little, tiny, incidental wounds went bad."

He gave a deliberately slovenly salute and turned for the door, whistling merrily. *Bastard. The evil, skinny little bastard. It was him, it was Queenie, deliberately injuring Apollo.*

Jack would have to tell Captain Thorne. Even though he knew that a dunking under the pump would be mild in comparison to what punishment the captain would unleash.

As if thinking aloud, Jack whispered, "A man could get his back broken if he's horsewhipped."

"And a new boy might get his skull smashed if he doesn't fall in line." Queenie — *Quentin* — lifted the latch once more. "You have one more chance, Jacky. I might still make you my lady-in-waiting."

"I think you'll find my name is *Jack*."

"Not anymore." With that he opened the door and wandered out into the sunlight with a cry of, "Who will help a poor Queenie shovel?"

Jack rolled down his sleeves. He was suddenly cold.

Chapter Five

"Care for a smoke?"

Wilfred had been sitting on a straw bale near the tack room, a tin mug of tea in his hand. He was about to light a roll-up. Another was lying in wait behind his ear.

"Not for me, thanks, Wilfred, but I wouldn't mind a cup of tea."

Wilfred tipped his head toward an office a few doors along.

"There's an urn. It's kept brewing all day. Sometimes it's even drinkable."

Jack returned in a moment with a tin mug of tea that closely resembled the color of ditchwater. It didn't taste much better, but it was better than nothing, and there were biscuits too. He leaned against the wall beside Wilfred and looked out across the yard.

"Busy day?" It seemed to Jack as if the hostility of the morning had blown away.

"Yeah…and you?"

"Could be worse."

"Ain't that the truth." Wilfred chuckled. "Look, about this morning... Don't mind old Queenie, will you? He's a bit...*theatrical*."

Jack studied the oily film on the surface of his tea.

"I'd noticed."

"He's a nice bloke, really."

"Look, earlier he said something about Apollo's injuries, and I—and it crossed my mind... Would Queenie...would he injure a horse on purpose, just for a lark? Even if he's nice, as you say?"

Wilfred raised his eyebrows.

"What, Queenie? Nah, mate, that's cobblers. He's all mouth is Trooper Charles. What you've got there with that Apollo is a half-wild creature—bet he bumps himself against the walls at the slightest thing. That's what it is, you mark my words."

"I hope that's true, even if..." Even if was a horrible thought that a horse could be so nervy and afraid. But still, something nagged at Jack. Unfounded, he knew. He'd look ridiculous if he even mentioned it. "You're good mates with Queenie, then?"

"Me and Queenie? Oh, yeah—he's great! A right laugh. I'd never met no one like him before! See, I reckon he got picked on something rotten at school, so I just sit back and let him queen it over everyone. Make him feel better about himself. You understand, don't you?"

Jack nodded.

"I keep an eye out for him, that's all I'm saying. You get rough sorts coming through here sometimes and they take one look at Queenie and... Well, I'm sure you can imagine, eh? My dad's an ostler in a pub, down by the docks. I can handle myself—down that way you only survive with your fists, or a smart mouth. And I've got my fists. Yeah?"

"An ostler? Were you following in his footsteps?"

"Oh, yeah! I love horses, I do. After all this is over, you know what I'm going to do? Get into horse racing. Bloody love all that."

Wilfred smiled, hugging himself.

"What'll you do after the war, Jack?"

"Go back to the farm. I don't really know anything else, truth be told."

"That sounds nice. A farm. Don't get many of them in East London!" Wilfred laughed and Jack joined in.

"I don't suppose you do, mate!"

"I'll tell you what," Wilfred dropped his voice to a cheeky whisper, "I'll not be seeing any more bloody fighting once I'm back home. No army for me!"

"Have you done any fighting since you've been in?" Jack brushed biscuit crumbs off the front of his jacket. "Ever been to…to the front?"

Wilfred shook his head keenly. "Not fighting, but I went out on a supply run a couple of weeks back. I don't ever want to go back and I wasn't there a half-hour!"

Jack tried not to wince. "We're lucky being here, aren't we? Much nicer than my last place — even if the officers still bark just as loud."

Even if my mattress stinks of piss.

"The noise up at the front — you can hear it from miles away." Wilfred shuddered. "Let's stick to our castle and our horses, even the loony ones!"

Jack clinked his mug against Wilfred's and they sat together in companionable silence, watching the activity in the yard. A clatter of hooves brought in a groom riding an officer's horse.

"I take it you ride?"

"I fall off more than I ride!" Wilfred laughed, nodding toward the groom. "And that one you're looking after, he won't let me anywhere near! Put me on a seaside donkey and I'll drop on my head."

"You should give it a go." Jack put his empty mug on the windowsill behind him. "Not on a donkey, I mean, but on one of the horses here. Maybe I could teach you? I've done it with kids from the village before now."

Wilfred looked at him. "You'd be taking on a bloody hopeless case, mate!"

"No, no, come on!" Jack stood and held his hand out to Wilfred. "Which is the sweetest, quietest horse here?"

"The sweetest happens to be one of the tallest." He cringed. "Further to drop!"

"You can't be nervous, Wilf. You've got to trust them. They're easier to handle anyway then, even just to comb their mane."

Jack put his hands in his pockets, looking out across the yard. One of the grooms larked about on a mounting block, jumping off the top step, arms and legs stretched out like a star.

"Tell you what, if it's heights that bother you—just for starters, why don't I give you a piggyback? It's what I do with the kids."

Wilfred frowned, clearly considering the unexpected offer. Then he said, "Is this a trick? You gonna drop me in the shit pile?"

"Why would I do that?" Willing to overlook what had passed between them earlier, Jack said, "You've been a mate to me since I arrived. I'd be a wally if I took to flinging you in the manure."

"Go on then, the gaffer don't mind!" He and Jack looked as one at the NCO who was laughing at the groom jesting on the mounting block. That gaffer didn't seem to mind much, which was probably exactly why Queenie enjoyed such freedom among his fellows.

"Right, come on then!" Jack was beaming. He could lark with the fellows as well as anyone, no matter what his father might have said. "Hop up onto the bale."

"Can't go unprepared!" Wilfred stood and bounded off into the tack room, leaving Jack to wonder what exactly he was doing. It was almost a relief that he didn't emerge carrying a saddle and bridle, though he had donned a tin helmet that was an inch or so too big and wobbled atop his skull, while a crop was tucked beneath his arm.

"Oh, you're a card, Wilf!"

Laughing, Jack positioned himself in front of the bale and leaned slightly forward with his bottom sticking out.

"Jump on!"

At the command, Wilf gingerly climbed onto Jack's back, clearly still not convinced he wasn't about to be dropped bottom-first onto the ground. He put his arms around Jack's neck and his legs around his waist. "Giddy up, horse!"

Jack held Wilf's legs tight. He was surprisingly heavy for a small lad, but Jack gamely walked into the yard with his burden.

"Ready?" And Jack went off at a jog.

Wilfred guffawed and Jack treated him to his repertoire of horse impressions, neighing and snorting like he did with the children at home.

"Faster, Wilf?" Jack was breathless but his exhilaration drove him on.

"Yeah, go on, let's have a gallop!" Wilfred tapped the crop to Jack's bottom lightly, his laughter growing louder.

Jack jolted at the touch, an image in his mind not of Wilfred, but Captain Thorne. The crop left a warm sting across Jack's flesh, but he pushed away all thought of the handsome officer. It wouldn't do to think of him now.

Jack tossed his head from side to side, so his hair shone like a glossy mane in the late afternoon sunlight. He neighed and careered at speed across the yard, galloping around the other grooms, who had stopped to laugh and cheer.

Wilfred clutched Jack's hair and clung on tighter.

"Into battle!" Wilfred waved the whip above his head. "Look out, Hun, we're coming for you!"

Jack made a trumpeting noise, trying to force his mind not to dwell on the captain at each switch of the crop in Wilfred's hand. He had to keep his feelings at bay. He would hide them behind his high-spirited gallivanting, happy as a child.

As they charged around the laughter died away, the claps slowed to nothing, but Jack barely noticed. Wilfred continued to howl and hoot and wave the crop, his arm tight around Jack's shoulder until he turned for one last lap of the yard.

There, one gloved hand gripping Apollo's bridle and the other bunched in a fist resting on his hip, was Captain Thorne. His face was pale with fury, as white as Apollo's coat, and his mouth was a tight, straight line.

"Don't stop on my account." His dark eyes moved over the yard, taking in each and every face there. Yet his voice was light, worryingly so. "Did I miss the announcement, chaps?"

Jack let Wilfred slip carefully to the ground. He went to rub his shoulder, but saluted instead.

"Captain Thorne, sir."

He was the man's groom, he should approach and take the horse. But it was as if his boots were filled with lead.

'The grooms here are a shower of layabouts, rascals and hooligans. Don't let them draw you into their ways.'

Jack remembered Thorne's warning. And he'd not listened. And now the captain's silent rage was aimed at Trooper Woodvine.

A dozen other hands darted up in salute but Thorne was addressing Jack, *his* man.

"I assume, since you're all no longer working, that the war is over. I'll ask again—" He didn't blink, his eyes boring into Jack. "Did I miss the announcement?"

Jack's mouth was almost too dry to speak.

"No...no, sir."

"Well, then, we find ourselves once again in an unfortunate situation." Thorne turned his attention to Wilfred, who had been doing his best to hide behind Jack. "Trooper Cole. You forgot to saddle your steed, bad form for a groom. Before you fall into your filthy blankets tonight, I want every saddle in the tack room polished and gleaming, and I mean *everything*. Get to it, and you might be done by midnight. Dismissed, Cole!"

Jack watched Wilfred shamble away, almost tripping over his own feet. The captain was staring at Jack. He could feel it on his skin, like a scald from a jet of steam. With trepidation, he looked up at him.

"Woodvine, come with me. The rest of you, back to work—playtime is over!"

Thorne strode away, leading Apollo along beside him.

For a moment, Jack hesitated. His hands were shaking. He was, he realized with shame, frightened. But he couldn't resist the pull of the captain. Even with the threat of punishment looming, Jack was in his thrall.

"After a ride, any mount needs his water!" They were heading to the pump, Jack knew, and Thorne drew the whip that was ever-present in his boot. He gestured toward the muddy ground and told him, "Kneel."

Jack's legs had locked. He couldn't sink to his knees. He merely trembled, staring at the sodden earth.

"It's… It's muddy, sir."

"Troo—" Thorne was silenced by the sudden rearing of Apollo, who gave a snort of utter terror, his rear hooves scraping back and sending his forelegs up with such a force that he nearly dragged the captain clear off his feet. The horse's great head snapped this way and that in his efforts to escape, his strong figure towering over them, nostrils flaring and eyes rolling.

Queenie stopped dead in his tracks where he had just rounded the corner of the building. He held up his hands and backed away out of sight, but Apollo wasn't so easily calmed and still yanked at the reins, despite his master's efforts to calm him.

"Settle down!" Thorne's arm was almost wrenched clean out of the socket as his mount fell forward then reared back again with such force that the horse came close to tottering over backward.

Seeing Apollo in distress again, Jack's sense of duty defeated whatever terror had risen up within him.

"Shhhh, handsome fellow… Shhhh… Calm now."

Avoiding looking directly at Apollo, Jack took a sidestep and grabbed the reins. His cooing and clicking seemed to calm the horse, who plunged his feet back down, but at something—was Queenie still there behind the wall?—Apollo reared again, almost taking Jack with him.

"It's your friend Jack!"

And at this, Apollo finally landed, blowing through his nostrils, a chuckle in his throat as he lifted his feet and put them down again. Jack rested his forehead against Apollo's cheek, still whispering to the horse, stroking him until he was calm. Jack smiled, and when he turned away from Apollo he found Captain Thorne staring at him.

"Sorry, sir. You asked me to kneel. I... My legs wouldn't—" With his free hand Jack rubbed at his shoulder. Thorne was silent for a long moment, his gaze fixed on Jack, lips slightly parted. Then he turned to stroke Apollo's nose and tucked the whip back into his boot.

"It was an ord—" Thorne blinked. He drew in a deep breath and looked to Jack once more, his brow furrowing with concern. "Are you hurt, Jack?"

Trooper Woodvine blinked into Captain Thorne's dark eyes. *Jack?*

"It's nothing, really. I passed the Army medical, so it can't be a problem, sir. It's just...I broke my shoulder. I was thrown from a horse, you see, and sometimes—but it's nothing. Honest. Worse things happen at sea and all that."

"Why the devil didn't you say? You can't possibly work with a horse like Apollo if you're struggling with injury. Get off up to your quarters and rest that shoulder. I'll have to think about this, Trooper."

"But—it's not... He came to me this morning, with my hands full of water, and he drank from them, soft as a foal. He... He..." Jack gave up trying to speak. He'd been given another order, to follow, not ignore. "Yes, sir. Sorry, Captain Thorne. I'll go upstairs now."

"Dismissed, Trooper Woodvine. We shall discuss your position later."

I don't want to leave.

But farmer's sons with gammy shoulders get found out in the end. Jack stared at the ground as he made his way across the stable yard, the other grooms keeping a wide berth. Up the rickety stairs he went to their quarters.

Jack threw himself face down on the bed, the dusty smell of the old pillow tickling his nose. He couldn't lie on his back or he'd see the photographs from home that he'd stuck on the wall. His mother with her frizzy fringe and leg-of-mutton sleeves, fashionable when she had posed for the photograph over twenty years ago. Woodvine Farm with Jack and his father stood before it, Jack in short trousers, beaming. Jack and his friend, at a photographer's studio at the seaside, straw hats and striped boating blazers, grinning with the bucket and spade that were props for child sitters. That same friend leaning against a chair of gnarled wood in a studio alone, the name of his ship on his cap tally. Jack on horseback—the horse that had thrown him when a thunderstorm had rolled in.

He didn't know how long he stayed there, his face buried against the blankets in that bed where a dead man had once wept and pissed away his last night before he was thrown into hell. He would soon be sent away too, he knew, because Captain Thorne didn't want a man with an injured shoulder anywhere near his horse, because Jack Woodvine couldn't follow orders or remember to salute or —

"Trooper Woodvine?"

"Captain."

Jack pushed himself up and turned to see Captain Thorne, incongruous in this grotty place. Jack's hand returned to his shoulder for a moment.

"I…I don't mind, you know, if you think it's best that I don't… If you want me transferred." The sentiment rang hollow. He did mind. He minded a lot.

"I was young once myself. I'm not so old now, you know. Trooper Cole has been relieved of his punishment." Thorne took off his cap and perched on the edge of Jack's bed. "You'll hear later there was a major push against us last night, we lost a lot of lads in the bombardment. Perhaps I was a little hard on you both. One shouldn't be emotional about such things… Keep a clear head and all that."

Despite the import of the captain's words, images played in Jack's head at the proximity of the captain, at the very thought of this man being on his bed. Holding him, pleasuring— No, he mustn't think of such things.

Jack's gaze flickered to his photograph collection. He would think about his friend Billy instead. Billy might be miles from a trench, but the sea wasn't any safer.

"Will…will we have to go to the front? To make up for the…the losses?"

"For now we shall stay safe in our castle." He set his cap down on the blanket and looked around the room. "Be honest with me about this shoulder, Trooper. Can you truly manage the work? If the answer's no I can have you moved onto the officers' household staff."

"I wouldn't want to be any trouble, Captain. It's... It twinges sometimes, that's all. And as time passes it does it less and less. It just needs a rub, that's all."

"I'd very much like to keep you, Trooper. Apollo has precious few friends." Thorne began to peel off the leather gloves. "Let's have a look at this shoulder then, Woodvine, don't be shy."

The captain was so close to Jack that his elbow accidentally brushed Thorne's thigh as he sat up.

"Let me just..."

Jack shrugged himself out of his jacket, not daring to look at the captain. He unbuttoned his shirt, willing his hands not to shake. As he skimmed it off, he caught Captain Thorne's gaze. His eye had fallen to Jack's hairless chest, taking in the slight muscles of his pectorals, his hardened nipples. The gaze went lower, to what could be seen of Jack's stomach above his high-waisted trousers. It had a gentle curve — fat laid down by his convalescence. Jack well knew that his body was nothing like the captain's, honed and muscular. He felt ashamed.

"I'll go on my front, sir?"

Thorne swallowed and replied, "I think where you already are will suffice, Trooper. Show me where it's painful?"

Jack took Thorne's hand and brought it up to his shoulder. It wasn't wrong. It wasn't strange at all, for Captain Thorne to take an interest in his groom's injury. It might, however, look a little unusual for anyone who happened to walk in.

And God willing, no one would.

"Just — just there, sir. The doctor said that when the shoulder broke, it scarred the muscle that was attached to it — it knots up sometimes. He said, '*You just have to knead it out, like bread.'* Can you… Can you feel…? It's a little lump, just there — under your middle finger."

Thorne's hand tensed as though Jack's skin was ice, then his fingers straightened until they were hovering above the shoulder. The captain cleared his throat and pressed his finger down against the lump, his handsome face clouding with concern. "Should I — Forgive me, Trooper, you're probably quite capable, but would you like me to help?"

"It's easier if someone else does it. You can do it harder than I can — perhaps."

"You'd better lie down, after all."

Jack rolled onto his front, this time his knee accidentally brushing the captain's. He rested his head on his pillow, his face turned toward Captain Thorne. He regretted it and wondered if he should look away, but there was something in the officer's expression that Jack could not tear his glance from. His concern — for his groom, for Jack.

"When Apollo was a youngster, he had the most dreadful health problems." Captain Thorne's hand returned to Jack's shoulder and began to knead the spot he had indicated, the soft palm moving with a firm assurance. "I had to massage *his* shoulder every morning and every evening or the poor chap couldn't move. He was set for the knacker's yard, but I was a determined sort of fellow. Our veterinarian believed I must have magic hands."

And the captain's face went suddenly very red indeed, his gaze dropping to watch his own hands work.

Jack's eyelids half-closed. He could feel the blood begin to flow again as the muscle unknotted.

"You did well with Apollo, Captain Thorne." He smiled, beginning to move slightly with the captain's touch. "I think…you must…have magic hands…sir."

The last word came out on a sigh.

"This is a fairytale castle, there must be *some* magic here somewhere."

"Well, I don't have a beanstalk, so it must be in your hands!"

Jack grinned at the captain. Was it possible that the stern man's eyes were dancing? That the man was actually smiling? Jack decided that he could afford to be cheeky.

"Did you really mean, sir, to drench me? Or just make me think that you would—to teach me a lesson? If I'd knelt, Captain Thorne, what would you have done?"

"Well, I wouldn't have consented to be your bride, Trooper!" Thorne actually laughed then, a bright, loud laugh that lit his entire face.

It took Jack by surprise, and after a moment's pause he laughed as well, trying not to shake too much in his hilarity and disturb the movement of the captain's touch on his body.

"I don't think I'll ever make much of a husband, sir."

"What age are you, Trooper? Too young to be thinking such sensible thoughts, surely?" Then, even as he continued to speak, Thorne's other hand came to rest on Jack's opposite shoulder, rubbing that too.

"Two-and-twenty. A month ago."

The captain's strong hands were eliciting bliss and Jack completely forgot that he was still facing him. His lips fell open as he gasped with pleasure.

"Twenty-two." Thorne's voice was lower, quieter. "If I had my way, I'd send every one of you young lads home. You haven't lived your lives yet."

"And have you lived?" Jack watched the captain through lowered lashes. "You cannot be so old—I doubt you're much beyond thirty."

"I stand on the cusp of thirty-one years on earth, Jack, and if I ever see England again, I intend to try to get to thirty-two one day."

"Then you're a young man still." Jack, so intensely happy, reached toward Thorne and patted him on the knee. "We'll see England again, I know it."

"If we do, I shall make you a promise, Woodvine." Thorne smiled, his gaze gentle when it settled on Jack's. "I'll take you along to the Oval and show you what real cricket looks like. And we'll toast every bloody one of those lads who lost their lives last night."

Jack bit his lip. How selfish he felt, reveling in the captain's touch, his sweet words, forgetting that even now they would still be burying the boys in makeshift graves. He didn't want to acknowledge the tide of tears that was blurring his vision, or the faces of the boys from his class at school, who would never see Shropshire again.

"We will, Captain Thorne. We bloody well will. We'll toast them all twice over, sir."

"I shall hold you to that, soldier!" Thorne nodded and sat back, lifting his hands from Jack's shoulders. "I've put Apollo in his stable but if you're up to it, he'd appreciate a rubdown. And I'll put in a request for a new mattress. This one appears to have known better days."

"Thank you, sir."

He patted the young man's shoulder and stood, peering up at Jack's photos before, perhaps suspecting this was an intrusion of sorts, he turned his attention to the less personal matter of books. With a murmur of approval Thorne scooped up a volume of poetry and opened it, sending a photograph fluttering down to rest atop the bed.

Jack had been buttoning his shirt. He grabbed for the photograph, but not fast enough.

It was the sort of photograph that could be bought cheaply from the sort of shops that traded from the sort of dark alleyways that were used as latrines. A young man of about Jack's age was kneeling on a vaguely tatty chaise longue, his trousers and underpants dragged down, his bottom exposed for all to see. In the foreground was a figure, a silhouette really, their face turned from the camera—woman or man, it was impossible to tell. They held up their arm, a whip in their hand. The image had been colorized, the blush on the young man's face matching the red stripe across his insubordinate buttocks.

Thorne said nothing but his mouth moved very slightly, teeth just worrying at his lower lip for a moment. He kept his eyes on the photo, then Jack saw his Adam's apple rise and fall with the effort of a dry-mouthed swallow as he held out his hand to return the picture to its owner.

Jack examined the captain's face, waiting for the words to come. *Unnatural desires.* But they didn't. Instead, Captain Thorne looked up from the photograph and gazed at Jack, his mouth fallen slightly open. And as they stared at each other—into each other—Jack felt as if his world had stopped. Jack saw something in Captain Thorne's eyes—a question, a reply and a promise.

"I swim at dusk each night, Trooper Woodvine." With that, Thorne replaced his cap on his head and picked up his gloves. "Once you've brushed Apollo, settle him in his stable. We're expecting a storm, I don't want him out in the paddock tonight."

"Yes, sir."

Jack lowered his gaze, but found himself confronted with a sight he hadn't expected, though he should have. Thorne tried to hide it as he pulled on the hem of his tunic, but the shape of his desire was all too obvious in the tight cut of his breeches.

"At ease—" Thorne laughed and flushed again. "You already are. Well, good afternoon, soldier."

With a brief nod he strode from the room and Jack heard him at the top of the stairs, already back in character with a bark at some unfortunate—"Get that bloody saddle out of the mud before I have you dunked in it, lad!"

'I swim at dusk each night.'

And so, Jack thought as he remembered Thorne's words, *shall I.*

Chapter Six

Queenie held court over dinner. Jack, sitting between Wilf and Bryn, wasn't intimidated. Whatever gossip Queenie thought he might have on Jack, it was nothing compared to what Captain Thorne had on Captain Marsh.

But thank goodness no one had come up to the grooms' quarters. *Imagine…a topless trooper, being massaged by a captain.*

A flush went over Jack's face as he thought of it, but he salted it away. *Never think about that – any of that – among the boys, never let it show.*

Heavy losses at the front, Captain Thorne had said. And though he'd put a gloss on it, it was obvious their own call to the front might not be too far away. The other boys told tales of officers who had been in the trenches and come back. Captain Thorne's name was often mentioned among them, but they made it sound like a miracle, not a possibility.

For some time after his accident, Jack had been tormented by the memory of his fall from the horse.

Not the pain that came after, but the second that played out in his mind as hours as he fell and the grip on his heart told him that he might die. Soon, he might receive his marching orders, and soon —

What if I never took the chance to go down to the stream?

And so he would go to the captain. He had to.

After dinner, Jack retrieved his pajamas from the tack room. He made a final check on Apollo then crossed the stable yard on his way to the paddock. He could already feel the cool water on his skin, could already see the naked captain in the clear water, could already feel... His heart was racing. He had to be calm. It wouldn't do...no, it wouldn't do at all for anyone to know, to look at his face and know.

"I'll get you smoking one day, Jack!"

Someone jumped down behind him from a wagon. It was Wilfred.

"Where are you off to, squire, this time of the evening?"

"Hello, Wilf. Just out for some fresh air. It's stuffy in our quarters."

Wilfred lit one of his ever-present roll-ups, ensuring that fresh air was but a memory for them both.

"Nice time of day for a walk, isn't it?"

Jack couldn't go a step farther.

"Look, Wilf, I'm so sorry about earlier. I...I had no idea..."

"No harm done, mate." He took a deep drag on the cigarette. "I'm just making a start on the first bleedin' saddle and in he struts, nice as you like and says no hard feelings! I tell you, these posh lads aren't all there."

Wilfred looked up at the sky, a deep orange glow on the horizon almost a fire in the distance. "There's a storm rolling in. Horses'll be making a right bloody racket tonight!"

Jack scuffed the toe of his boot on a loose stone. He rubbed absentmindedly at his shoulder.

"They've all been brought in, haven't they?" He stared along the path to the paddock, picturing Captain Thorne at his bath. "We…we don't need to go back to the paddock?"

"Got them in before tea so it's an easy night for us, mate!" Wilfred took another draw on the roll-up. "Feet up and a good kip!"

"That's all right, then." Jack forced himself to turn back toward the stable block. "Early bed for the boys!"

* * * *

Jack must've fallen asleep, although he couldn't remember doing so. The storm was close now, rain hammering on the panes, leaking in through the cracks in the glass and splashing against his face. He lay on his back, eyes wide, watching the flashes of lightning on the whitewashed walls, counting until the rumbles. Nearer…nearer…

Snorts and whinnies drifted up from the stables and Jack wondered who else, apart from himself and the horses, was awake.

Jack's first instinct was to go to Apollo and stay there as long as the horse needed him—all night if he had to. He pulled his boots and his jacket on over his pajamas. Then he yanked the blanket off his bed, took up the pillow and went as quietly as he could past the beds of sleeping grooms. Not that his stealth was necessary. Everything was drowned out by the storm.

He had to run across the yard, splashing through the fast-forming puddles to reach Apollo's stable. Although it was late at night, regular flashes of lightning illuminated his way.

As he came up to the stable door, he had the strangest idea that someone was singing. Not Queenie, it couldn't be. The voice was soft and deep.

Then there was a pistol in Jack's face.

"I think we've had quite enough of this mischief, don't you?" Jack was sure it was Captain Thorne's voice, but only a forearm — a *naked* forearm — and hand were visible in the darkness of the stable. "Are you here to retrieve your glove or leave my mount with another *innocent* scratch?"

Jack tried to raise his hands but couldn't risk dropping his meager bedding in the wet.

"Sir," he whispered. "It's me, Trooper Woodvine."

"Woodvine?" The gun was lowered immediately. "What the devil are you doing out here, soldier?"

"To check on Apollo. The storm, you see. I've brought half my bed down with me. I was going to stay with him."

He heard Thorne give a soft laugh and admit, "I had the same idea. Poor old Apollo's going to be crowded out of his own stable at this rate!"

"How is he?" Jack squeezed around the stable door as Thorne opened it for him. "Is your foot any easier?"

Just then the stable was lit with a bright lightning flash, so lurid that everything was tinged with green and purple. And right in front of him, illuminated only for a moment in that brightness, was Captain Thorne, his torso bare.

"Apollo is surprisingly calm, and I managed not to get stung tonight." There was a change in the air then, the captain stepping away with a rustle of straw. "And caught no poetic troopers hiding in the foliage. How's that shoulder?"

"It feels much better, actually. You took out all the stiffness. I suppose you really do have magic hands." Jack threw down his bedding and stroked Apollo, whispering to him. The thought of the captain's hands on him returned to his mind and it filled his body with warmth.

But Thorne seemed distant.

"I did want to come to the stream, you know." It was all that Jack could think of to say, his voice heavy with the weight of his yearning.

"Look, Woodvine, I was out of line this afternoon, I realize that. I was still in the air after news of the casualties. Some men are—" Thorne paused and Jack heard him take a deep breath. "I'm not some sort of odd fellow. I hope there was no misunderstanding."

Lightning flashed again, showing Jack that the captain had turned his back to him. Why had he become so unreachable?

"What could I have possibly misunderstood?" Jack leaned his face to Apollo's cheek. "How were you out of line? I liked it, all right. I liked feeling your hands on me. There. Throw me out of the regiment, sir, send me to the Glasshouse, give me a dishonorable discharge, but it's true. I have *unnatural desires*, sir, but—but it's how the Lord made me. And I *was* going to go to the stream, because you asked me to and because I…because I…"

The thunder rumbled so loudly overhead that had Jack said anything, neither of them would have heard.

He turned back to the horse, whispering, calming him. What had passed between them surely hadn't been in Jack's mind. Surely it had been real.

"I wouldn't want you to come down to the stream because an officer requested it." Another sound of movement suggested that Thorne had turned once more, and his voice was just a little louder, closer. "I hoped you might want to."

Jack stepped away from Apollo. He couldn't see Thorne in the darkness but he knew he was there. His heat and scent were not easily hidden.

Jack threw off his jacket and started to undo the shirt of his pajamas. The rain was even heavier now, hissing against the ground, rattling through the gutters, the rich smell of wet earth rising about them.

"I want you, Thorne."

"I'm your captain." Thorne's voice was low, breathless, suffused with longing. Then there was another sound, the rasp of a lighter striking, and there, in the darkness, glowed the dim flame of a lantern. It flickered and flared brighter as Thorne closed the stable door, shutting out the night.

"And I'm your groom. I'm your Jack."

The stable wasn't spacious but now it seemed even smaller now that Jack was standing just a few feet from Thorne. The captain looked away and reached up to attach the lantern to a hook in the ceiling, the intimate flame illuminating him, clad only in breeches, the usually immaculate man looking slightly, gloriously disordered amid the straw.

"I don't fraternize, Trooper. Never have. It doesn't befit an officer." Yet still there came no order to return to quarters, no admonishment. Still those dark eyes blazed into Jack's own, filled with fire.

"What if…what if we had met some other way? If there'd never been this wretched war. And you'd — you'd come to Shropshire. To buy a horse from my farm. And we met, and we talked, and you weren't an officer, and you weren't my captain, and we…and we…" Jack moved a step closer, dropping the shirt of his pajamas in the straw. "There's a very nice stream on the farm, utterly private. We could have… There would have been nothing to stop us."

"I don't believe in unnatural desires, Woodvine." There was certainty in those words, yet just for a moment Thorne's gaze dropped to take in Jack's naked torso. "Our so-called leaders have opened hell itself, the world's ending every bloody day, boys fresh out of school blown to kingdom come for the sake of what? Six feet of mud and a squabble that was never ours to begin with. *That's* unnatural."

Then he reached out and asked in a voice that was low with desire, "Will you stay?"

Jack nodded, taking Thorne's strong hand. With a gentle movement of his arm the captain drew Jack closer until they were just inches apart beneath the lantern's dancing light, the thunder crashing somewhere in another world.

Slowly, Jack laid his fingertips on Thorne's chest, staring into the coal-dark eyes that gazed down on him. He was aware of Thorne's every breath, every heartbeat. He trailed his touch across that muscular body until he cupped Thorne's strong jaw. He tried to move his face nearer to Thorne's but he stopped, hesitant.

"Thorne… I've never kissed anyone before. I don't know what to do."

"Are you suggesting, Woodvine, that I'm some sort of tart?"

Jack's hand slipped from the captain's face.

"No! Never, I didn't say that, sir."

"Forgive my dry humor, I only meant to tease." Thorne lifted his free hand to stroke Jack's face and smiled a devilish smile, quite unlike any expression Jack had seen him wear previously. "Alas, I've been lacking in opportunities to be a tart."

"But you…" Jack returned his hand to Thorne's torso. "You could have anyone for the asking."

"I was a sensible sort at school." The captain gave a pantomimed pout, sliding his hand into Jack's hair. "Then I joined up and how does one even *begin* — A few fumbles do not a tart make."

He drew Jack closer, close enough that he could finally press his lips to Jack's cheek.

Jack reached around Thorne's waist, holding him. He followed Thorne's lead, trying to kiss his cheek, but his lips could only reach his determined chin. Thorne gave a soft chuckle and lowered his head to capture Jack's lips with his own, murmuring a gentle encouragement.

Jack sighed against Thorne's mouth, the captain's full, soft lips opening a little under his own. Jack was overwhelmed not just by Thorne's scent but by his taste, so intimate, so warm. He felt the softness of Thorne's tongue as it tenderly swept his mouth, teasing Jack to part his lips farther.

He pulled away, laying his head on Thorne's shoulder, his mouth against Thorne's neck. He swept his hands over his captain's perfect torso, all the while very aware that Thorne's desire was pressing against him.

"I made myself a bit of a bed in the straw. It's yours tonight." Thorne whispered into his hair, glancing up at a violent crash of thunder, though Apollo didn't seem to notice. "You need to keep that shoulder of yours rested."

"Don't go... I don't want to sleep on my own — *Captain R. B. Thorne.*"

He looked up at the man in his arms, impossibly handsome, but for this moment, his. That devilish look was there again, and slowly Thorne lowered his mouth to Jack's. Softly at first, but as another roll of thunder split the air Jack yielded to Thorne and to his passion. Their kiss was eager, desperate, almost clumsy in its fervor. The force of Jack's ardor, of Thorne's, left him breathless, and it was only the captain's strong arms around him that stopped Jack from falling.

The captain was the first to move, his arms still around Jack's waist as he eased them both down into the straw, covered as it was by his own blankets. The kiss didn't lessen but grew more intense, if that was even possible, Thorne's tongue moving against his own, their bodies tight together. Jack was atop him now, that strong torso beneath his own, the hardness of Thorne's erection pressing insistently against him.

As Jack kissed, he sank his fingers into Thorne's thick, dark hair, the spicy scent of his pomade headier than ever. Thorne ran his hand down Jack's back, leaving a trail of fire on Jack's skin. He skimmed his hand over the fabric of Jack's pajamas, caressing, feathering his touch to the dimple just before the rise of his buttocks, and swept over the curve of Jack's bottom. Jack moved his hips against Thorne as though he would buck like an excitable colt, but Thorne stilled him, seizing Jack's buttock in his powerful grip.

Jack slipped his hand from the captain's hair and twined his fingers with Thorne's where they lay over his buttock, encouraging Thorne's grip to be even firmer. When Thorne answered, clenching the flesh through the fabric, Jack moaned into their kiss, a stifled cry of pleasure and need.

In reply, the captain slid his free hand up into Jack's hair, holding their mouths together so the kiss couldn't end, the gentlest of murmurs coaxing him on. Then Thorne released Jack's buttock and, with their hands still together, he lifted his palm and brought it down on Jack's arse in a firm slap.

As heat burned across Jack's buttock, lightning flashed again, leaving him with the most intense awareness of being alive. He was exquisitely poised on the brink of pleasure and pain, all senses alert. The slap had done nothing to satiate him. It only made his yearning all the keener.

"Harder," he breathed.

"Harder," Thorne growled, stilling his hand, "*Captain.*"

"Harder, Captain Thorne — sir."

Thorne's hand came down again, harder this time, his palm landing against Jack's buttock with a resounding *slap*.

"Thank you, Captain." In gratitude, Jack ran his mouth over Thorne's neck and across his chest, his tongue darting out to taste the hardness of his nipple. He took the tight bud in his mouth.

Captain Thorne — *Captain R. B. Thorne* — so perfectly turned out, so proper, arched his back and parted his lips to let out a moan of sheer, wanton pleasure. He slapped his hand down again and Jack felt his fingers pulling at the thin pajamas, roughly pushing them down to expose his bottom.

Jack redoubled his efforts, grazing his teeth gently against Thorne's nipple, his bare skin trembling in anticipation of the captain's touch. He pressed his hips against Thorne's, shifting until their erections were against each other, only two layers of fabric between them.

The captain's moans grew more breathless. His hand lifted again but it didn't fall, the moment of anticipation teased out until it was as exquisite as it was unbearable. Still Thorne clutched at Jack's hair, his sculpted back arching up from the blankets.

"Please, Captain — I beg you!"

A delicious shiver began to run through Jack, his slight body trembling against Thorne's muscular figure as it arched from the makeshift bed. Jack ran his hand down Thorne's side, caressing the toned flesh that strained to Jack's touch.

"You'll wait, Trooper, until your captain's ready." And still the hand didn't fall, still Jack longed for that sweet sensation.

"If you wish, my Captain...my handsome Captain." Jack returned his mouth to Thorne's nipple, his teeth a little more insistent. He settled his wandering hand on the captain's waist as he steadied himself for what must come. And Captain Thorne thundered his hand down onto Jack's bared arse as a flash of lightning lit the stable. It was hard, sharp and a dream come true.

Jack trembled into bliss, into a whiteness brighter than any thunderbolt. A tightness that had been building in the very core of his being unraveled in a moment and sent him hurtling into ecstasy. He dropped back onto Thorne's chest, panting for breath, a sheen of perspiration glossing his skin.

He felt the captain's hand stroke over his bottom, tender and gentle, then Thorne's voice was ice as he asked, "Did I give you permission to orgasm, soldier?"

Jack raised his face from Thorne's chest, blinking languorously. A lock of hair had fallen over his forehead. His lips dropped open.

"No, sir, you didn't, sir. Sorry, Captain."

Thorne's eyes were gentle in the lamplight and he quirked the hint of a smile before he looked pointedly down toward his own chest. "As you were, Trooper. You have a job to finish."

Jack took Thorne's nipple in his mouth, kissing, suckling, teasing with his tongue. He stroked the other, tweaking gently. But, responding to another moan from Thorne, another arch of his back, Jack twisted the nipple between finger and thumb.

Looking up again into Thorne's dark eyes, Jack whispered, "I want to give you pleasure, sir, as you have given me."

"You have a mischievous look, Woodvine," he said. "What's on your mind, soldier?"

The hand that had so obediently waited at Thorne's waist spoke for Jack as he dipped his fingertips under the waistband of Thorne's breeches.

"Do I have permission to touch you, sir?"

"Granted, Trooper." He brushed their lips together, the captain's tongue just touching Jack's. "Make sure I enjoy it."

Jack broke away from Thorne's mouth, pushing himself up to straddle the captain's firm thighs. Meeting his gaze, Jack gave him a salute. Not a cheeky, lopsided salute—a salute worthy of any parade ground.

His chest rising and falling with each breath, Jack ran his hands slowly about Thorne's stomach, the muscles twitching at his touch. His eyes darting between Thorne's gaze and his own hands, Jack unfastened the top button of Thorne's breeches. He felt Thorne shift beneath him, but Jack remained firm.

Another button, and another, until they were unfastened. Jack carefully peeled back the fabric and Captain Thorne's erection rose up before him.

He stroked through the clustering dark hair and gently brushed his fingertips against the impressive erection. Thorne shifted again, touching Jack's shoulders, combing fingers through Jack's hair. Jack took the erection in a light grip, gradually tightening his hold until Thorne's mouth fell open and he moaned. Jack stroked, awkward at first, but soon he found a rhythm, which Thorne's hips began to match.

"Does this please you, Captain Thorne?"

"Don't be bloody impertinent in front of Apollo," Thorne warned him. "You'll go over my damned knee."

Jack's hips jolted a little at the thought of it. How he adored his captain, who at this moment was struggling to look stern as waves of pleasure crossed and recrossed his face.

"Yes, sir—I will go over your knee whenever you wish."

Thorne's voice was stolen by a moan. He pushed his hips hard, urging Jack's hand on faster, arching again.

Jack found pleasure of his own in bringing Thorne to his bliss. His wrist had become a blur as he worked his fist and Jack pressed his legs ever more tightly against

Thorne's to stop the man's bucking from flinging him off. He wasn't going to be thrown by *this* stallion.

Where had that immaculate soldier gone, with his clipped tones and his sharp manner? What had become of the captain who seemed so *together*, so collected and proper as he went about his duties?

He was still here beneath the abandoned moans and straining muscles, but for now he had truly allowed himself to leave duty behind.

Thorne's hips rose from the blankets, and with a deep cry he fountained over Jack's hand.

"Jack — " It was a gasp and Thorne closed his hand on Jack's shoulder, bringing him into that strong embrace. "My darling Jack…"

Entirely unresisting, Jack fell into Thorne's powerful arms. He rested his cheek on Thorne's shoulder and for several minutes, while the storm still raged on outside, they were at peace. Jack's whole world was a bed of straw in a low-lit stable, and the warmth of Thorne's body.

He didn't move when Thorne drew a blanket over their entwined bodies, the only sounds those of their breathing and the occasional movement of Apollo's hooves as he too rested.

"My beautiful Jack," Thorne murmured, stroking his chestnut hair. "Thank you…"

Jack gazed at his captain, his eyelashes touching Thorne's firm jaw as he blinked in the soft glow of the lantern.

"Me?" Jack laughed softly. "I'm not beautiful, Thorne. But you… You are the most handsome man I've ever seen. I'm so… I'm so puny."

"That's nonsense," he murmured. "You weren't so puny piggybacking that lad around earlier."

Jack blushed at the mention of his transgression, and Thorne must've seen as his gentle smile intensified.

"I do that at home all the time, with the children from the village, in case you were wondering. I pretend to be a horse, and sometimes it helps them learn to ride, but honestly, it's just fun." Jack bit his lip, a giggle in his throat. "You'll think me a softy for that, I'm sure!"

"We all need help on occasion, even battle-hardened old captains." The captain glanced toward Apollo. "A couple of years after I left Sandhurst, I took a fall and smashed my leg. I hardly dared look at a horse while I was convalescing, the thought of riding one left me terrified."

He gave a shy smile and reached up to ruffle one hand back through his pomaded hair. "And then I met this weak, angry little gray foal who was bound for the knackers and what else could I do but take him in? Apollo and I got our confidence together."

Jack lifted his head, staring at Thorne in amazement.

"I would never have guessed! If only I'd known you then, I should have given you a piggyback too. Which leg was it?"

"The left. It healed, but—" He laughed a little shyly. "My father's a born horseman and was convinced I just needed a push to get back to it. And though I would never have expected it, he was right. I just had to find the courage to try."

Jack reached under the blanket for Thorne's left leg. He stroked over the tight breeches and felt the taut muscle under his fingers. It was a wonder that a limb so perfect could once have been broken.

"My mother put me on a pony when I was three. Maybe I was too little, but it was her way, you see.

Horses were second nature to her." Jack was aware of the sad note in his voice. "She had gypsy blood."

"When did you lose your mother?"

"I shouldn't have mentioned…" Jack paused for a moment. He hadn't wanted to speak of anything sad. But he was safe in Thorne's arms. "I was four. She died in childbirth with my sister. Father doesn't speak of her, so I never do either."

"Was your sister—" He felt a tension in Thorne's chest, the captain clearly not sure whether it was safe to pursue this, but he was on the road now, he could hardly turn back. "Did your sister survive?"

"She only lived a couple of hours. I saw her. Such a little thing. So small. I used to talk to her afterward, though she wasn't really there. Father didn't give her a name, but I called her Rose, because it was summer and the blooms were out in the garden."

"You shouldn't be here, Jack, not in a place like this." Thorne held him closer than ever, placing a gentle kiss to his hair. "You should be at home in your village—"

"No, I shouldn't—I should be here. My life is no more important than anyone else's. I have to do my bit. And if I don't…maybe there won't be a village for me to come home to anyway." As Jack stroked his fingers through Thorne's hair, a fond smile came to his lips. "And I would never have met you, either."

He gazed into Thorne's glittering dark eyes. As he went to kiss him, he whispered, "We mustn't be sad. We have each other now. If you'll have me."

"I don't make a habit of rolling about in the hay, Trooper, so I'd say you can take this as a yes." Thorne smiled. "But I won't be able to give you an easy ride, you know that?"

Jack ran his kisses about Thorne's face, hands in Thorne's hair, disordering it even more. "Wouldn't it be boring if everything was easy?" He winked. "Sorry for ruining your perfect hair without permission, sir."

"Oh, that's all—" And Thorne blinked, and the bright smile on his face became a fierce look. "What the devil have you been up to, soldier?"

"Running my hands through your lovely hair, Captain."

"I'm known as a vain man among the officers, how dare you presume to even *touch* my hair?" He pushed himself to sit against the hay. "Am I to teach you a lesson?"

Jack sat up and saluted

"Yes, sir, Captain Thorne. I'm a very bad soldier, sir."

"Will I put you over my knee, Woodvine?"

"Will you please, sir?"

"You'll find my clothes over there." Thorne nodded to the dark corner opposite. "Bring them to me, Trooper Woodvine. An officer should be properly attired to hand out discipline."

Jack stood and pulled up his pajamas. He saluted again, heading into the dingy corner to gather up the neatly folded uniform, which carried with it the inevitable masculine scent of its owner. Bearing it in his arms, he trod his way through the straw, skirting around the sleeping Apollo, and stood, awaiting his next order.

"Your uniform, sir."

The captain, however, rose to his feet and fastened his breeches. Then he turned and bent over to further bank up the straw, leaving Jack with the distinct impression that this was a show for his benefit, that his sigh when

Thorne had stooped to retrieve the glove earlier hadn't gone unnoticed.

"Sir?" Jack's heart was thudding so heavily that he was convinced Thorne could hear it.

"Set it down, then I want to see you standing to attention as if the king is in residence. Go to it, Trooper!"

As soon as Jack laid the clothes on the straw, Thorne began to dress, rightly assuming that his order would be followed. Even though Jack was clad in nothing more than the lower half of his pajamas and a pair of boots, his stance was unimpeachable. And he held it, his body straining to keep taut and still.

As he dressed, Thorne stroked each item, touching away any straw and any sign of a crease. The fabric swished against his skin and he held Jack's gaze as he buttoned his shirt and tucked it into his waistband. The muscled torso might have been lost to sight, but in its place was the immaculate captain, tie perfect without the aid of a mirror, tunic displaying his neat waist and strong shoulders, cap on as if he had used a spirit-level. And finally he picked up the gloves.

It was all for Jack to gaze on, in a way that he couldn't in the stable yard. He didn't have to wrestle with his reaction now, or feel ashamed about what betraying looks might dance across his features at the sight of such a man as Captain R. B. Thorne. Even standing to attention so rigidly that it was as if he had a broom handle to his spine, he could allow his eyes to wander, his cheeks to pinken and his mouth to open just enough to emit a pleased sigh. His body stirred into arousal again.

"At ease." Thorne linked his gloved fingers behind his back as Jack finally relaxed the salute. "Strip."

Despite standing still, Jack nearly stumbled over at the command. He somehow managed to stop himself from shaking.

"Yes, sir."

Jack turned away from the captain and removed his boots. He brought down his pajamas, his bottom on show as he bent to remove them. Then he turned back to face the captain and for the first time in his life someone other than himself saw his erection. For a moment, for a pointless moment, he was about to cup it in his hands, but he didn't. He dropped his arms to his sides and looked into Captain Thorne's eyes. And waited.

"Come here?" Thorne's voice was soft, one hand held out to Jack.

Barefoot, Jack approached carefully through the straw. He took Thorne's hand.

"Captain Thorne, sir?"

"I don't want—" He lifted Jack's hand to his lips and kissed it in a gentlemanly gesture. "I wouldn't want you unhappy or feeling as though you can't say no because of rank or any of that nonsense."

"Thank you, Thorne." He nodded, Jack again for a moment, not Trooper Woodvine.

Jack touched his fingers to Thorne's cheek. For a second the captain's eyes closed and his lips brushed Jack's fingertips, sending a shiver through him. Then he took a slight step back and drew in a tight breath.

"Creeping about the yard after dark, spying on an officer as he dresses, naked in the presence of your senior. This is no trifling matter, soldier."

"Sorry, sir."

"'Sorry, sir', he says. It's a bloody poor show!" Thorne settled on the banked straw and told Jack, "Over my knee, Trooper Woodvine, let's see if we can spank some discipline into you."

Jack approached, standing in front of Thorne. Realizing that his erection was pointing at the captain in a rather impertinent manner, he shifted to the side to kneel over his officer's lap. The captain caught hold of his hair and guided him down. Jack's erection rested up against Thorne's thigh as he lay there across his knee, his buttocks exposed to the captain's will. He kept as still as he could, trying to temper his excited breaths.

Jack heard Thorne flex his fingers, heard the leather glove creak, smelled the soft scent of straw and rain and his captain's delicate fragrance, saw the faint flash of lightning around the door. Still the storm rumbled on, still the world kept turning, yet here in this small stable, they might have been the last people left on earth. There was a disturbance in the air as Thorne raised his hand and Jack closed his eyes, feeling the rasp of uniform against his skin, anticipating the wonderful moment of contact.

"Rank insubordination!" Thorne's leather-clad hand landed on his bare skin with a hard slap.

Jack moaned his pleasure through gritted teeth. It stung, but all sensation focused in on that one point – a place on his skin where he'd been slapped by an officer.

"Sorry, Captain Thorne…"

"You don't sound sorry." And another spank landed, ringing through the stable. "Get in line, Trooper!"

"Oh…oh…!"

Jack was incapable of speech. He had longed for someone to take him and spank him, but he hadn't known that it could be like this. The affection through the humiliation, the delicate balance of pleasure and pain. There came just one more smack, the warm leather hitting his buttock hard and fast. Then, just as surely as he had played the furious officer, Thorne was gathering Jack in his arms, urging him into his lap.

His touch was gentle now and he slipped his uniformed arm around Jack's naked waist, steadying him. Jack rested his head on Thorne's shoulder, a tremble running through him as he let himself be held.

"Thank you," Jack whispered. "Thank you so much. You can't imagine...how long I... No one has ever... Thank you, R. B. Thorne."

"Was that enough? I didn't want to hurt you, but I don't want you thinking it's not enough either." One of those gloved hands slid down Jack's torso to rest on his thigh.

Jack smiled. "It was splendid."

Thorne returned the smile then pressed his lips to Jack's throat, softly caressing. His hand, meanwhile, slid from where it was resting on his waist until he could stroke his fingers over Jack's rejuvenated erection.

Jack's breath caught in his throat as Thorne touched him. He began to say his captain's name, but then, his arm slipping around Thorne's waist, he asked, "What does R B stand for? I tried to guess when I saw it on Apollo's girth. I know what I would like it to be, but...will you tell me?"

"What would you *like* it to be?" Thorne's hand continued to stroke, fingers tightening just a little. "What suits a captain of my estimable character?"

"I do have a name in mind, a good, strong name... Like a hero in a Scottish story. I think..." Jack grinned at him. "I think your name is Robert."

"I'm going to keep you in suspense" — Thorne's hand began to move harder against him, each stroke swift and sure — "for a little longer."

Jack gave himself over to this new experience, allowing someone else to pleasure him. He whimpered, helpless, and the name came out again.

"Robert...Robert... Robert..."

Embarrassed that he might have settled on the wrong name, he pressed his face to Thorne's shoulder. The name appeared on his lips again, his hips starting to rise from Thorne's lap as his bliss began to shiver through him again, and Jack bit down on Thorne's epaulette to silence himself.

"Come on, soldier," Thorne's voice was a growl against his ear, breathless and heated with desire. "Don't hold back."

"Robert...? Oh... Robert!"

There were tears in Jack's eyes as his orgasm claimed him and he shuddered through pure paradise, falling but not falling because he was safe in his captain's arms. And there Captain Thorne held him, cradled him, placing soft kisses on Jack's jaw, kissing his way to his lips to whisper, "It's Robert."

Jack sighed, a laugh in his throat.

"See, I can whisper the horses and I can whisper the officers too...but I haven't a clue what the B. stands for."

"That's my one remaining mystery — " Thorne held up his hand as Apollo's head bolted upright and the horse drew his hood back in one fretful, frightened movement. "Get round behind the door, someone's outside."

Chapter Seven

Trooper Quentin Charles, Queenie, the pride of the regiment, the prettiest boy in Oxford, the exotic bird who kept Edmund Marsh smiling in return for an easy war, was furious. Behind his tapestries he had lain awake, staring from the window toward the turrets of the chateau where Marsh's light burned, illuminating the man who had *squeezed Jacky's cheek*. Little Jacky, the wide-eyed new boy with the chestnut hair, the one who could keep that fucking horse quiet, who had gone running to Captain Thorne telling his nasty little stories.

Oh, they might pretend that he was innocent, that he wasn't a filthy tale-teller, but Queenie knew better. He had seen plenty of boys come through the doors to the dormitory and plenty leave and he knew people. He knew that Jack Woodvine had found that glove, had run to his Captain Thorne, and he was willing to forgive all that because everyone had to learn the ropes, but to make a play for Marsh?

No.

Queenie didn't care for Edmund Marsh—who would, with his wandering eye and paunch, his drunken jabberings about the horrors of the trenches?—but a boy had to keep himself in smokes somehow. Then along came Jack Woodvine and all of a sudden the man who supplied those smokes was pinching his cheeks and batting his eyes and talking about *the new boy this, the new boy that*.

Queenie swung his legs round, feeling the complaint in his muscles from the shoveling, a sting in his heart from the humiliation. Oh, Captain Thorne would be the finest prey if a boy could only find the bait. Wouldn't it make up for every shovel of shit he threw onto the muck heap to have the captain kneeling there before him, Quentin Charles' cock firmly between those perfect, full lips? Wouldn't it be the victory of victories to be able to tell Captain Thorne, 'You're not my type of girl'?

Yet Captain Thorne wasn't one for the chaps. Queenie had realized that when his every effort to seduce the handsome devil had fallen on stony ground. So he'd moved along to Edmund Marsh, sad, lonely, drunk, pathetic…*rich*.

A dream lover for Queenie Charles.

Captain Thorne throwing him under the pump, covering him in freezing water, forcing him to shovel shit and—

That was all it took to propel Queenie from where he lay, fully clothed, atop his bedcovers. He snatched up the crop that he had sharpened to an arrow point and drew back the lacquered screen to creep into the dormitory.

And there was an empty bed in the ranks.

Creeping about again, little Jacky?

You'll be creeping about in the morning all right when the damn horse is found with its eye pecked through.

Queenie crept through the sleeping grooms and through the door. Under the cover of the storm he stole across the yard toward Apollo's stable, blood boiling at the thought of that pinched cheek, that water pump, that shit pile. He could still hear the laughter of the other troopers, the sneer of Captain Thorne's voice, and worst of all, he could still see the faraway look in Edmund Marsh's eye when he talked of his beloved new arrival.

Before Queenie could open the door it swung wide, just missing colliding with him, and there stood Captain Thorne, fully dressed, a pistol in his hand.

"Trooper Charles, good evening." Thorne's voice was calm, sure. "Return to your quarters, soldier, we'll discuss this in the morning."

"The storm—" He looked up into the sky, heavy raindrops falling on his face as he realized he hadn't felt them at all until now. "I wanted to check on the horses, Capt—"

"To quarters, Charles, and leave your whip with me. Now!"

Queenie opened his mouth to protest again but could muster only an outraged gasp as Thorne snatched the sharpened crop. He took a step back, glancing to the chateau again, then said, "Of course, sir." With a snapped salute, Queenie turned and headed back toward the sleeping quarters.

He had no intention of going back to bed, of course, and instead slipped around the block and out onto the driveway. Then he was running, blind with anger, with humiliation, his boots splashing through the puddles as he raced toward the chateau.

Only when Queenie reached the enormous, closed doors did he stop. He drew back his foot and kicked the door hard, shouting, "Open up!"

The door opened a crack, an NCO peering out. He had, he must have, recognized the voice, a voice he had heard innumerable times.

"Trooper Charles? I suppose you'll be wanting to come in?"

The door opened no wider.

"Is Woodvine in here? Is he upstairs?" Queenie jammed his boot into the door.

"Who the hell is Woodvine?"

"I'm have an appointment with Captain Marsh, open this bloody door!" He gave it a pointless shove. "Now, Officer, now!"

"Another appointment with Captain Marsh, eh, Trooper? Right you are, then…"

There was a metallic scrape as the enormous wooden doors were fully unlocked and swung open.

"Keep the noise down, though, eh, Trooper?" The NCO smirked as Queenie ran past him.

He flew upstairs, taking them two at a time, sure that he would find *the new boy* there in Edmund Marsh's bed. And if he did, oh, tales would be told without a doubt. Tales told, careers ended, the trench stronger to the tune of one trooper and one captain. Upstairs he went from one landing to the next, dripping rainwater on the priceless woven carpets, treading mud into the solid oak boards of the corridor along which he had once danced, teasing Marsh with the tips of those silk scarves.

'If you can catch me, I'm yours…'

At the door to Marsh's room Queenie finally paused, mustering his rage, then he threw the door open and burst into the room with a cry of, "How *dare* you!"

Marsh was smoking in an armchair by the fire, whiskey in his hand. Had it been almost any other man, it would have presented a still life of consummate gentlemanly elegance.

But it was Captain Marsh in this scenario, and he rolled his eyes at Queenie, his moist, saggy mouth fountaining a desultory stream of smoke.

"What a pleasant surprise! My dear Queenie, my boy...and I *dare*, yes, I do *dare*, to sit in my armchair and smoke—yes, I do—while you suffer in your garret with those wretched, sweaty roughs... Come and sit on the arm of my chair and let me beg my forgiveness of you, my darling boy, my sweet, fragrant little pansy."

Queenie positively surged into the room on a tide of nervous fury. He flicked his gaze this way and that as though he might spy his rival secreted away somewhere. He kicked the door shut with his muddy boot, smearing dirt over woodwork that had once been admired by Madame de Pompadour or some other powdered floozy.

"You filthy, dirty, nasty little maggot!"

Marsh recoiled and fumbled with his crystal glass, the cigarette nearly falling from his fingers.

"What is it, m' boy, m' sweet, m' pretty lass?"

A few lopes carried him across the room and he seized Marsh's plump cheek between his thumb and forefinger, pinching and twisting hard. "Whose cheek did you pinch, Marsh? Not your Queenie's!"

Marsh grabbed Queenie's slender wrist, trying to hold him off, but the vicious tweak went on. With an ill-concealed groan of pain, Marsh said, "What is this, m' Queenie says I've been untrue? That I'd never be, my bonny lad!"

Booze and cigarette thrown aside, he slipped his free arm about Queenie's waist.

"Sit on m' knee, laddy, let Uncle Marsh give you a kiss."

He pouted his wet lips at him, as appetizing as a saggy fish. Queenie met the look with a scowl then twisted his lips into a smile more radiant than any painted cherub's. He released Marsh's face and leaned forward as though a kiss might be forthcoming then, with a force belying his dainty ways, he drew back his hand and slapped Marsh hard across the face.

"Did you pinch its face, Marsh?" He stared at the officer, barely even breathing. "And you know that Queenie always knows when Marsh tells fibs. Did. You. Pinch. Its. Face?"

Holding his hand to his face, Marsh stared at Queenie. Queenie, who had to be pleased, or would tell everyone about his officer's predilections.

His voice was measured, careful and quiet. "What did that rustic little yokel say, Trooper?"

"I want him moved, sent off to the trenches where he belongs. And where is he now?" Queenie snatched up Marsh's glass and drained it in one gulp. "How dare he gad about as though he owns *my* yard? He's not in his bed, Marsh. Have you had him up here? Have you been sucking him too?"

"I—I've been alone all evening. You wore me out last night, boy! I was sitting here contemplating your pretty little cock, and then, as if by magic, you appeared! As though merely thinking of your dear little appendage summons you into my presence. My jaw's still clicking!

But if you want your Uncle Marsh to suck you again, you need only say."

"And dear, handsome Captain Thorne is sleeping in the stable like Mary herself," Queenie's voice dripped with venom. "Do you know what he did to me today, Marsh?"

"*Did* to you?" Marsh spluttered. "What the devil are you saying, girlie?"

"He dragged me out of my bed and put me under the pump. Then he had me shoveling shit all day!"

Spittle shot from Marsh's flabby lips. "The fucker did that? Why did you not tell me at once, dear boy! I'll have the ruddy bastard horsewhipped!"

"He's down in the stable with that beast of his." Queenie finally deigned to perch on the arm of the chair. "And his man is who knows where with who knows who. You wouldn't betray your girl, Marsh, would you? Not your Queenie?"

"Of course I wouldn't. Thorne's apple-cheeked lad… Well… I wouldn't be surprised if he's gone off to the whorehouse with the lads from the depot down the road. Break the virgin lad in, I suspect. Initiate him. He'll still be drunk next week, and he won't know where he's left his trousers!" Marsh put his arm around Queenie's slender waist and reached to the front of his jodhpurs. "Have you a little present there for Uncle Marsh to suck?"

He tossed his head and sniffed, looking down his nose at Marsh. What a pathetic, ridiculous sort of man this was, but a stepping stone to better things when the war was over. No man like this — married, respectable — would hesitate to find his lover a place to live or a new wardrobe of clothes, let alone an entry into society, when they were back on civvy street. Wouldn't it be a cheap price to pay to keep *Mrs.* Marsh, the lady with the money, in the dark, after all?

"That's it, slip off the chair… Come and stand between my knees. Let me unbutton you… Oh, yes, that's it…that's it… And what would you like from Uncle Marsh, eh? A new bed, eh? I could get you that. Perhaps you'll let me join you on it!"

"A new bed, yes," Queenie agreed, though he didn't really care one way or the other about that. "And I want a glass of wine, Marsh, and then I may consider letting you embrace me."

Queenie, unbuttoned, gave Marsh a tantalizing hint of what lay within, the flat, pale stomach, the almost-blond hairs. Used to a fleet of servants, Marsh would have to shift for himself. He rose from the armchair and Queenie was in it a half-second later, crossing one elegant leg over the other, not acknowledging Marsh at all.

"The red's been warming by the fire, boy. It's a vintage from the cellars. Expensive, I shouldn't wonder — you'd like that, yes?"

Queenie waved a hand to suggest that he didn't care one way or the other about that either. Sitting here watching the fire burn, he knew without a doubt that this was the life, and that he had to get out of the stables and on to the officers' staff once and for all. He would be Marsh's batman, his chap, and do nothing all day long. Of course, this wasn't the first time such an idea had occurred to him and off went Marsh to make his case and each time the answer was *no.*

'Captain Thorne has concerns about Trooper Charles joining the chateau staff.'

'Captain Thorne thinks Trooper Charles is lazy.'

And what did Marsh do other than tell him *why* he was still stuck in the attic over the stables? Nothing, because he was pathetic. Instead he nodded and crawled away, touching his forelock to the plummy Captain Thorne.

"I want to be on the chateau staff." Queenie pouted.

"I've tried m' best, laddy, but… Here's your wine, pet." Marsh passed Queenie a tumbler of dark ruby liquid and ruffled his hair. "One day, maybe…"

Marsh knelt before the armchair, puckering his moist lips at Queenie. As Queenie drank, looking over Marsh's head, the officer stroked his hand up Queenie's slender leg to the unbuttoned fly.

"Get on with it if you're doing it," Queenie told him. "You look ridiculous."

Marsh shuffled in between Queenie's legs, a hand in the groom's jodhpurs and one in his own. The wet mouth found its way to Queenie's unenthusiastic cock and up and down Marsh's head bobbed, a sad little groan puffing from his lips each time, his knees creaking against the teak floor. Finally, after ten long minutes had ticked past on the ormolu clock on the mantelpiece beside a photograph of Mrs. Marsh and their son, the debased officer reached his vague climax.

Marsh looked up at the pretty boy with cheekbones like knives as Queenie slapped him across the face. A hard, vicious slap from the boy he paid for his silence.

"I need some cigarettes."

Holding his hand to his cheek, Marsh heaved himself back to his feet and passed Queenie the large silver box, the kind that French grand-mères kept almond biscuits in for their visitors. It was stuffed full of gold-tipped cigarettes handmade to his own specifications by a tobacconist just off Bond Street. Queenie dug his fingers into the box and took a handful before turning his gaze on Marsh and blessing him with a cold smile.

"You may finish me off with your hand later. I shall sleep here tonight."

Marsh had moved off to the bed, shrugging himself out of his uniform.

"Will you never let me bum you?" There was no hope in his tone — he had asked the question many times before. On this occasion, though, Queenie didn't even deign to speak his refusal — he merely gave Marsh a withering, pitiful look and shook his head.

"Thought not." Marsh put on his hairnet and yawned.

Queenie turned back to the fire, smiling to himself as a thunderclap sounded overhead.

Chapter Eight

Jack, concealing his nudity as best he could under a blanket, had only breathed out when Thorne had holstered his gun. But he didn't dare speak. Still Apollo fretted and snorted, ears flat, eyes wide, but he couldn't risk going to the horse with Queenie so close, even when the captain closed the stable door and stood beneath the lantern, his face pale with annoyance.

"The mystery is solved," was all he said as he flung the sharpened crop to the floor. Then he laid his gloved hand on Apollo's nose and told him, "Calm, lad, calm."

"Has he gone?" Jack could only manage a whisper. "I just don't understand how a groom could intentionally wound a horse. *Why* does he do it?"

Thorne shook his head and pressed his cheek to the horse's soft face, closing his eyes. "It's for tomorrow. I won't have tonight spoiled."

Jack put his arms around Thorne, touching his lips to the nape of his neck. How many nights would they have together? No, tonight couldn't be spoiled.

The blanket slowly slipped off Jack, but he made no attempt to grab it.

"My gypsy," Thorne whispered. He turned in Jack's embrace, slipping those strong arms around his waist. "Apollo tells me he likes you. It's a rare compliment."

"Will you tell him I like him too? And will you tell him that I won't let any harm come to him, ever?"

Jack began to unfasten the belt on Thorne's tunic, his eyes never leaving his lover's.

"I believe he already knows." Thorne stroked Jack's face with his gloved fingers. "He adored you from the first."

"A big strong creature like him and a slip of a lad like me...perhaps we belong together." Jack leaned into the touch as he unfastened the shiny buttons on Thorne's tunic, seeing in those dark, sparkling eyes a vision of a future. A place of peace, and...yes, the possibility of love.

"He's not so fearsome as people think." He let his palm linger on Jack's cheek, throat moving when he swallowed. "And I would rather he were safe at home."

Jack kissed Thorne gently.

"We can't lose hope... We mustn't ever lose hope."

Together, they removed Thorne's tunic. Together, they unraveled his tie and unbuttoned his shirt. Together, they took off his boots and skimmed off his breeches. Together, they lay naked in each other's arms.

And those kisses, those lingering, deep, loving kisses that might go on forever, Thorne's arms around Jack as though that alone would see them safe through the maelstrom.

The storm was still rumbling on outside, but fainter now. Worn out from love, he and his captain fell asleep.

* * * *

The fresh air of the morning woke Jack. His head pillowed by Thorne's shoulder, he was warm and content. He was waking in his bed on the farm at home.

But how could Thorne be there, in Shropshire? How could either of them, when this wasn't Woodvine Farm at all?

"Darling..." Jack, caught up in the sleeping man's strong arm, couldn't move. "Darling...no one's about yet. Perhaps —"

Thorne replied in a murmur and fluttered open his eyes to gaze sleepily at Jack. They brightened immediately, even as he gave a slow blink.

"Good morning, gypsy," he murmured gently. Then he pressed a kiss to Jack's hair, shifting beneath the blankets.

Jack tried to cling on to the warm, safe feeling of being home. A feeling he'd not had since he had crossed the Shropshire border.

"Good morning, Captain. Good morning." Jack kissed him lightly on the mouth, his voice soft with affection. "Good morning, *Robert*."

"I can see you might be trouble." Thorne gave a hint of a mischievous smile and reached up with one toned arm, stretching it above his head. "I shall keep an eye on you, Trooper."

Jack reached under the blankets and tickled Thorne's stomach, intent on making him laugh.

"But, Captain, if you keep those lovely eyes of yours on me, then how am I to concentrate on the task in hand? I'll be terribly distracted, sir."

"You must learn to keep yourself focused" — Thorne seized Jack's hand and twined their fingers together —

"because I might find myself being rather stern about the yard today."

Jack squeezed his hand tightly against Thorne's.

"I'm very fond of my stern captain." He kissed the firm jaw. "Even if he shoves me under the pump."

Thorne gave a rather theatrical sigh and glanced toward the utterly sedate horse. "Your good pal got you out of that particular fix."

"I know he only did it because of Queenie, but for a moment, I did wonder..." Jack grinned at Thorne.

In reply his captain raised his immaculate eyebrow, the look on his face one of good-humored disbelief.

"I could do with a bath, actually. Perhaps you should dunk me with a bar of soap." He tossed his head, his fringe flopping back from his forehead. Jack was aware that Thorne had a liking for his chestnut hair. "Do you think I'd suit pomade, sir, or is that only for the officers?"

"I think you're perfect just as you are, Trooper Woodvine. Unlike your vain captain, you were just made that way."

Jack brought their linked hands to his stomach.

"Perfect...really?" His eyes were alight. No one had ever said that to him before — legs too long, eyes too big, hair untamable. "Even with my little round tum?"

"It's perfect too." He kissed Jack's forehead.

"Permission to stay all day in this very spot with you, sir, just exactly as we are now?"

"My God, I wish I could grant that." Thorne shifted his lips lower, brushing Jack's own.

"How — how long do we have together?"

"Don't think about it..."

They kissed with exquisite tenderness, hands roaming to caress delicate skin, sighs captured by passionate lips. Desperate not to let go, Jack embraced his captain tightly, his leg draped over Thorne's waist to hold him near.

"I don't want this to end," Jack sighed. "I wish... Oh, Robert, I wish you could always be with me. I wish you could hold my hand in the stable yard, in front of everyone, and that it wouldn't matter to anyone but us."

"Don't..." His voice was soft, imploring, and he held Jack tighter than ever. "I wish it too..."

Just as their mouths were about to meet again an imperious bark split the morning peace. Outside in the stable yard, one of the officers shouted, "Trooper Pritchard! Wake up, you scrawny ginger bastard, and fetch me my horse!"

"Poor old Bryn!" Jack's eyes sprang wide with alarm. "Oh, heck, Robert, what time is it?"

"Get dressed." Thorne kissed him urgently. "And follow my lead."

Jack flung back the covers. He found his boots and his pajama trousers easily enough, but his jacket took some effort to locate. Eventually, he discovered it under Apollo's hoof and he charmed the horse into lifting his leg so that he could reach it. He pulled his uniform jacket, still damp from last night's rain, over the top. His clothes and his hair were laced with straw. It was certainly not a look that would pass muster.

"Ready, Rober—I mean, ready, sir." Jack saluted.

And Thorne was immaculate, dressed in his uniform, cap perfectly in place, gloves covering the hands that had been so soft on Jack's skin just moments earlier. He brushed the last of the straw from his shoulder, returned the salute sharply and kissed Jack's cheek.

"You're trying my patience, Trooper!" Thorne threw the door open onto the brightly lit yard. "Buck bloody up!"

"Sorry, sir!" Jack tried his best to sound like a woebegone groom, even as Thorne's strident bark excited him. He blinked in the sudden sunlight, his legs unsteady.

"When the hell did you last have a bloody wash?" Thorne seized his arm and ran one disapproving hand through his chestnut hair. "Have you *any* respect for your king's uniform?"

"Sorry, Captain Thorne, they had no hot water at my last barracks, and I've been too busy here to —"

"And you're too delicate for cold, are you? A wilting flower on the vine?"

"No, sir. Sorry, sir!"

"A delicate" — he put his face very close to Jack's and bellowed — "English! Bloom?"

Jack gasped and rocked back on feet.

"No, sir!"

"No, sir! You're a slovenly little bugger, what are you?"

A gentle pink stain came to Jack's cheeks. "A slovenly little — little bugger, sir."

"Pump! Now!" And the captain strode off toward the water pump, the crop tucked beneath his arm as he went.

Jack marched across the stable yard. He saw an audience gathering at the windows of the grooms' quarters. Someone whistled. There was a shout of, "Woodvine's going for a dunking!" and laughter. Raucous, relieved laughter because it wasn't them going under the pump.

But Jack, wearing the expressionless mask of a soldier, was gleeful with anticipation.

Thorne drew himself to his full height and swished the whip toward the muddy ground with a command of, "Kneel!"

This time Jack fell at once to the soaking earth, panting, his head bowed, his hands clutched behind his back. Thorne's dark eyes were fixed on him as he reached for the pump handle and sent a shower of freezing water over *his* gypsy.

Jack shivered—from the cold of the water, from the surge of exhilaration that rushed through him.

"S-s-sir…sir! Oh, Captain Thorne!"

"Salute your officer, soldier!"

Jack gave Thorne a shaky salute, his lips trembling. He looked from Thorne up to the pump above his head then back to Thorne again.

"Please… Captain Thorne, sir. I am still dirty. Will you drench me again, sir?"

"Hold the bloody salute!" And he cranked the pump handle again.

Jack shuddered as the freezing torrent gushed over him, still saluting. He looked up, his face split wide with a glorious smile for his captain. Thorne gave the slightest ghost of a wink and bellowed, "Care to share the joke, soldier?"

"Th-this w-water is c-colder th-than at my last b-b-barracks b-bathroom, sir. Am—am I—c-clean enough n-now, C-Captain Thorne?"

"Do you think you are, Trooper?" He touched the whip to Jack's salute. "At ease!"

Jack dropped the salute. He was still shivering, water dripping from his fringe, his eyelashes, the tip of his nose. Crystal drops gathered on his trembling lip to splash onto the toes of Captain Thorne's boots.

"Thank you, Captain Thorne. I shan't abandon my bathing ever again, sir."

"Get upstairs, now!"

"Yes, sir!"

Jack pushed himself up to his feet, and with a swift glance backward at the dark, scowling eyes of his captain, marched quickly away. He could feel Thorne's eyes on him, warming him with the strength of his desire. But he didn't dare look back.

He heard boots on the ground, his heart skipping at the sound of the captain—*his* captain—following.

And that barking voice, commanding, "Get a bloody move on!"

So, with Captain Robert Thorne at his heels and his heart pounding like a military drum, Jack climbed his muddy way up the stairs and into the attic. Here the grooms turned to look at him as one but any jests, any catcalls, were silenced by the appearance of Thorne in his wake.

"Dressed and out, everyone, unless you all want a dunking!" Thorne cracked the whip against his boot. "Breakfast, then work, we've got guests coming today!"

The grooms who were already dressed scarpered downstairs. Those wandering in their pajamas were into their uniforms in seconds and cleared out as fast as they could. Soon the quarters were empty save for the sodden Jack and the immaculate captain.

Settling his gaze on Thorne, Jack removed his cold, saturated clothes.

"Have I been a very bad groom, Captain Thorne?"

"Marvelously so, soldier. Get yourself into the bath." Thorne's voice had softened a little but he corrected himself and growled, "Now!"

Jack jolted at the command. With militaristic efficiency he collected his soap and towel from the cabinet beside his bed and, naked, marched with Thorne close after him to the end of the room. Behind the door was a corridor that smelled strongly of disinfectant, leading to the grooms' washing facilities. The slap of the captain's footsteps echoed off the tiles.

Jack went to the farthest bathroom along. When he turned on the taps, somewhere a boiler clanked into life. There was a murky tinge to the water, but it was at least warm. He bent down to push in the plug, suppressing a sigh at the sweep of the captain's light touch across his buttocks.

Jack looked up at his captain through the steam, waiting for a command.

"In!" He pointed the whip toward the bath. "Come on now, soldier, are you afraid of a little bit of water?"

"No, sir."

Thorne's voice was a furious, clipped, public school, ponies-and-privilege shout when he bellowed, "Get in the bloody bath, Woodvine, now!"

Jack's long legs carried him into the stained enamel tub, the water up to his waist but rising higher. He took his lump of carbolic soap and lathered it up as best he could before smoothing the bubbles along his arms and across his chest and stomach, into his armpits and around the back of his neck. He pointedly avoided his groin, which was flourishing again.

His gaze never left Thorne's. He saw the captain doing his best to maintain his stern persona, but a muscle twitched in his jaw, his dark eyes glittering with desire.

"And that hair!" The whip cracked with a fierce *thwack* against his polished boot. Yet the captain's tone betrayed him, deeper, breathless.

With mimed effort, Jack combed his fingers through the damp knots.

"Yes, sir!"

He took a deep breath, remembering his bare chest being measured, expanded and relaxed, at his sign-up, and plunged himself under the water. And he stayed under, the warm water revitalizing him as he rubbed his scalp. He wondered how long Thorne could wait for him to resurface.

Barely a couple of seconds had passed before the bathtub rang with the impact of the cracked whip and a bark of, "Trooper!"

Jack stayed under, blowing a stream of insolent bubbles to the surface. The bath rang again and he felt gloved fingers tight in his hair. When Thorne pulled, there was little force but it was just enough to give the impression of an apoplectic senior officer who was fast approaching the end of a very short tether.

Gasping, Jack pushed himself back up, his hand over the captain's on his hair.

"I was washing my hair, sir." Water gathered on his eyelashes as he spoke his innocent words.

And Thorne leaned forward and kissed the water droplets away, caressing Jack's jaw with his hand.

"I forgot to bring my comb, sir."

"You're an insolent bloody fellow." Thorne released Jack's hair and reached into his pocket. From it he retrieved an elegant comb fashioned from tortoiseshell, which he brandished like the whip that was currently tucked into his boot.

"Shall I oblige?"

"If you please, sir."

When the captain's hand touched Jack's hair to smooth it, the leather was warm, supple on his scalp. There was no roughness in the gentle sweeps of the comb, each tangle in Jack's soft hair subject to his officer's tender teases and attentions. Jack sank into the sensation of being utterly cared for, of a role where there was no war on the horizon, no pretty young men with violence in their blood, nothing but his captain and him, sharing this stolen moment in a cold, grimy bathroom.

His voice was barely a whisper as he murmured, "You're very kind, sir, to an insubordinate fellow such as I."

"I'm a fool, Trooper." He tapped one finger to Jack's scalp. "Don't make the mistake of thinking this absolves you from another spanking later."

Jack stroked his soapy hand lightly to Thorne's jaw.

"Jolly good, sir. I shall await your command."

His eye darted toward Thorne's whip, then he glanced away. Thorne reached down to touch the handle that nestled against the side of his knee and asked, "Something to say?"

Jack turned to clutch both hands against the side of the tub nearest Thorne. He rested his chin on the cold enamel, his glance moving between the whip and Thorne's eyes. How could he ask without sounding ridiculous?

"Later, will you spank me with your hand, or…" Jack breathed deeply to force out the words. "Or…with your whip, sir?"

"I believe such impertinence" — he dropped his voice, gaze fixing on Jack's wide eyes — "will require a taste of the whip."

Jack nodded, his skin tingling at the promise.

"Of course, sir."

"Any further impertinence today and you'll taste it even harder tonight. Understand?"

"Righty-bloody-ho, sir!" Jack saluted, and plunged back down under the water.

"Insolent little blighter!" The captain's voice was dulled by water, his hand slapping hard against the bath.

Jack came up again. He tried to still his laughter, having decided to be as insolent as he possibly could. One elbow leaned casually on the side of the bath, with his free hand Jack lightly touched his erection, which peeped over the surface of the water. He pouted a smile at his captain and closed his hand around it, stroking, stroking, all the time pretending that the hand was not his own.

"Leave a captain to do a captain's job," Thorne murmured. Then his gloved hand closed over Jack's, encouraging him to move harder.

Jack's gasp was one of both surprise and pleasure. He was caught up by the captain's pace, amazed at the intensity of the vigorous caress by another's hand. And not just any hand, but the leather-clad hand of his captain. He moved his hips to increase the pleasure, the water splashing about him as he bucked. He wanted to cry out Thorne's name, but he didn't dare. He couldn't trust his voice not to give him away.

Thorne's lips found Jack's then, possessing him with a long, deep kiss. His hand grew tighter, urging him on toward his climax.

Swooning into his bliss, Jack's eyes closed and he was at once utterly within and without himself, tumbling through a bright white furnace of delight. As he laid his head back on the side of the bath, he looked up at his captain and sighed.

"Robert...my darling Robert..."

"My beautiful gypsy." Thorne leaned forward to kiss him, reluctance in every word that followed. "And now we have to pretend all over again. Real life calls."

Chapter Nine

As Jack worked, he was aware of a flurry in the ranks. The larking of yesterday had gone and even Queenie was behaving, all of the grooms working — or at least, doing their best to appear so. There was a tense energy discernible in the stable yard, which seemed to be bleeding over from the chateau. Every so often an officer would stride in, bark, then stride away again, or gallop off at great speed. Not that this was unusual, but it was impossible not to feel the tension in the air.

The atmosphere had a noticeable effect on Apollo, whose ears twitched, dissatisfied grunts vibrating in his throat. Jack was relieved when he saw Thorne marching toward the stable. Hopefully he'd be riding out on Apollo so the horse would be spared.

Was this it? Are we about to be sent to the front?

"Gentleman, into the yard!" He tucked his whip beneath his arm. "Fall in, quick now!"

Horses were tethered, brooms propped against stable doors, buckets left where the grooms had been standing. Despite their usual rabbly behavior, they formed neat columns and stood to attention before the captain. Perhaps not as neatly as most soldiers, who wouldn't be smeared with horse manure or have straw in unusual places. But to Jack, whose place was at the back of one of the lines, it was an oddly impressive sight.

"General Bowes-Fitzgerald has graced our little castle with his presence!" Thorne walked back and forth at the head of the columns, looking along each one with a stern eye. He paused before Queenie to pick away and discard a piece of straw from his shoulder. Queenie twitched just a little, no doubt wondering when news of his own punishment would fall. "He's on his way to speak to you and I want to see you all *perfect*! Sharp salutes, shoulders back, make your officers proud."

Thorne glanced back between the stables, where a long avenue wound its way to the chateau. He straightened his already poker-straight back and shouted, "Attention!"

And those columns, with their messy grooms and whiff of manure, snapped to attention just in time to welcome the general.

Bowes-Fitzgerald swept into the courtyard at the head of his own entourage of three uniformed attendants. He exchanged a salute with Captain Thorne and turned to the soldiers, a slight smile on his narrow face. It was the awkward smile of a headmaster addressing the new boys at the start of turn, an effort at avuncularity by a man to whom such notions were a mystery.

"At ease," he told them with a gesture of his hand. "My goodness, what a lot of new faces! How is our Captain Thorne treating you, chaps?"

Nobody answered, of course, but this clearly pleased the general. He gestured to one of his attendants, the man stepping forward to hand Bowes-Fitzgerald a piece of paper.

Jack heard, from a couple of rows ahead of him, a strangulated wheeze of panic. It was snipped off quickly by a dry cough.

"Well now, here we are. What news have I for you gents?" He cleared his throat and held the paper at arm's length before bringing it closer and moving it away again as though playing the trombone, squinting to focus. "Today marks the birthday of our estimable monarch, His Majesty King George."

He looked to the men. A quick raise of Thorne's eyebrows encouraged his soldiers to make suitably patriotic noises.

"And to celebrate this happy occasion and, of course, our continued dominance at the front, you are all required to pop on your finest" — he looked at the men again — "your cleanest togs, and join your officers for a celebration of His Majesty's glorious reign up at the *big house*!"

Another quirk of Thorne's eyebrows assured a smattering of appreciative laughter for the general's effort at humor.

"So there we are." He handed the paper back to his attendant. "Sev— Nineteen hundred hours sharp and fun for all."

He tried another smile, quickly covering its awkwardness with a salute. Then the general turned and, with a nod to the captain, ambled away from the yard.

As soon as he was out of sight, muttered exclamations of "Bloody hell!" rang out from among the rows, even with the looming presence of Captain Thorne before them.

A voice near Jack said, "I thought he was bloody well going to send us to the front!"

Jack tipped his head very slightly to one side so that he could see Captain Thorne, wondering if he would be able to detect any reaction in his face. But the visor of Thorne's cap was shadowing the handsome officer's eyes, and it was with effort that Jack tore his gaze away and fixed it to the back of the groom's head in front of him.

Trooper Woodvine would be going to the chateau, to the holy of holies, the place where only the officers could go. The place where his lover slept.

Thorne's upper lip was quirking, a prelude to a bark, but it didn't silence the continued chatter that was rippling through the ordered lines.

"Dismissed! I want this place perfect, and if anyone steps out of line, they're going nowhere!" Thorne sealed the command then with a gesture of his hand. "Back to work!"

As the columns fell apart, Queenie stepped forward, saying something to Thorne. He met the inaudible words with a shake of his head and said, "I don't have time for it, Trooper. About your business!"

Queenie nodded and turned to walk away, his face set with annoyance, and perhaps just a touch of anxiety about that looming punishment.

The tension had gone from the air, replaced by a restrained holiday atmosphere. As Jack combed Apollo's mane, the horse was noticeably calmer.

"I hope we didn't keep you awake," he whispered. "I'll look after your dad, I promise. Just as I'll look after you."

Leaving Apollo in the stable, Jack approached Thorne. The captain was turning back to the chateau, but on his long legs Jack was able to catch the officer up.

"Captain Thorne, sir — will you be riding today?"

Jack knew his manner was unimpeachable. He was the deferential trooper, the dutiful groom. When Thorne turned to reply, Jack saw the perfect example of a captain with better things to do, wearied by all these bothersome soldiers.

"Turn him out to grass, Trooper. The general has requested my company today."

"Yes, sir!"

Trooper Woodvine snapped him a salute, even as a futile stab of frustration entered his heart. But why torture himself? He would see his captain later.

Jack hurried back to Apollo.

Chapter Ten

During his short time in the service of the Crown, Jack had learned that there was always one soldier in the barracks whose uniform was perfect, a lad who by some dint of fate had the magic of neatness in his fingertips. In the grooms' quarters, this was one Trooper Burney, whose mother, had anyone asked — and Jack did — ran a laundry. Burney was always complimented on how well his uniform looked, which was quite a feat for a groom. A canny soldier would enlist him when their own uniform required attention and pay with money or cigarettes or dirty postcards.

Jack handed over his uniform and some money, and Burney set to work. Not a piece of straw was left, not a crease or mere speck of dust. It was, Jack decided, money well spent.

Jack shaved, a ritual that he performed twice a week, if that, the peppermint of his shaving cream giving his face a delightful sting. He polished his boots using a dab of Apollo's hoof oil and, with Bryn's aid, pomaded his hair.

"You look bloody dashing, you do!" Bryn clapped Jack on the shoulder as they headed up to the chateau. "I've got a lovely sister, by the way – but I'll have to keep my eye on her if she ever sees you."

A staff car was pulled up on the gravel near the door and large candles burned on the porch, even though the June evening wasn't dark. There was already the sound of conversation and laughter from inside, and faintly on the breeze, music.

"They haven't hired an orchestra, have they?"

"They might have kidnapped some of the old fellows from the village to play. You ever been to one of these bashes before, Jack?"

"Nope!"

They followed the stream of soldiers over the marble-floored hall, the grooms staring about at the opulence of the place. A glass chandelier hung down from the high ceiling and an enormous stone staircase wound up into unseen heights. Portraits of sitters in ruffs, lace collars or powdered wigs covered the walls. Gallivanting cherubs swung from glass bunches of fruit. Gold touched the mirror frames, the well-scrubbed faces of the troopers reflecting back. A bloody rabble, they were. Interlopers in a fairy palace.

The troopers went through an enormous pair of double doors and here was the source of the music and the laughter, the party in full swing for the king. Obsequious household staff bore bottles so that an officer should never suffer the indignity of an empty glass, and there were trays of dainties that Jack had never seen before in his life. Where were the stew and dumplings that had been his fare ever since he had left home?

A band of elderly Frenchmen were set up on gold chairs in a horseshoe, their instruments battered but cared-for. Just as Jack and Bryn found their way in, the musicians struck up a tune and a blushing local girl with a rose in her hair started to sing. Jack recognized the song but he couldn't have named it for worlds. It made his heart swoon.

And through a gap in the milling crowd of uniforms, Jack saw Captain Thorne.

He had never seen anything like it in all his days, certainly not in the Shropshire countryside. Like all of the officers, his captain wore full mess dress, vivid red and jet black, gold buttons and braid and epaulettes like flames beneath the glittering chandelier. There was no cap on Thorne's head and his hair was, of course, immaculate. He was like something Jack might see on the cinema screens when he made his rare forays out to the pictures.

And this man, this perfect, handsome officer, was his.

Thorne was deep in conversation with the general, smiling at some tortured witticism from the older chap like a good soldier should. His hands were knitted behind his straight back and when his gaze casually fell on Jack, Captain Robert Thorne smiled.

And it was *marvelous*.

"He's an arrogant bugger, your captain, isn't he?" Bryn laughed and turned to greet Wilfred, who had just arrived.

But Jack barely heard him. He approached Thorne, drawn like metal filings to a magnet, and gave him a perfect salute.

"Good evening, Captain Thorne, sir. Good evening, General Bowes-Fitzgerald, sir."

"Trooper Woodvine, good evening!" The two men saluted in turn and Thorne turned placed his hand on Jack's shoulder. "This is the chap I was telling you about, sir, the young man who has proved more than a match for Apollo."

"Well, it's about bloody time." The general took a sip of wine from the glass he held, the liquid a deep, dark red. "Do you know, lad, I believe we might have this bloody war won if you boys put the same effort into it as his horse does into stamping on the grooms. What do you say, eh, young man? Couldn't we? Eh?"

Loyalty fizzed in Jack's belly. He took a moment to reply, ensuring that he didn't wag his finger at the general for insulting his horse.

"Ha ha, sir. Of course!"

"Of course, sir!" Bowes-Fitzgerald echoed. "Send a few thousand Apollos off to the trenches, stomp those Hun into the mud, what?"

Jack saw a muscle twitch in Thorne's jaw.

"I'm not sure he'd be too handy with a machine gun, though, sir. On account of him not having any fingers."

"Get the triggers ready for those big hooves instead!" Still holding the glass, the general pantomimed a spirited performance of a man with a machine gun, as though such men weren't dying in thousands mere minutes from there. "Well, Thorne, what a smart young lad he is. A credit to his master."

"Thank you, sir." Thorne gave a courtly nod of acknowledgement. "Woodvine's an asset to the regiment, one of our shining stars."

Jack, aware that his mouth was hanging open, pressed his lips together tightly and executed a sharp salute.

"Thank you, sir!" His focus was hovering somewhere on the middle distance. He couldn't look at Thorne. Not with all these people here.

"A good couple of chaps." Bowes-Fitzgerald gave a lazy salute that the captain met with one of those whipcrack salutes of his own. "Enjoy the bash, I shall go and say a few words to your fellows. Buck them along, eh?"

With that he pottered away, leaving the two men alone in the crowd.

Jack allowed himself a second to give Thorne an appreciative glance. He could have stared at him in that getup for hours — days — and never, ever been bored.

"You look splendid," Jack whispered. He wanted to add, *Robert*, but that really was a step too far. Thinking even his first comment was too much, he corrected himself. "That is, the party is splendid — isn't it, sir?"

"As it should be for the king," was Thorne's perfectly proper reply. "You all look tremendously smart. Well done, soldier."

"Thank you, sir." Jack wanted to ask Thorne's opinion on his hair. But as he caught sight of himself in a mirror on the other side of the wall, he noticed that a strand of his hair had come loose. He could feel his cheeks redden. "Sorry that my hair's still untidy, sir. I did try."

With a look that suggested nothing more than a senior officer attempting to show a more human side to his groom, Thorne reached out and gently placed the strand back in position.

"There you are, Woodvine." He smiled and dropped his voice. "You look lovely."

There was a surge in the crowd, allowing Jack to lean against Thorne for a moment. As if it were mere accident, to avoid losing his balance as the revelers shifted, Jack pressed his palm against Thorne's upper arm and as quickly withdrew.

Just as Jack was congratulating himself on that surreptitious touch going unseen, he noticed Queenie. And Queenie had noticed him. But whether the vicious groom had realized what that palm on Thorne's arm signified was another thing entirely.

But what did one touch on the arm matter when Queenie had turned up rouged and enveloped in silk scarves?

He was like a butterfly fluttering in his colorful fabrics, dazzling against the plain, dull khaki uniform. His gaze met Jack's but the look told him nothing, then Queenie turned away and, with a bray of laughter, made his way through the crowd toward them.

"Isn't this *fun!*" He saluted Thorne. "I must say, dashing good of you not to take the misunderstanding last night any further, sir. I let myself down, but no harm was intended."

How did Queenie get away with it? With all his viciousness, his thoroughly unsoldier-like appearance, his cheeking to the officers. Was Captain Marsh really so important?

"It's not a question of it going no further." Thorne sniffed. "I've made a report. It's out of my hands now."

He glanced across to the general and Queenie followed his gaze, his pretty face slowly lightening. This time, Jack knew, Quentin Charles' smile was genuine, and it was triumphant.

"Righty-oh!" He bowed. "Do enjoy your party, gents. I shall go and say hello to our guest of honor."

And with that he pranced away, placing one hand on Bowes-Fitzgerald's shoulder as soon as he was within touching distance.

Jack stared. *Of all the insubordination! A trooper, being so familiar with a general?*

"Sir, where's Captain Marsh? Shouldn't he stop Queenie? What sort of a carry-on is *that?*" Which, Jack knew, was rich coming from the trooper who had frolicked in a bath that very morning, but at least that hadn't been in the ballroom of a chateau.

"Trooper!" Despite the stern tone, however, there was a gleam of affection in Thorne's eyes. It dimmed when he, too, looked to Queenie and the general, whose pale, liver-spotted hand was resting lightly on the young man's slender elbow. "Sometimes, one simply has to accept the unacceptable."

He nodded toward the musicians, the young lady by now trilling a gentle song and flashing her knees at the soldiers who were admiring her. "Enjoy the entertainment, have a glass of something and for one evening, forget that we're at war."

"I'm not accustomed to drinking, sir." But as a silver salver went by, Jack helped himself to some wine and took a swallow. He spluttered and nearly managed to spray red wine onto Thorne's face. "Gosh, sorry, Captain Thorne."

"You'll get used to it by the third glass, I'm sure." Thorne patted his arm. "You'd better go and see your pals, Trooper, people will talk."

"Yes, sir." Jack saluted, wine glass in one hand, and drifted over to Bryn and Wilfred.

His friends were laughing, Wilfred slapping his hand on his thigh from the excess of his mirth.

"Hahaha, oh, bloody hell, you nearly spat in Thorne's face! There'd be another dunking in that for you, hahaha!"

Jack took another mouthful of wine, this time with ease. His mind was elsewhere. "Probably."

Chapter Eleven

As the evening wore on and the wine flowed, Queenie Charles was left in no doubt that he need fear no punishment, regardless of what Captain Thorne might wish. He knew how to turn a general to his favor, how to bat his eyelashes, to tinkle his laughter and touch just the right spots on a man who was no stranger to his charms. Queenie might not fall into bed for the likes of Edmund Marsh, but for a gentleman like General Bowes-Fitzgerald, the same Bowes-Fitzgerald whom he had once encountered at a rather intimate members-only club in Islington, there was no such hesitation.

He hadn't been General Bowes-Fitzgerald then, of course, but a nameless gent who'd claimed to be visiting the city on business from somewhere conveniently out of town. He had asked Queenie to call him *daddy* and so, on the first day that Queenie had laid eyes on the almighty general, he'd known that his life in the army might turn out to be rather easy. Not quite so easy as he might like, of course, for his *daddy* was a tricky man to get hold of, yet here was the key to a place on the officers' household staff, to leave behind the stinking stables and the crowded attic and move into the castle at last.

And when he was living in his castle, what other mysteries might be revealed? Might he learn if something more than professional admiration lay behind that touch to Thorne's arm? Might he discover where Jack Woodvine had been last night if he hadn't been in the attic, nor with Marsh, who obviously intended to make the poor little lamb his victim one day soon?

Perhaps, he mused as he looked from Jack to Thorne, the two men studiously avoiding each other as they stuck to their own classes, they were *both* in that stable. The horse had been misbehaving, but with far less fire than the moments when Jack Woodvine *wasn't* there.

When Marsh finally arrived in the ballroom, Queenie turned his back on the general and kept it like that, every ounce of attention devoted to ignoring his so-called daddy, to showing General Bowes-Fitzgerald that he wasn't an unimportant little nobody when compared to the grooms who were his comrades-in-arms. Besides, he knew that nothing sent his no-longer-unnamed gent wild for his touch like being ignored.

The sky was ink-black by the time Queenie decided it was the right moment for him to show the gathered men and those village girls who had somehow secured an invite exactly what entertainment meant. He retied the scarves around his neck until they were a riot of bows and silk, drained his glass of wine and wandered through the crowd toward the band.

Queenie exchanged a few words with the musicians and, satisfied that they would be capable of not embarrassing him, cleared his throat and began to sing.

"*Si*," he paused until heads began to turn in the direction of the young man with the young woman's voice, "*Mi chiamano Mimi, ma il mio nome e Lucia.*"

And as he sang, as he embodied Puccini's tragic heroine, he lifted one scarf, toying with it, making a prop of it that swept his forehead, his face, swirled daintily in the air. He could have any man in this room now, Queenie knew, and the women too, but it was the general whose eyes were fixed on him most intently, whose tongue licked along his thin lips, who *might* receive Queenie's favors tonight.

"*Lei m'intende?*" As he sang, he slid his gaze over to Marsh, seeing nothing there to challenge the promise of his tall, slim general. His white-haired general who liked to be spat on, who liked to be screamed at, to be trodden on.

Come on, Marshy, Queenie silently crowed. *Show me that you're worth singing to and I might grant you a kiss.*

Marsh, his watery eyes looking first one way then another, assuming he was unseen, blew Queenie a kiss. A kiss that carried a trail of tobacco smoke with it. An officer standing beside him had seen and Marsh laughed it off, a dismissive flap of his hand in Queenie's direction. *It was all a jest, a joke, he had a wife and a son for heaven's sake. Ho-ho-ho, what a lark – cross-dressing is what the Army's all about. No fairies or pansies in the Army, of course not! No, not at all!*

Queenie pantomimed catching the kiss in the palm of his hand. He opened his clenched fingers as though examining an exotic insect then, not missing a note, squeezed his fist tight to crush that imagined creature.

When he opened his palm a second time, he mimed blowing the dust from his fingers before going back to his song.

And Thorne was looking at him, no more than a glance before it was over, that untouchable captain turning away to talk to another officer. Still Queenie continued to look, moving his gaze to Jack to see if he betrayed anything worth knowing or if it was just the cod-eye of the foolish lad.

Jack was trying to push back his ridiculous forelock which had defeated the pomade that he had unaccountably chosen to wear. His face had turned very pink, but the room was not so warm as all that and Jack was standing near an open window with Bryn and Wilfred. And as Jack continued to toy with his hair, the direction of the new boy's gaze was all too obvious. It was *almost* subtle, catching its target and drifting away again, but to the practiced eye of an invert like Queenie it was all too obvious.

The lanky rustic was mooning over Captain Thorne! Of all the ludicrous notions, how could he possibly have imagined these two were a couple – if Queenie couldn't catch the captain, then what chance did an unworldly calf like *Jacky* have? It was utterly laughable. The thought of the two of them together, the vain, sophisticated peacock of a captain embracing a farmer's freckled son, was too ridiculous for words.

Queenie's eye roamed again, this time fixing on Captain Thorne. The officer would sneer at that look from *Jacky*, and Queenie would enjoy it.

The moment, when it came, was delicious, as Queenie anticipated the crushing of that *absurd* look. Thorne turned slightly, just enough to meet Jacky's gaze, yet there was no sneer, no roll of those dark, blazing eyes, but instead quite the opposite. Queenie saw the exact moment that the gazes of the peacock and the rustic met, and as if it were scripted, each raised his glass to his lips at precisely the same moment. A kiss exchanged across a room, a moment shared with a hundred spectators and with none all at once. It was almost enough to make Queenie Charles miss a note.

Almost, but not quite.

He reached the end of his aria with a flourish, pushed along by the joy of the applause but more than anything by the secret that he, Jacky and Captain Thorne now shared.

Chapter Twelve

At midnight the party was officially ended by the sudden silencing of the band and the barking of an NCO.

"Three cheers for his majesty, George V!"

Glasses were raised, and with ruddy-faced bonhomie, the room cheered, "Hip-hip—hooray! Hip-hip—hooray! Hip-hip—hooray!"

Having done his bit for the king, the NCO then bellowed orders at the grooms—it was time for the encroachers, the rabble from the lower orders, to head back to their quarters.

Jack, unable to see Thorne as the party broke up, scuffed his way back to the stables with Wilfred and Bryn. Wilfred had drunk heroic quantities of booze and yet could still stand. As they crossed the yard, Jack broke off to check on Apollo.

The horse was dozing, his stable peaceful. Jack, not wishing to disturb the stallion from his sleep, made little fuss, tucking his blanket around him as though he were a child.

The moon in its cloudless sky cast a silver glow across the yard. Rather than go up to the attic and his narrow bed, Jack felt himself drawn back to the chateau. Not taking the front door—how could he?—Jack wandered into the garden and marveled again at the carved stone figures on the long switched-off fountain. Neptune, balancing on one foot upon the back of a fish, several nudes twined about him. The moonlight gave the stone figures a strange cast, as if they were almost alive. Perhaps they were, and had been frozen for some long-forgotten transgression, or at the vengeance of a foe.

As Jack stared up at the fountain, as still as a stone figure himself, he heard a footstep. He glanced round, his heart racing for a moment. On the warm evening air he detected that unmistakably masculine scent of the captain.

"Did you enjoy yourself tonight, Trooper?" Thorne's voice was formal, infused with just a touch of wine-flavored merriment.

"I had a wonderful time, sir."

Jack watched as Thorne emerged from the shadows, the moonlight throwing silver over his chiseled features.

"I...I just came back from checking on Apollo. I wanted to look at the fountain again." Jack realized how guileless that made him sound and he bit his lip. "Did you—did you enjoy yourself, Captain?"

"It was pleasant enough." He moved to stand beside Jack and dropped his voice. "It was torture, because I had to stand with a damned general when I wanted to dance with *you*."

A thrill ran through Jack and he put out his hand, but brought it back again.

"Are we alone?" he whispered.

Thorne's answer was to take Jack's hand in his own and bring it to his lips, holding it there for a long moment.

"You could dance with me now, perhaps?"

But even as Jack said it, it seemed a daft suggestion. The moonlight glare was so strong that anyone who happened to look out from an upper window of the chateau would see them. Even as the thought occurred to him there came the sound of singing on the breeze. He knew the voice right away as that of Trooper Queenie, trilling another of his operatic arias.

Thorne pressed a finger to his lips and gestured for Jack to move toward the chateau, away from the sound of Queenie's song and the gentle, appreciative cooing of an upper-class bray.

Jack followed and Thorne took his hand, leading him around the edge of the building, away from the sound of Queenie and his general. Entering the chateau via the kitchens, lit only by what moonlight could peer in the windows, they hurried onward. A large door set into a wall in the servants' quarters revealed a staircase. Jack paused, his heart pounding. He was convinced that Thorne must be able to hear it.

"Upstairs?" Jack whispered.

"If you'd like to." Thorne brushed Jack's pomaded forelock back once again. "I hope you would."

"I would… I would, more than anything in all the world, Robert."

The stairs wound higher and higher, as if ascending a castle turret. Narrow slit windows threw lines of moonlight over the stair, but otherwise they were in darkness. Finally, Thorne grasped a large metal handle on a door and pushed it open.

The corridor was a world away from the practical plain back stairs. The carpet was thick underfoot and everywhere Jack looked were gold and flourishes, carvings and paintings, cherubs peering down from a fake sky on the ceiling. As eager as he was to be safe in Thorne's bedroom, he slowed to a dawdle as he stared.

He dared not say a word, but he was too breathless from this strange world to utter anything.

Thorne took a key from his pocket and slipped his arm about Jack's waist as he unlocked a gold-framed door. He brought them inside and closed the door behind them. It was entirely dark, except for a few points of light where the moonlight was doing its best to come in around the curtains.

Not letting go of Jack's hand, Thorne lit the candles around the room and finally the gas lamps over the mantelpiece. As each candle shuddered into life, Jack stared, his eyes wider and wider.

"You—you sleep *here*?"

Jack had never seen a room like this before in all his days. A vast carved marble fireplace, with an elaborate painted screen in front of it, velvet armchairs and sofas with gold frames, cascades of luxurious fabrics, a huge gramophone, dark, polished tables, a wardrobe—or perhaps the entrance to another room, for its doors were so vast—and incongruous, hanging on it, Thorne's breeches and khaki tunic.

And the bed. Which Jack had tried not to look at. One could almost imagine Napoleon reclining on it, planning a military maneuver while choosing himself a wife. It was the biggest bed Jack had ever seen. The natural swirls in the dark wood had been polished to a shine with gold garnishing the top of each bedpost. On it, pulled taut with military precision, was a beautiful embroidered quilt.

"Gosh — this really is quite a room."

"Rather fussy, though, don't you think?" Thorne shrugged in response to his own question. "Do you like it?"

"*Like* it?"

Jack stood in the center of the room and turned and turned, his arms flung out wide. He threw back his head and laughed. Dizzied, he fell into an armchair. The piano shawl that had been draped over it slipped off and cascaded over his shoulders.

Thorne laughed too, dropping to one knee before Jack's chair. The gold braid shone in the candles and he bowed his head, peering up at Jack through his eyelashes to ask, "My beautiful gypsy, would you consent to dance with this old soldier?"

Jack grinned and took Thorne's hand, palm upward.

"I'll have to see if that's in your fortune, won't I?" He narrowed his eyes at the elegant hand and traced his fingertip across the palm. "You have a long life ahead of you. And…" Jack swallowed. He wasn't playing. He knew very well what he saw. "But you'll know sadness too. Perhaps you already have. And then, this line, here, it's a deep crease — this is love. You'll love very deeply, but this line *here*…" Jack looked up from the hand and squeezed it tightly in his own. He couldn't look at it anymore. "Oh, it's a lot of silly — I wouldn't listen to all that. And you know your future can change, just as the lines fade or deepen. It doesn't have to be — Oh, let's dance, Robert, now that there's no one around besides us!"

"What did you see, Jack?" Thorne's voice was quiet.

"It's your fate line, where it crosses your heart line, it— But please don't… You could read anything into it. My mind's playing tricks, that's all."

Jack was tempted to look at his own palm, but stopped himself with a laugh.

"You can't read your own—I don't know why I tried."

"I don't believe in fate. Apollo's fate was the knacker's, it didn't happen." Thorne kissed Jack's hand fiercely. "We make our own fate, you showed me that yesterday."

Jack ran his fingers through Thorne's hair, gazing in quiet wonder at his ardor.

"Now, Robert, what about that dance?"

Thorne rose to his feet and drew Jack to his. He pulled him tenderly into his embrace and kissed him, chasing away the memory of those lines in his palm. Jack responded, his mouth soft and yielding. They swayed as if to a song that neither could hear but both remembered.

It was some minutes before Thorne whispered, "Why don't you choose our song?"

"Would you like something happy or sad?"

"Not sad, not for us."

"Only, sad things are sometimes the most beautiful."

Jack slipped out of Thorne's arms and went to the gramophone, where he could see a pile of records. There were pieces from opera, and chamber music, and symphonies. There were popular tunes from music halls, there were folk songs.

Jack pulled out a record and held it to his chest, hoping Thorne would guess what he'd chosen.

"You slipped away from this amazing room to sleep with me on a pile of straw." He looked up at Thorne. "You know there's a song about that?"

In a gentle tenor Thorne sang a line from the song, of a milk-white steed and a lord in search of his bride. His gaze was filled with affection and he smiled. "*My raggle-taggle gypsy, Jack Woodvine.*"

Jack beamed and held out the record to him.

"I've got this one at home! Honest, I have. The self-same recording. I love this woman's voice… Antonia Sheridan. I take the gramophone up to my room and I listen to her singing it over and over again. I feel like I'm there with her in the song. I can see it all — the lord and the gypsy and the lady, and the milk-white steed. And Dad and Mrs. Byatt bang on my door, but I don't care and I fling the windows wide and sing it!"

Jack started to crank up the gramophone, peering over his shoulder at the look of amusement on Thorne's face.

"Am I a bit too silly?" Jack wondered if he should temper his enthusiasm.

"Do you think she has a decent voice, this Sheridan woman?" He put one hand on his hip, eyes widening as he waited for a response.

"*Decent*? Oh, I think she's *smashing*!"

"I'll be sure to let her know." Thorne passed a hand over his already perfect hair. "She'll be pleased to hear that the most beautiful chap in Shropshire thinks she's smashing!"

"You know — you know *her?*" He completely missed Thorne's compliment and breathed the singer's name as though it were an ancient prayer. "Antonia Sheridan — *the* Antonia Sheridan?"

Jack dropped the needle onto the record and a fiddle started to play. Light as a breeze, sweet as a nightingale, Antonia Sheridan's voice could be heard, as if summoned by Jack's imploring. He grabbed Thorne's hand and dragged him to stand beside him in front of the gramophone's horn.

"I love her," Jack confided.

"So do I." Thorne said it with such gravity. "Quite a woman."

"Well, she is marvelous! Who couldn't love that voice?" Jack, his arms around Thorne, swayed in time with the lilting melody. "It sounds silly, but sometimes when I feel sad, I pretend that there was a mistake and that Miss Sheridan is actually my mother, but she had to leave me on the farm when I was a baby so that she could pursue her career."

"I hope she isn't your mother." Thorne kissed his cheek, holding him close as they began a lilting dance. "I'd hate to find out that we were brothers."

"That *would* be awkwa—" Jack held Thorne at arm's length and gaped. "Wha—? What did you just say? You're—she's—what? She's your mum? But surely she's too young!"

"Oh, she's going to love you, darling, if you tell her that!" Thorne turned to show Jack his profile and told him, "Everyone says I have a look of her. She's rather prettier than I am, of course."

"I would never have guessed if you hadn't said— Oh, lor', I feel so embarrassed now."

Jack had indeed gone very pink again. He rested his head on Thorne's shoulder as if he was hearing a lullaby.

"But...she does sing very beautifully, doesn't she?"

"She does." Thorne kissed his hair. "She taught me, I'm teaching Apollo. He's not putting much effort into his lessons, though."

Jack chuckled and was about to lean in toward Thorne to kiss his mouth when he looked back at the gramophone.

"We… We can't do that in front of *Miss Sheridan*, can we?"

"We can probably go *that* far. I might draw the line at spanking your bare arse, though."

Jack pushed himself up onto his tiptoes and Thorne bent to Jack's lips. Their kiss began tenderly enough, but as Jack ran his hands about Thorne's jacket, his gold buttons and braiding, he felt a pull of irresistible desire and their kiss deepened. And still they danced to that song that was theirs, their lips together, bodies pressed tight to each other.

They were still dancing when the needle traveled off the record and the disc hissed as it turned. Thorne held Jack in his arms as the dance continued, and in that rich tenor, sang their song once more. Jack gazed up at his captain, lost entirely in the depths of his dark eyes.

"I don't sing as well as she does," he murmured, quirking a small, bashful smile.

"You're better than me. I squeak like a choirboy."

"You have many other talents." He brushed his fingertips over Jack's face.

"Such as…?" Jack gave Thorne a deliberately cheeky smile. "Being rather naughty with my captain?"

"Poetry, taming willful stallions, being naughty with your captain." He grinned at the last of the three. "What do you think of the old mess dress, eh? The *only* reason I joined the army, don't you know!"

"You look so bloody handsome in that get-up, Captain Thorne! I've never seen — I mean, not that you don't look handsome in the khaki. Or…or not wearing anything at all. But…this! Gosh."

Jack ran his fingertips over the shining gold buttons.

"I saw you, and I had to remind myself to breathe."

Thorne glanced down as though he had forgotten what he was wearing, then returned his gaze to Jack's. "I wonder, Trooper Woodvine, if you would do me the honor of falling asleep in my arms again?"

"I would, most certainly. But I'm not tired yet."

"And how would you propose that we tire you out?"

"I didn't ask your permission to pomade my hair. I suspect my captain might want to punish me for that?"

"He might," Thorne agreed. "Jack— I've been thinking all day about you, about what we —" He drew in a deep breath and Jack smiled as his captain set his jaw, clearly about to broach something that was causing even *him* a little embarrassment. "The whip. Are you sure that's what you want?"

Jack threaded his fingers through Thorne's.

"Will it hurt? Only, I keep thinking about it. What it would feel like on my skin. I just… I trust you, Robert. And if you switch it over my buttocks once and it hurts then I'll know. And if I *like* it…then…"

"*Lightly*, I'm not having you unable to sit down for a bloody week, Trooper!"

"Well, I wouldn't want that either!" Jack turned to look at the bed. His voice heavy with desire, he asked, "Shall I undress?"

"Shall I undress, *sir*!" Thorne thundered, stepping ably into the character who would wield the whip.

Jack stood to attention.

"Shall I undress, Captain Thorne, sir?"

Thorne snapped an answering salute. "Undress, on the bed and let's have a look at that arse, Trooper. At the double!"

Then he turned away from Jack and crossed the room to where two pairs of polished boots were neatly standing with their toes to the wall, the crop handle protruding from one. He pulled it out and swished as though testing the heft, the air *swooshing* as it was disturbed. At the sound, Jack's fingers fumbled on his buttons.

Once he was naked, Jack neatly folded his clothes and put them on a delicate wooden table. He climbed onto the bed, the silk eiderdown soft against his bare hands and knees. He crawled toward the headboard and knelt up, holding on to the antique wood as he looked over his shoulder.

"This is a wanton display, soldier," Thorne told him in a tight, stern voice and the crop sliced through the air once more. "Standing before a general with pomade in your hair without permission from your captain? Poor show, Woodvine. Jolly poor show indeed."

The crop swished through the fizzing air, candles flickering at the disturbance. It landed across Jack's bare bottom with the force of Captain Thorne's more moderate spanks.

Jack moaned at the hot tingle that washed across his skin. It was just as he'd hoped it would feel. He clung more tightly to the bed, poking his buttocks out just a little farther toward his captain.

"Sorry, sir…" Jack couldn't look away. Thorne had undone the first few buttons on his jacket. He now looked rakish as well as handsome. "Did you like my pomade, though, sir?"

"Damn it, man, don't be so bloody impertinent!" He swung the crop again, landing it with the same force. "I thought you looked very dapper, Trooper!"

Through gritted teeth, Jack replied, "I'm glad you think so, sir." He took a rasping breath. "I wanted to look handsome for you."

"You're already beautiful. Leave something for the rest of us?" Thorne rested one knee on the mattress and leaned down toward the bed, placing a soft kiss to the point where the crop had landed.

Jack gave a fluttering sigh.

"Captain…" he murmured. "Will you please spank me harder?"

"With my hand?" Another kiss soothed the crop mark. "Or with the whip?"

There was a pause. The room filled with a viscous silence.

"With the whip, sir."

In a second the captain was on his feet again, his fingers nipping at a couple more of the tiny gold buttons that fastened his mess tunic. Then he drew back the crop and brought it down with increased force, his hand lingering to stroke and soothe the point of impact.

Jack gave a cry of pain, which immediately turned into a sigh of pleasure. He sagged against the headboard.

"Will you hold me, Captain?"

"Christ, Jack, I'm sorry." Thorne threw the whip down and pulled Jack into his arms, pressing kisses to his face, his lips, his hair. "I'm so sorry…"

"Don't be…it was splendid… But I just needed you to hold me. If that's all right." He felt the captain smile against his hair, and the strength of Thorne's embrace increased, drawing Jack's naked body to that mess dress that had left him enchanted.

"What do you have on under all that, Robert? You've undone all those buttons but you don't appear to be wearing a shirt."

"I can assure you I was properly attired at His Majesty's party." He laughed bashfully. "When you went down to the yard, though, I thought I might shed a few layers just for your sake."

Kissing Thorne with surging enthusiasm, Jack stroked his hand inside the jacket, unbuttoning him farther with his other. He looked up at his handiwork — the stunning red and golden tunic hanging open, Thorne's muscular torso on view.

"You — *you* — Captain Robert B. — whatever that stands for — Thorne... You are too bloody handsome for words!"

"I'm not doing too badly for thirty." Thorne laughed and settled back on the bed with Jack still help in his arms. He crossed his legs at the ankle and told him, "I've been accused of arrogance in the past, you know. Can you believe such a thing?"

"*Yes!*" Jack caressed the bare skin, dipping his fingertips below the waistband of Thorne's trousers. Hoping to force an answer via the art of distraction, he asked, "What does that B. stand for?"

Thorne gave a lilting, longing sigh and Jack realized that he had won, that it had taken so very little to finally undo Captain Robert B. Thorne in the end.

"It stands for," Thorne breathed, closing his eyes in blissful anticipation, "*Bloody handsome*. Is there any wonder I'm arrogant?" Then he opened one eyelid, watching Jack with merry amusement.

"I've tried to work it out, but short of it being Bertie — and I can't quite see that — I reckon it's actually some old toff's surname!"

"You'll *never* guess that one, but I assure you that it's *not* Bertie."

Jack stroked his fingertips over the hard shape in the front of Thorne's trousers. Just as Thorne moved his hips forward into Jack's touch, Jack pulled his hand away.

"Go on, tell me…"

He saw admiration and surprise mingle in his lover's eyes in the moment before Thorne said gravely, "Trooper, are you toying with your captain?"

Jack shone him a lopsided grin.

"Now would I do that?"

"One might almost imagine you'd *like* to go over my knee again." Thorne lifted one immaculate eyebrow, his handsome face set in a look of pursed-lip anticipation. "But that can't be the case, surely?"

Adopting a two-pronged attack, Jack scattered one hand through Thorne's perfect coiffure and feathered the other over that shape in his trousers.

"I appear to have ruined your hair, Captain."

"It would appear so." Thorne slipped his fingers beneath Jack's chin and tilted his head up a little. Then, as his lips pressed to Jack's, he lifted his free hand and brought it down with a resounding *slap* on his derrière.

Jack gave an involuntary grunt of satisfaction, losing himself in their kiss. He reached for Thorne's waistband again, slipping his fingers inside against that hard, flat stomach, twisting and sliding down to touch the warmth of his erection. In response, Thorne's breath quickened, grew hoarser, and Jack marveled that he could tease out such a reply from this man who seemed so controlled, so logical. The captain's fingers tightened against his buttock, kneading the soft, supple flesh beneath his palm in the moments before he lifted his hand and slapped it down again.

Jack fell out of the kiss, sighing, stroking Thorne's erection within the tightness of his still-fastened trousers.

"Do it again!"

"Address your captain in the proper manner, Trooper." Thorne whispered it, though, a delicious, warm command against Jack's ear.

"Captain Thorne, do it again — sir."

Jack had managed to pop open the fastening on Thorne's trousers and he took his lover's hard length in his fist, stroking as best he could with their bodies so closely pressed together. Thorne spanked him harder still, the warmth of desire flooding through Jack's blood as Thorne's hand fell again, even as his captain moaned wantonly into the kiss.

Looping his leg over Thorne's hip to keep him close, Jack shuddered, trying to hold Thorne's face to his, desperate not to break the delicious kiss which seemed to have no end. And there, just a nudge between his buttocks, was the intimate touch of the very tip of Thorne's finger. Jack's hips moved a fraction backward, encouraging the approach.

"Whatever happ—" Thorne silenced himself with a kiss, hunger and desperation in every moment of it. His finger pressed a little deeper, his body rising toward Jack.

Jack's hips twitched and rolled against the incursion. He wanted this, had hoped for it, had never thought he would ever find a man who could — oh, but it was true — *love* him like this.

"Robert... Robert... I know we only met the other day, but I feel as if I've spent my whole life up to this very moment...missing you. You dear, darling man, my handsome captain, you complete me. But now we've found each other, we might only have a little while." Tears were rising in Jack's eyes. In his mind, he saw again Thorne's palm, the fate line cutting through the line of heart. Severing asunder. "I live a hundred years in every second we have together. I want you. So bloody much I can scarce breathe. Robert, my darling captain...will you make love to your trooper, to your Jack?"

"Jack—" Thorne caught the word in a swallow and let his forehead rest against Jack's for a long moment, their gazes locked on each other. He drew in a deep breath, kissing Jack's closed lips. "No matter what happens, what that palm of mine told you— The first time Apollo saw you, he adored you, Jack, with all his heart."

"And I adore him, with all my heart...with all my soul."

Then Thorne was kissing him as though they might never see each other again, as though the massed forces of the German army were at that moment marching along the driveway to the chateau to tear them from each other's arms. He felt himself being eased back against the soft eiderdown, heard the whisper of fabric as the captain shed the opulent mess jacket, then Thorne's arms were strong around him once more, the warmth of his naked skin enveloping Jack.

For a few moments, perhaps a few days—maybe, God willing, for more years ahead of them both than they could count—they would be together. Limbs tangling, safe and loved and adored. Jack could feel the captain's intimate touch again and he gasped until he had no breath left at the intensity of the pleasure he felt, at what it meant for this stern man to uncoil, just for him.

"Jack…" His lips brushed down Jack's throat, nuzzling and tasting. "My beautiful love."

Ruffling his hands through Thorne's hair, Jack skimmed his bare ankle down his lover's still-trousered leg. "Robert…let's shove protocol away, let your trooper give you an order! I want you naked… I want to feel your skin against mine."

"Yes, sir!" The captain left him with a kiss and sat up to discard first one boot then the other. His eyes didn't leave Jack as he slipped from the bed and slid the breeches down, taking his time with each movement.

Jack propped himself up against the pillows and cushions, an arm thrown casually back, framing his head. He watched, and he savored every second. The naked body he had first seen emerging from a stream, the naked body that he had clung to through the night of the storm. And now, the naked body that was appearing just for him.

Thorne had the physique of the Neptune on the fountain, toned and perfect, hewn and hard. Unlike Neptune, there were whispers of dark hair garlanding Thorne's torso and on his strong legs and arms. And very much unlike Neptune indeed, the real man of flesh bore a splendid erection of impressive dimensions.

Jack whispered, "Can I give you another order?"

"Sir!" Jack snapped a salute.

"Get back up onto this bed right now and ravish me, Captain."

"Never commence ravishment without checking your kit, Trooper Woodvine," Thorne told him. Then he crossed to an ornate dressing table on which a vast triple mirror afforded Jack a look at Thorne once more, of both that torso that stilled his heart and the broad, muscular back exposed to him. The table's polished surface was home to a rainbow of glass bottles and small, bright jars and it was one of these that he picked up before he returned to where Jack waited. Thorne's gaze settled on him once more and he placed the emerald green jar down beside the bed then, with the softest kiss to Jack's brow, slipped down to the bottom of the bed, where he bent his head to kiss Jack's feet.

Jack watched, spellbound, as his lover kissed across the bottom of his feet. Slowly, Thorne made his way to Jack's ankles, running his tongue in circles around the delicate bones. Jack's body stirred in response to the tantalizing caresses and Thorne kissed ever farther, his cheek brushing for a moment against the blond hairs on Jack's legs, which in his desire were goosebumped. Higher still, inexorably Thorne came on, kissing Jack's kneecaps, licking around to kiss the soft skin behind. Jack emitted a cry of joy at that, never thinking that it could be so tender to the touch. But perhaps it was only the touch of *this* man that could induce such warm intensity to flow in Jack's veins.

Thorne was now between Jack's long legs, kissing his way along the tops of Jack's slender thighs. His skin was on fire wherever Thorne's lips and hands fell. Thorne went lower, kissing the soft flesh of Jack's inner thighs.

Putting his hands about Jack's waist, Thorne looked deeply into Jack's eyes. Then, with a moan in his throat, touched his tongue to Jack's erection. In one slow, sinuous motion, the captain swirled his tongue from the tip of Jack's cock to the base, softly stroking and teasing him before he retraced his path. Jack lifted his hips toward Thorne's touch and stroked his tongue down and up once more. All the while, Thorne's blazing dark eyes held him in their thrall.

Then, slowly, gently, Thorne took just the tip of Jack's erection between his pouting lips, as he slid lower, taking him fully into his mouth. All the time that magical tongue was teasing and tasting, driving Jack on through sensations he would hardly have dared to imagine, let alone dream of experiencing.

Jack clutched the headboard as his hips rose again from the bed. Little sparks ran to and fro over Jack's skin and with his free hand he caressed Robert's face, his hair, his neck.

"Darling Robert... My Captain... Oh, how I—" *I love you.* But the words wouldn't form in his mouth. He could barely string a thought together with the increasing speed of the captain's mouth, his lips and tongue carrying Jack far from the world, the war, the threat of that severed line on his palm. Thorne's hands were as sure in their touch as his lips and with one palm still gripping his hip, the other slipped round his waist and lower, his fingers pressing softly between Jack's buttocks again.

Jack fought against his body's insistence on collapsing into bliss, wanting the sensations to never end. But Thorne's touch, turning so gently inside him, undid him. All of Jack's muscles clenched at once then sprang back at his release and he saw nothing but an intense whiteness, as if a hundred doves had been set free from their cote together.

He shuddered, moaning Robert's names—*Thorne, Captain, Robert, my love.*

Thorne embraced him, kissing Jack's hair, and nuzzled close to his neck. Nothing could hurt them here, safe in this fairytale palace, in those strong arms, the sweet spice of his skin lingering in the air.

For a moment Jack thought he had drifted off to sleep. Thorne had turned him onto his side and when Jack's eyes opened, he realized that he had been watching him.

"I wasn't asleep, not really…" Jack reached to kiss him. There was a lingering impression in his marrow that he had had a dream. A desolate space of mud…a woman in a strange cap…the lane that led up to the farm…a gray horse in a field…a strong arm about his waist.

"You must be exhausted." Thorne stroked his hair, his voice just a whisper. "Thank you, Jack, for sharing tonight with me."

"I don't want to sleep. Not while I'm with you. I don't want to waste a second. And besides…" Jack looked down, and with a smirk held Thorne's gaze. "I can't be *that* tired."

"What an eager soldier you are, Woodvine." Thorne laughed. He skimmed one hand over Jack's shoulder and inward to his nipple, teasing it between finger and thumb. His touch was as sure as it was gentle, tweaking and caressing the soft, stiff peak.

Jack murmured into the kiss, rocking with pleasure against Thorne. He reached down between their bodies to stroke Thorne's erection, deriving pleasure from his response. Delicious groans came from Thorne's throat, making Jack stroke him faster, his grip tighter.

A moment after Thorne lifted his hand from where it was resting on Jack's back, he heard the sound of glass chinking on glass as the captain lifted the lid from that small, emerald green jar and set it down on the table. A lightly spiced scent filled the air and he recognized it as one of those that made up Thorne's fragrance, the perfume that would forever send him into the memory of this man's arms, no matter where life had taken them.

"Are you going to ravish me, sir?"

"Would it be a terrible disappointment if I made love to you instead?"

Jack felt himself go rather pink. His captain, making *love* to him.

"Not at all…not at all."

"That's not a *no* to ravishment, by the way." The captain's face lit up with a wolfish smile in the moments before their lips met and Jack sighed at the sensation of Thorne's tongue exploring their kiss, claiming him once more. When he felt his lover's hand on his buttock this time he gave a gasp of pleased surprise at the sensation of the jar's contents against his bare skin. It was a soft, scented cream, though it was nothing like the sensible cold lotions that he had seen Mrs. Byatt rub into her hands after she had finished the laundry, as exotic as the housekeeper's were domestic.

Captain R. B. Thorne worked his elegant, strong hands about Jack's buttocks with the same assured deftness as he had massaged Jack's shoulders. But this was a world away from the grooms' attic quarters, as Jack and Thorne lay together naked on the exquisite silk quilt. He could quite happily have spent what remained of the night like this, but knowing it was the prelude to something else made Jack's enjoyment all the more intense.

The captain's second incursion was as gentle as the first, but the lotion made the sensation even smoother.

Gently he moved, stroking and exploring, the soft silence punctuated only by their shared breaths and those occasional, enchanting moans. Jack caught Thorne's rhythm and moved his hips against him.

"Another, Robert... Am I greedy to want another?"

Thorne was admirably quick to grant the request, the two fingers moving with confidence as the captain's kisses grew even fiercer.

Jack's entire world had collapsed in on this one place, this enormous bed where two bodies met, where lust and affection combined, where unsung need was met. Tomorrow might soon brighten at the window, but tomorrow could go hang.

Cupping Thorne's jaw as he kissed him, Jack slipped his mouth away for a moment. He was almost breathless as he ran his touch along Thorne's erection. "Darling, darling Robert—I'm ready."

And he knew that Thorne was too.

"My beautiful gypsy," Thorne murmured, very gently withdrawing his hand and returning it to rest on Jack's hip. He eased Jack back against the luxuriant pillows and Jack looked up into his lover's dark eyes as the captain moved over him, seeing passion flaring in the depths.

The hand that rested on Jack's hip lifted him slightly before Thorne's lips were at his ear, nuzzling and tasting. He toyed with Jack's nipple even as he pressed their bodies closer.

Jack was alert to the closeness of their bodies, to the heat of his skin. So softly that Jack almost couldn't discern the moment at which it happened, Thorne nudged just a little and their bodies were joined. He paused for a moment, as if allowing Jack to become accustomed to the new sensation, then as he moved slowly farther inside him, it seemed to Jack impossible that they could ever be severed.

'We make our own fate.'

It was true—Jack had made the choice not to hide from how he felt, from what everyone else said was wrong. He had found someone who felt the same, and it was his chance to love and be loved. Even if they only had a sliver of time.

But what if it was fate, after all? Because how else had they found each other?

Perhaps they wouldn't be lost after all. Fate and the universe could not be so cruel.

There was poetry in every kiss, every touch, a gentle unheard music between them in the tender rhythm of his captain's movements. If this was his last night on earth, he could think of no better way to spend it, and no one with whom he would rather share his last breath, his last kiss.

The stern captain had almost vanished, present only in the might of Thorne's love, his determination rendered delicate by Jack. A peacock tamed by a horse-whisperer.

Jack embraced him with his arms around his shoulders, his legs canted up and crossed about his waist. There was no possible way to be closer.

Thorne's hand closed around Jack's erection, matching the pace and rhythm of their hips, as sure as a virtuoso. Their shadows danced as one in the candlelight, their breaths and sighs a shared song.

Not quite knowing where his body ended and his lover's began, Jack felt a spasm of bliss catch them both. Jack's vision was filled with stars, brighter than the glass drops of the chateau's chandeliers, a galaxy of suns and stars and other worlds. He was pulled shuddering into a luminous place, and Thorne was there with him.

Long moments — was it minutes? — of bliss passed as he lay there, Captain Robert B. Thorne's strong arms around him, their lips still exchanging the softest kisses. Eventually Thorne shifted just enough to bring his mouth against Jack's ear and whisper one word, full of mischief and sheer joy.

"Brereton."

"Brereton?" Jack shook with laughter. He adopted a mock-nasal tone. "I say, old boy, my name is *Brereton*. I have two thousand pounds invested in the three-per-cent consuls and a Palladian mansion with a fine stable of horses!"

Even as he said it, however, Jack wondered if he should joke. Perhaps Thorne — Captain Robert Brereton Thorne — really did have all the trappings of a life that Jack could never begin to understand. For a moment a rueful twinge caught him, but as it was, that very same man with the plummy middle name was lying naked on top of him, their sweat cooling on each other's skin. The trappings of rank and class didn't matter here.

"Sorry, dear old Robert, darling... I didn't mean to mock. My middle name's Forrester — as you probably saw on my papers, along with my height and my god-knows-what. I should emigrate to Canada and become a lumberjack."

"You don't follow politics, do you, Jack?" Thorne lifted his head to look down at him with dancing eyes. "Strictly speaking, I'm not *only* Captain Robert Brereton Thorne. I'm Captain *the Honorable* Robert Brereton Thorne. You should probably bow to me and carry my sedan chair around the fleshpots of Paris."

"Well, you're not very honorable at the moment, are you, romping with a groom? In fact, I'd say you're Captain *the Extremely Dishonorable and Rakish* Robert Brereton Thorne right now."

"I'm exceptionally honorable. Dishonorable would have been a quick roll in the hay!" Thorne laughed. "This is the bed in which Paul Barras got his first look of Josephine's garters. It's history, Trooper!"

With his arm still around Jack's shoulders, Thorne shifted to settle on the mattress. As he dragged the soft blankets over their naked skin, he told him, "My father is Viscount Brereton, so I shall tell Mother that you think her voice is splendid and Father that you think his name is absurd."

"I somehow doubt he'll care for the opinion of a farmer's lad from the back of beyond. He won't be shedding any tears over me. Unless I steal you away from a marriage to a princess."

"He married an actress of dubious and slightly confusing Portuguese heritage. I'll wager you didn't know that Antonia was anything but an English rose." Thorne smiled. "They were very scandalous once upon a time."

"I had no idea! And you, the son of scandal. Well, perhaps I should've guessed." Jack snuggled into Thorne's body, safe there, comforted. "There's nothing scandalous at all about my family. Even my mother's gypsy blood goes unremarked. Although… I have sometimes wondered about Mrs. Byatt and my dad!" As Jack began to doze, his voice seemed to come from some distance away. "Of course, you'd have to meet them both to find that amusing… And I'm not quite sure what I'd say to introduce you to them."

"I should tell you that I'm the younger son," he heard Thorne murmur lightly. "You'll never be a viscountess."

Chapter Thirteen

In rooms that had once housed the doomed monarchs of the Bourbon dynasty, their grandest inhabitant now sat against the pillows in an opulent four-poster bed, elegantly smoking an expensive cigarette. Queenie felt far more at home here than he ever had in dull old Oxford or gray old London, and it was right that he be on the arm of a general. At least until a field marshal came up for grabs. He glanced at Bowes-Fitzgerald, his head resting on the pillow beside Queenie, and thought how old the general was looking these days — far older than he had during their assignations in the pre-war city.

Perhaps it was the war, perhaps it was the fact that Queenie Charles had been kicking him in the balls with an army boot for the better part of five minutes, or perhaps it was the strain of being walked around the rococo suite on the end of a silk scarf that had been fashioned into a dog's leash, but whatever the cause, he had aged by a decade since he'd shed his uniform.

"Daddy." Queenie pouted his most beautiful pout and danced his fingers through the general's white hair. If his *real* daddy had been a general perhaps he wouldn't be here at all, but Alfred Charles was a clerk, a nobody, so his son was a manure-shoveling groom. "Your Queenie is *not* a happy little thing."

"Yes, my lady, what is it?"

"Look at my hands." He held them out, showing off his pale, smooth palms and elegant fingers, the nails almost pristine but not quite. "I'm not made to shovel shit, am I? It occurs to me that I'm made for chateau life!"

"My elegant Dotty-Dolly, my lovely girl." The general clasped Queenie's hands and pressed them to his mouth. He winced slightly as he shifted on the pillows. "You have claws, too."

"They are not half so sharp as Captain Thorne's temper." His pout grew more dramatic. "He has been very cruel to me, Daddy, because I wanted to stay true to you. I know he has been spreading the most nasty rumors about me, you cannot believe anything he tells you!"

"A report has come across my desk from Thorne, about certain…" Bowes-Fitzgerald cleared his throat. "I don't have to read it, Dotty-Dolly. Would you like Daddy to tear it up for candle-spills?"

"And perhaps just a little, tiny signature from my daddy might move me into the chateau? I'd be so much happier polishing an officer's cap badge than shoveling up muck in a nasty old yard." Queenie leaned down to kiss the general's forehead, breathing in the scent of cigar smoke. "And might I have a little room to call my own? I talk so loudly in my sleep, and I say all sorts of silly things!"

Bowes-Fitzgerald's mouth became a tight, bloodless line. "Well, we can't have that, can we, what? A transfer for my dear Dotty-Dolly… That can be arranged…oh yes — into the chateau you shall go, my darling!"

"My adorable, darling daddy!" Queenie snuggled to the general and took a drag on his cigarette. Into the chateau indeed, one more step away from the trenches, one more step toward England.

Chapter Fourteen

As the weeks passed by and the birthday of the king became a happy memory, the new châtelaine of Chateau de Desgravier settled happily into his role. Queenie performed the light duties that were required of him, polishing the occasional boot, pouring the occasional bottle of wine and delivering the occasional message but, all in all, being the general's little dolly was far preferable to being Edmund Marsh's favorite *girl*.

He still treated Marsh to the odd liaison, of course, for Daddy didn't provide cigarettes or bottles of booze and was a rare sight indeed at the chateau. Captain Marsh, however, was a permanent fixture, and Queenie could see that he was adored.

Queenie could see many things from his position at the top of the domestic tree. He saw the midnight escapes of Captain Thorne, noticed how much longer his dusk swims had become, understood why there was sometimes an excess of straw on the rugs of the captain's room, almost as though a groom had thrown down his dirty clothes there. From Wilf came reports of Thorne's regular meetings with Jacky, of Jacky's absence from the attic at dusk, of the smell of a certain exotic scent about the stables.

Then there was the new mattress and the news that Jacky, that little rustic piglet, was making his sty in what had been Queenie's bed. It was no longer contained in its improvised boudoir of tapestry and chinoiserie, of course, but it was still the finest bed in a poor selection. News of an intrigue was hardly worth wasting one's excitement on, but this — this went too far for Trooper Charles, and he burned with it. Burned with the thought that the yokel might win the peacock when he, the prettiest boy in the regiment, had never been afforded so much as a second glance.

Tonight, though, there would be no secret liaisons for anyone, because tonight the officers were dining together and Queenie was enjoying an evening of leisure. His appointed task had been to lay the table and once that was done it was a glass of port, a cigarette or two and a wander down to the yard to see Wilf, just like old times.

Now he and Wilf were perched on the paddock fence watching the few horses that still grazed there as night rolled in. Someone would be down for them soon, but for now the pasture was theirs and the two young men watched the animals lazily chew the grass, the groom and the gentleman's gentleman each smoking what was left of their cigarettes.

"So yeah, I reckon they were at it this afternoon, if you can believe that." Wilfred exhaled, smoke curling from his nostrils. "Thorney had his pansy walk up the avenue with him. He didn't ride off, no, he made a big show, waving his bloody whip about, shouting, '*You'll walk my horse for me, Trooper! Take the reins!'* And Jacky's all simpering and fluttering his eyes at him, *Yes, Captain Thorne, sir, no, Captain Thorne, sir, three bags full, sir.* I had to take the barrow out about ten minutes after. And you know there's that summerhouse? Or whatever it is. Posh shed, up the drive? No one ever uses it. Well—I only spotted Apollo tethered to a tree near it, didn't I? And the door was half-open. I didn't see in, mind—I was too far away, and I'm not sure as I'd like to see, quite frankly. But I hid. Jacky came out first, whistling some folksy-sounding tune. Two minutes later, large as life, Thorney appears, and he's only combing his bloody hair!"

Wilfred tipped back his head and emitted a raucous guffaw.

"My God!" Yet even as Queenie brayed a laugh, he wondered how that thick, dark hair would feel beneath his fingers. Not oily and thinning like Marsh's, he was sure, Marsh with his filthy stained pillowcases and the flakes on his collar. "Thorne had him up at the big house on Sunday afternoon after service. He was carrying on about this and that, making a great old hoohah, and marched him off into the office."

Queenie sucked in his slender cheeks and leaned a little closer. "Obviously, one had a little bob down to the keyhole and what do you think? He'd *covered* it. Now, why would a chap cover a keyhole if a chap had nothing to hide?"

"After church? Bloody hell! Bet he had Jacky on his knees at *prayer* before his captain, eh? God, if Thorne came at me with his fairy cock, I'd bite the damned thing off."

"You'd never get a new mattress that way, Wilfie!"

Wilfred appeared to think that this was the funniest joke that had ever been told, and nearly fell backward off the fence.

"Evening, fellows."

The gate creaked open to admit Trooper Bryn Pritchard. His red hair caught the evening light, glowing like amber. He held his hand up to his eyes, like a visor against the sinking sun, and peered across the paddock for his captain's horse.

Wilfred was still laughing. "Did someone order carrots, Trooper Charles?"

"One has no need of leeks either, boy-o." Queenie howled with laughter. "Trooper Bryny, little Bryn-Bryn, what would *you* do if Captain Thorne waved his cock at you after church?"

"Come on, lads, what's all this talk? I'm only here to fetch Owain." Bryn locked the gate again. He walked a few paces and, as if he almost hoped his tormentors wouldn't hear, said, "And you can cut it out with the carrots, and the leeks—I've heard it all before, thank you very much. I didn't laugh then, either."

"What would you do—" It took Wilfred a few attempts because he was already laughing at his own joke. "What would you do...if Captain Thorne made you crawl across the stable yard with a daffodil up your arse?"

"What the hell is the matter with you two?" Bryn shook his head. He almost walked away, but then he returned, pointing his finger at Wilfred. "Do I laugh at you because you're a Cockney, do I? Short-arsed Cockney with half a brain cell in his skull? Do I laugh at Quentin because he calls himself Queenie and acts like a girl? I bloody well don't, and I'm bloody sick of you two. What the hell you find so funny about Wales,

I'll never know. We've got a big red dragon on our flag, and one day it'll burn both your arses off!"

"You come here closer and say that." Wilfred swung himself off the fence with the controlled power of an orangutan shifting from a tree branch. "You come here, Taffy Pritchard, and you *fucking* well say that!"

Queenie clapped his hands as Bryn took awkward steps back and forth in the dusty paddock, Wilfred squaring up to him with his fists raised, teeth bared like a bulldog.

"Go on, Wilfie, give him a proper good going over!" Queenie clapped again and sat forward on the fence, his eyes growing wider. If he acted like a girl, it was a very *special* sort of a girl—a girl who took no nonsense from Welsh peasants.

"Come 'ere." Wilfred's voice was a growl, born of brawls on the Wapping docks. He curled his finger toward Bryn.

"Now, come on, Wilfred—let's just shake hands, eh?" Bryn extended his square hand to him. "We'll not beat the Hun if we're at each other's throats, will we?"

The gesture of peace was lost on Wilfred. Bryn's gentlemanly, vulnerable pose left him open to his aggressor. Within a couple of steps, Wilfred swung his arm forward and punched Bryn so hard that he almost toppled backward. He staggered, holding his hand to his nose, blood fountaining from his face. Dazed, he looked up, beyond the two bullies on the fence.

"Bryn!"

It was Jack.

He vaulted the fence in one leap and ran to his friend, producing a handkerchief from his pocket and pressing it to Bryn's face.

"What the hell's going on, Bryn? Were these two—?"

Wilfred, having drawn blood, was not satisfied. He beckoned to Jack with hands like flippers.

"You want some and all, do you, pansy boy?"

"I'm not talking to you, Wilf—me and Bryn will actually do some work and bring the horses in, and we'll leave you two to have your mothers' meeting."

Wilfred swung his arm again just as Jack turned to walk away. It caught Jack at the nape of the neck and he fell forward. Bryn couldn't catch him, still surprised from his own blow, and Jack landed face down on the ground.

"Fairy faggot, bet you're used to biting the ground, aren't you?" Wilfred took a short run-up and gave Jack a hard kick between the legs.

Jack groaned and rolled over onto his back, trying to rub at his nape where the first blow had fallen. Wilfred went in for another kick between Jack's legs and Jack could only shout silently in his pain.

"Leave off him, Wilf, you shit!"

Bryn tried to grasp at Wilfred but the little bruiser was too nimble on his feet to catch, even if sprays of Bryn's blood spattered over Wilfred's shirt. Queenie, stately and proper as a princess at her toilette, slipped down from the fence and stooped to gather up a long, fallen branch that lay beneath the overhanging trees. As he approached Bryn from behind he drew the thick branch back and whipped it hard across the Welshman's knees, sending him crashing to the ground with a cry of pain. Then he strolled to where Jack was prone on the ground and watched him as a cat might watch an injured mouse, his head cocked neatly to one side.

"There's one queen in the castle." Queenie drew back the heavy branch and thrashed it down against Jack's stomach with each subsequent word. "And. His. Name. Is. Queenie. Charles."

He punctuated the statement by slamming his foot into Jack's ribs and, just to drive the point on, spat a thick wad of tobacco-colored spittle into his face. Then he went down on one knee and whispered, "I'll piss on more than your bed if I see you in my castle again, Jacky-boy."

As he rose to his feet once more he called, "Wilf, old chap, do you want to give him a bit of a kicking? Don't break anything, though, we don't want him sent home before the Hun have had a shot!"

Wilfred laughed and got straight to it, kicking Jack as if it was great sport, just a Sunday afternoon football kick-about with his mates back home. Jack groaned at each kick, trying to roll away from Wilfred's feet. But he couldn't get away.

Bryn crawled across the paddock toward them, the blood no longer flowing, red clots drying on his face.

"Why are you doing this?"

Queenie stood back, chewing thoughtfully on one of his nails, his other hand loose in his pocket. He toyed idly with the penknife he found there, his gaze fixed unblinking on Jack, the man who Captain Thorne had taken to bed. The man who he hated more than any German. He wondered now what Jack had seen, conjuring images of the captain wearing only the red silk robe that hung on his door. Or would he wear his cap with it, set at an angle that was *just* the wrong side of rakish? Had he seen that stern, handsome man lounging in that opulent bed, firelight dancing on his skin, dark eyes blinking, *imploring*?

How did one see any of *that* when one was being sucked by Edmund Marsh and fucked by General Bowes-Fitzgerald?

How did one snare the prince, when one had netted the ugly sister and Baron Hardup?

He pulled the knife from his pocket, a flick of his thumbnail releasing the blade. Bryn, his lungs filling with air, bellowed at a volume that would have put many officers' parade ground barks to shame.

"Jesus Christ! *Jack!* Quentin's got a bloody knife!"

But Wilfred's kicks still thudded home and Jack couldn't move away.

And Queenie had a choice. An eye might be lost accidentally during a bit of silly play-boxing in the paddock, mightn't it? All these branches and — But then Jacky would never see the trenches, and he knew from his regular patrols of the officers' quarters that the day was coming, that some of their chaps would be headed to the front sooner rather than later.

'Got to get the numbers up,' Daddy had sighed. *'Keep the boys on their toes.'*

Still he stood there, the blade in his hand, weighing up his choices of taking an eye and sending a man to the trenches and all the terrors they held, but the peacock wouldn't, *couldn't* love a cripple, could he? And his boy would be sent away and —

A pistol shot split the birdsong and Queenie was suddenly back in the paddock, the blade flipped back into the handle and in his pocket in a second. He turned toward the sound and watched Captain Thorne — who else? — running toward the fence, his gun still drawn. His gloved hand closed on the wooden rail and he hauled himself up and over into the paddock, his face white with rage.

No. Queenie smiled inwardly. *With horror. The horror of a man who has just found his lover bleeding on the ground. The horror of a man who knows his general will do nothing.*

"Oh, shit—oh, shit!" All the strength had gone from Wilfred's stocky legs. His knees buckled as he raised his hands in a sign of surrender. "Just a josh, Captain, between the boys, eh—eh, Jack, my mate Jacky?"

Wilfred gave Jack a thumbs-up. Bryn was trying to help Jack to his feet, but he shivered for breath and couldn't stand.

Bryn shot Wilfred a look that could curdle milk from two miles away.

"Just a joke, sir. Just the lads, eh, messing about. That's right, me and my mates, Shroppy Jack and Taffy Bryn." Wilfred finally managed a salute.

"A bit of horseplay, as General B.F. might say." Queenie gave a leisurely salute, though his heart was hammering. "No harm meant, though I can see now that Wilf did get a bit carried away! It was only meant as—"

"Get to your quarters, the pair of you." Thorne's quiet, seething delivery of that particular line threw even Queenie, who had been waiting for an explosion. There was a moment of silence before the artillery landed when Captain Thorne bellowed with enough volume to clear the birds from the trees, "Quarters, now! I'll make sure you're both shipped as far forward as I can bloody get you without sending you into the Kaiser's lavatory with a bayonet up your arse!"

Queenie *did* salute then, for the first time feeling the unfamiliar shiver of doubt in his belly. He turned and began to stroll away, refusing to wonder what would happen if his general *didn't* save his Queenie, if this time he really *had* crossed some sort of unseen line. At the gate he threw down the branch. Only then did he realize that Wilfred was following.

Chapter Fifteen

Jack was aware only of the arms that were around him. They didn't belong to his Robert, but to a lad, who smelled of carbolic soap.

"Bryn... Bryn..."

He clutched his friend and heard him say, "Captain Thorne, he's in a bad way, sir. I got a punch, and then Jack got worse for helping a pal. I tried to stop them, of course I did, but..."

"What about you, Trooper Pritchard?" Thorne was looking at Jack as he spoke, his hands hovering above his body as though afraid to touch him for fear of doing any more injury. "Are you walking wounded?"

"I'm a bit dazed, sir... The bleeding's stopped. I'll shove my head under the pump and I'll be right as rain again, I don't doubt."

"You'll do nothing of the sort." He finally looked at Bryn. "Get up to the chateau and tell the doctor we're on our way. Have him look you over while you're up there and tell him you have Captain Thorne's permission to have a glass of the good brandy."

"Thank you, sir!"

Bryn nodded to Captain Thorne and whispered, "Jack, will you let go of me now—Captain Thorne's here."

Jack released his friend and Bryn hopped to his feet and gave a salute. Then he bent down to Jack again, holding out the handkerchief he'd been given.

"Ah, Jack, pal, I got blood on your hanky. Sorry…"

Jack reached up for it, regardless of the blood, and squeezed it into his palm.

"It's all right, Bryn…it's all right…"

Bryn hurried away and Jack fell into Thorne's arms, at last allowing himself to cry. The captain cradled him close, pressing gentle kisses to his hair and forehead. With infinite care he gathered the young man into his embrace and told him, "It's going to be all right, darling, I promise."

Thorne stood and lifted Jack into his arms, carrying him like a groom might carry a bride. They set off across the paddock, the captain softly humming a gentle melody to his lover.

Through his agony, Jack held his gaze on Thorne. Each breath hurt as if his ribs were cutting through his lungs. Speech was excruciating, but he had to sound the alarm.

"He called me a pansy…a fairy faggot… It was vile. And Queenie… Queenie says he's the—the only queen in the castle… Robert! They *know!*" Jack started to cry. "And I haven't brought the horses in from the paddock."

"They know nothing." Thorne kissed the tears from his eyes as they walked. "And the horses will enjoy the last of the evening, they'll have no complaints."

Jack struggled on with his breathing.

"It hurts, sir… It hurts so much. I'm afraid."

"Don't be frightened." He carefully unhooked the gate and crossed over to the path, fastening the latch behind them. "We'll have the doctor patch you up then put you to bed. I won't leave you."

He resumed the soft melody then, though there was a tremble to that usually so confident voice.

The front door of the chateau was already held open for them. Jack had an impression of the huge chandelier and the elaborate rococo gold leaf. Through corridors they hurried, Jack hovering on a knife-edge of pain. But it wasn't the exquisite pain of a controlled leather glove or a whip across his buttocks or the backs of his thighs, always followed by a caress. This was like his throw from the horse, a bombardment of agony that he couldn't escape.

There were voices, Thorne's barked orders, the sound of running.

"Ah, Captain Thorne and young Woodvine — Trooper Pritchard told us you were on your way." Then the sound of footsteps receding and growing louder as Thorne followed, eventually settling Jack down on a soft bed. "Let's have a look at the damage, shall we?"

Jack clenched his teeth as someone with a delicate but deliberate touch palpated him through his clothes.

"Bruising, I shouldn't wonder. Hurts like billy-oh, and no blood to show for it, either — unlike poor Taffy. Sent him off to the kitchen for a dish of something hearty."

"Bryn, his bloody name's Bryn…" For his troubles, Jack flinched from a renewed spike of pain.

A familiar touch caressed his cheek and a deep soft voice whispered against his ear, "I'll stay with you."

Jack felt strong arms around him, was aware of the comforting scent of Thorne's nearby.

"Don't leave me, don't ever leave me…"

"Poor chap's getting frantic. This'll sort things out — sedation, what?"

There was a scrape of metal, a rattle of glass bottles. Jack's sleeve was rolled up and the skin patted. Jack opened his eyes for long enough to see an enormous metal syringe looming before him.

"No…no, don't…"

"Nonsense, soldier! Captain Thorne, will you look at those good, fine veins. Stop squirming, Trooper! Captain, will you please help me hold him down, he's wriggling like a good 'un."

"Doctor." Thorne drew in a deep breath, his voice calm. "I don't think sedating Jack is going to do any of us much good, do you? Can we just make him comfortable and settle him?"

"*Settle* him? Good lord… Well, he does seem a little calmer now. Is anyone going to sit up with him — you? This is a morphine pill, and I shall give you one and one only. If the pain gets bad, then he takes it. If after that it gets any worse, then you know where my quarters are. Brandy might help the poor bugger, too. Good evening, Captain. And Trooper…"

The door closed softly behind him.

He felt a soft hand on his brow, soothing and gentle, and the captain whispered, "It's all right, darling…"

Jack lay still for a while, aware only of the sound of their mutual breathing.

"Did you mean it…when you said you'd send them to the front?"

"Don't worry about them, leave it to me."

"Is that…is that punishment now? Will they send me?"

"It's the last place on earth you'll be going." Thorne's lips were soft against his cheek. "Of course I won't send them to the front. I'd ship the lot of you home if I could."

"You won't go there either, will you?"

"I've already served my time out there." There was another kiss, softer still, and a whisper of, "I'll do my very best not to go back."

Jack opened his eyes a little and gripped Thorne's hand.

"We will go back to England, you, me and Apollo. And nothing bad will ever happen to us." He grinned at Thorne. "I saw it in the tea leaves, so it must be true."

"It must," Thorne whispered, then he blinked rapidly, as though to clear something from his eyes. "I'll never let anyone hurt you, Jack, not ever again."

"I love you."

It was a murmur so soft that it could have been a whisper of fabric or the wind stirring the branches outside.

"I love you," was the answering whisper. "My gypsy."

In the distance were the sounds of chateau life. A slammed door, far-off footsteps, the inevitable bellowed order. But in this room, it was still and quiet.

"I think I can sleep now, it doesn't hurt as much. Will you…will you sing me to sleep?"

"I can't promise to be as tuneful as Mother, but I shall do my best." And the captain, always so proper and unbending, began to softly sing, telling once more the tale of the lover born to privilege who gave it all up for the love of a gypsy.

As Jack touched his eyelids together again, Woodvine Farm came unbidden to his mind. A figure in khaki striding to the gate. But Thorne's tender cadence had him in its thrall, and just as the figure's face swam into focus, Jack slipped into sleep.

Chapter Sixteen

Over the next few days, Jack didn't stray far from that comfortable bed at the chateau and it didn't escape Queenie's attention that, at every opportunity he could seize, Captain Thorne was there beside him. Of course he was sure there was always an excuse, a question about Apollo, an update on some imagined *issue*, a little bit of fiction to grease the wheels of romance.

For his part, Queenie was confined tight to his quarters and given more pairs of boots to polish than he had ever seen in his life. If that was to be his punishment, though, so be it – it was certainly worth it to see Jack Woodvine bleed.

He had no doubt that he would face nothing worse, that General Daddy would see him right, so, when he was summoned to meet Thorne in the same office where he had covered the keyhole, Queenie took his time as he ambled along the hallways to that closed door.

He saw Wilfred from the end of the corridor and recognized the look of a man who was waiting to be marked for execution. And maybe, for Wilfred Cole, he was.

"Hello, Wilfy!" Queenie slipped his hands into his pockets and leaned one shoulder on the wall. "Have you been trapped in the attic all this time?"

There were dark bags under Wilfred's eyes, made darker by the pallor of his skin. He glowered at Queenie with hatred.

"Maybe I should've sucked some cocks too."

Queenie's innards flinched but he shrugged and breezed, "It's one way to make your mother proud."

Wilfred's lip quivered. "I'm my mother's only boy."

"Then perhaps, Wilfy, you shouldn't have let yourself be so easily led." And as the words left his lips Queenie felt something twist and snap inside him, the severing of a last thread he hadn't even known was there.

"I looked out for you, you git. I tried to protect you 'cos you were my mate. Do you know that? And all you did was use me. Like you use every-bloody-one else. You think you're so much better than the rest of us, but you ain't. Even if you don't shovel shit no more, you're still cleaning it off the officers' boots." Wilfred extended his yellow tongue, his voice low and threatening. "*Licking* it off, like the little whore you are."

"How do you know that I haven't made a representation on your behalf? I might have saved your rotten old bacon!" He waited for the flicker of doubt that he knew would cross Wilf's face before confirming, "I haven't, of course."

Wilfred's lip curled into a snarl. "Nah, course you ain't—it's hard to speak with a cock in your gob, you fucking fairy."

The office door swung inward then and Queenie greeted Captain Thorne with his usual leisurely salute, recognizing and relishing the look of loathing that he saw there. It was a reaction, after all, and that meant that he had made an impact.

"Cole, Charles." Thorne saluted in turn. "Come in."

Queenie strolled through the door and stood before the desk, giving a rather good impression of a chap at attention. Wilfred shuffled in behind. Queenie had a feeling that he might be going home, that some magic had been worked and that all of this — polishing boots and saluting — was about to become a memory that would soon be danced away.

When Cole was safely beside him Queenie heard the door close and the sound of the captain's boots approaching. Thorne set his cap on the desk beside his neatly paired gloves and took his seat in a rococo chair studded with carved cherubs strumming lyres, the king on his throne — no, Queenie knew, not the king, for that was Queenie Charles.

Thorne knitted his hands on the blotter, his dark eyes flitting over a piece of paper that lay before him. Then he lifted his gaze and said, "Gentlemen."

"Captain Thorne, sir." Wilfred stared at him with eyes like peeled boiled eggs, the quiver returning to his lip. "G-good morning, sir."

"Trooper Cole." Thorne looked only to Wilfred, leaving Queenie to lazily gaze over his head and out into the grounds. "The morning after the incident involving Trooper Woodvine, I received orders regarding your deployment. As a result of those orders, I made no report on your behavior. Your record remains clear."

He drew in a breath and Queenie fixed Thorne with his gaze, because he knew without a doubt what was about to be said, or at least some variation on it.

"Thank you, sir. I'm...I'm very sorry for what happened, sir." Wilfred almost sounded contrite.

"You fell in with bad company. I can't excuse it, Cole, but sometimes we must recognize a malign influence and withdraw from it. A lesson I hope you shall carry with you."

Queenie met Thorne's gaze before his glance flickered back to Wilfred.

Wilfred lowered his chin to his chest. "Yes, sir. I will, sir."

"A number of men from our little band have been summoned to Ypres to join the battalion." Even Queenie's mouth fell open, a cold stone of fear plummeting into his belly for just a second. "You are one of those fellows, Trooper. You'll leave for Passchendaele at first light."

Wilfred went even paler. But then he lifted his head and looked straight into Captain Thorne's eyes. There was a smile beginning on his lips and he saluted.

"Wipers, Captain Thorne? Ready to do my bit, sir, for King, Country and Empire."

Thorne rose from his chair and saluted in return. "You blotted your copybook once and only once, Trooper Cole. I have no doubt you will make us all proud to call you a brother-in-arms."

Then, to Queenie's shock, the down-the-line, protocol-observing captain extended his hand to Wilf. "May good fortune go with you, Wilfred."

"Thank you, sir!" Excitement thrummed in his voice as he energetically clasped Thorne's hand. "Shall I go and pack right now, write a letter to my mum? Am I allowed to — she'll be so proud of me, sir, when I tell her."

"Of course. You're dismissed, lad!"

Queenie glanced to his former friend, his one-time protector and said, "Good luck, Wilfy. Give Fritz a kiss from me!"

Wilfred looked back at Queenie, no longer as a boy, but as a man. Not with hatred in his eyes, only tired scorn. Queenie was beneath the contempt of the ostler's son who planned to be a hero. He banged the door shut sharply behind him and his confident stride echoed away down the corridor.

"Trooper Charles." Thorne remained on his feet, his eyes on Queenie as he slid his hands into the discarded leather gloves. "Are you amused at Trooper Cole's new deployment?"

Queenie smirked and tipped his head to one side to display his swanlike neck. A coquettish touch, which Daddy and Marsh liked so well. An irresistible invitation for them to dot their kisses to his porcelain skin. But it had never worked on Captain Thorne. *One last try, though.*

"Perhaps it's a look of relief, Thorney, old boy. Because I know *I* shan't be scrubbing about in a muddy trench with an oik like Cole."

Queenie rested one hand on his hip, the smirk twisting his mouth even further. Leather stretched against Thorne's knuckles as he clenched and unclenched his hands.

"What's the time of my ferry, then, Cap'n? Is it a paddle-boat cruiser? I'd like that. I'll stand on deck, my prettiest scarf fluttering in the wind, and I'll blow kisses to all of you as the white cliffs of Dover hove into view." Twirling his wrist, Queenie trilled, "*My bonnie lies over the ocean…my bonnie lies over the sea…*"

Thorne's hand darted out and landed with a ringing slap on Queenie's pale cheek, hard enough to twist his head sharply to the side. "You're not going home to Blighty, Trooper Charles. Instead, you are to spend the rest of the war carrying bags and shining shoes for General Bowes-Fitzgerald. No doubt your life will be an easy one, though I can't tell you how much I wish it were otherwise."

Queenie blinked, the world lost for a moment behind a screen of tears as he recoiled from the sting. Furious at his humiliation. Furious that he wasn't going home after all.

"But...but I was *promised*—"

His gaze dropped to his feet, but all he could see was Marsh crouched between his knees, all he could feel was the general's wrinkly old arse under the toe of his boot. Even if there was to be no trench for Trooper Charles, the queen would remain a servant.

"You leave at dawn on Friday and believe me, it isn't a moment too soon for me." Thorne met his gaze and bawled, "Dismissed!"

Queenie began to back out of the room, clutching his hand to his slap-reddened cheek. He dragged his arm across his sniveling nose.

"I'll tell him, I'll tell Bowes-Fitzgerald, I will! I'll tell him what you did to me!"

"You'll just be one more pretty young chap on a staff that's bursting with them." Thorne returned to his seat. "I really don't think he'll care."

Queenie attempted a flounce as pulled open the door, but his humiliation was more painful than the slap. *'One more pretty young chap.'*

There was nothing remarkable about a rare and precious orchid when placed in a hothouse with two hundred others, Queenie knew, and the thought sent a chill through him.

"Good day, sir!" Quentin mumbled, and went out into the plush corridor alone.

Chapter Seventeen

The evening was coming on, the clouds glowing orange as they gathered in the sky. Jack's elbow was on the sill as he watched the heavens change, the golden light illuminating his face and the delicate embroidery of the shawl around his bare shoulders. One pajamaed knee was drawn up to his chest, his notebook resting on it as he paused from his poem, awaiting the arrival of the gloaming.

Jack glanced back at the bed, where Captain Thorne watched him through sleepy eyes. One arm was pillowed beneath his head and beneath the blankets, which were pulled up to his waist, his knees were bent. Against them, atop the simple bedspread, was the sketchpad at which he worked, delicately shading the drawing that he had been busy with since Jack took up his seat beside the window.

Jack folded back the cover of his notebook and started to write. His pencil stub in its metal holder moved across the page as his words came out in a torrent. It was a poem for his fellow soldiers who, yesterday morning, he had seen being loaded into a wagon from this very window. How would this mellow sunset seem to them, in their dugout, the golden light striking the barbed wire and the twisted metal in no man's land?

He was barely even aware of Thorne lighting a cigarette before returning to his work. Jack struggled to recall a time when he had felt so contented as he did now, with each happy in his own world, one with his pictures, the other with his words.

Jack laid his pencil on the windowsill and read his words over, both hands gripping his long fringe. He put down his notepad and glanced outside again.

"I do hope they're all right..." He turned to look at his captain.

Thorne put down his sketchpad and pencil and reached across to rest his cigarette on the edge of the ashtray. He set his bare feet down on the thin rug that covered the floorboards and pulled the blanket from the bed, wrapping it around his waist before he crossed the room to where Jack sat.

"What're you working on?"

"It's nothing, really. I was just thinking. About Wilf and the others."

The failing light struck Thorne's eyes and they glowed like agate.

"I wrote—" Thorne swallowed the words. "Will you read it to me?"

"I don't think I can." Jack looked outside again. Without turning to Thorne, he passed him the notebook. "But only that page...you're not allowed to look at anything else in there. I wouldn't want to subject you to my unfinished doggerel."

Long moments of silence passed while Thorne read but Jack's gaze remained focused on the sky outside, the last birds fluttering through the clouds on their way back to the safety of their nests.

Jack's handwriting was a whirl of loops, a result of the speed at which he wrote. It wasn't really a poem at all, if one were strict about such things. Just some words, which had seemed right at the time.

When the gloaming comes,
I shall think of you, my friends.
Golden light of evening,
The mellow end of day,
May it make you smile a while,
To know not far away,
Your friends think fondly of you,
At the closing of the day.

"Not enough explosions for *The Morning Post*, I suspect." Jack's gaze was fixed on the square piece of sky that he could see from his window.

"Possibly." Thorne closed the book and turned, his reflection receding as he walked away from the window. He paused before the mirror, looking into the glass.

Jack picked up his pencil again and scratched at his scalp with its tip.

"Oh dear, was it really that bad? There's another I don't mind you reading. About Apollo! But I'm stuck on the last line. Maybe you'd know the right word?"

"I probably won't, but I can try," was Thorne's murmured reply, his gaze still on his own reflection. "I'm going gray, darling. Just like my father."

Tucking the pencil behind his ear, Jack crossed the room to Thorne. He slipped his arms around Thorne's waist and kissed the nape of his strong neck.

"You've got the odd bit of silver right here — I noticed it the other day. I rather like it, I must say. My distinguished gentleman lover."

Jack rested his chin on Thorne's shoulder and caught the glance of his reflection.

"Your poem was wonderful — now tell me what you've been writing about that pony of mine."

"You sure I won't sound silly?"

Thorne's reflection offered the faintest ghost of a smile and he slipped the book into Jack's fingers. "Why don't we try it and see?"

Jack retreated. He was encroaching on something. Shadowy, half-realized notions presented themselves to him, but they were too ill-formed for him to grasp.

He perched on the edge of the bed and flipped to the right page. Even if Thorne wouldn't share what was bothering him, at least Jack could try to cheer him up.

"It's not the best poem in the world. I wrote it one afternoon, in the paddock. I bought some nice paper so I could write a fair copy and give it to you as a present, but the last line just won't come. Are you ready?"

Thorne drew himself up to his full height and swallowed, setting his jaw. Then he ran his palm back over his hair, silver strands and all. It was like watching a man putting on his Sunday best or a woman applying her rouge, donning a mask before they could face the world. When the captain turned to give Jack his attention he wore a brighter smile and said, "I'm ready."

You're not, Jack thought. But he painted on a smile and, in a voice honed by the masters at the grammar, recited,

Lone in the field stands the white charger,

A more fearsome creature could never be known.
He'll bite and he'll kick, for he is a fighter,
A toss of his mane and a glare; he's alone.

But I do not fear the fearsome white charger,
To me he is sweetness, to me he is mild.
To me he is sunlight, and wind breathing over –

"And that's where I'm stuck. Something-something child, to rhyme with 'mild'?"

It was only then that Jack looked up from his notebook.

"My white charger." Thorne smiled, a faraway look crossing his eyes. "Not so lonesome anymore, eh?"

"I was worried, lying here…who would look after him. But I'm glad that Bryn's stepped in. If we're not careful, Apollo will be the most popular horse at the chateau!"

That was, Jack admitted to himself, a dramatically outside possibility.

"I think your young friend is even a little less afraid of me than he was, though he still flinches when I call him to attention." Thorne was clearly considering the matter of the poem. He folded his arms over his broad chest and clicked his tongue.

Jack grinned. "I think everyone flinches when you call them to attention. Although I have different reasons…"

Jack laid his poems down on the bed and noticed that Thorne's sketchpad was lying open. There was a near-finished sketch of a young man sitting by a window, and Jack angled his head to look at it, smiling when he realized that it was of him.

"And who's this chap you've been drawing, then?"

"Oh, just some terribly seductive gypsy sort that I know." Thorne was casual as ever until, with a sudden burst of speed, he bolted for the bed, his arm already outstretched to seize the pad. Jack was quicker and he snatched the sketchbook away, leaving Thorne to tumble down onto the mattress, though he managed to catch one arm around Jack's waist as he went.

"I can't escape!" Jack laughed, playfully slapping Thorne's arm. "I must say, you've made me look very…well, I'm sure I can't look quite like *that*. Almost beautiful."

"Then I'll start again on a new page, because you *are* beautiful. Almost isn't good enough."

Jack narrowed his eyes at him. "Is this the first picture you've done of me? And remember, I'm holding your sketchbook, so I'll find out!"

"Give me back my pad!" Thorne laughed, dotting a kiss to Jack's shoulder.

Jack locked his legs around Thorne's. "Not until you answer me!"

"There may be one or two others…"

"May I see them?" Jack asked, surprised and flattered.

"They're really just little sketches." Thorne kissed Jack's cheek and sighed contentedly. "They're in the back of the book."

Jack rolled onto his side. He turned the book as if it was a valuable artwork and took care not to open any other page. He knew well the excruciating sensation of someone seeing one's work.

He chewed the side of his finger as he looked at the drawings. There was Apollo by the stream, Jack leaning close to the horse, one hand on his mane as he brushed him. Jack's fringe had fallen over his face, mirroring

Apollo's forelock, his long legs not unlike the stallion's. Another showed Jack perched on the paddock fence, his head turned at an angle as if he was looking at the sky. Perhaps he had been. Limbs braced as if he was about to jump down, his face radiant with a smile.

He studied each pencil stroke on the page, individual lines that were nothing by themselves, but brought together by Thorne had turned into something that almost breathed.

Jack closed the pad. He reached toward Thorne and tenderly caressed his face. No one who knew Thorne only as the whip-cracking officer with the spine-chilling bark could guess that he had such a talent, such an eye.

"They're ever so good."

"I love you." Thorne shifted to rest his head on Jack's shoulder. "Your poem hit me— I think about them all the time, you know, the chaps we send on. I wonder why they're going and why I'm still here, what the future might hold."

Jack pressed his mouth to Thorne's neck.

"It's not your fault. You mustn't blame yourself… Wilf had such a big smile on his face when he left—did you see? I saw him from the window. He hopped up in that wagon and was waving his goodbyes—he *wanted* to go. I wrote him a note… I said I forgave him, because I knew he hadn't been behind it, not really. And he replied and said he was sorry."

They lay in silence for a while.

"I haven't been outside for ages." Jack lifted his head, turning toward the window. "I'm like the Lady of Shalott. *I am half sick of shadows.*"

"But, unlike her, you *do* have a knight." Thorne held him close. "Loyal and true."

"Let's walk down to the stream, then. It's a lovely evening."

Chapter Eighteen

Captain Robert Thorne showed no sign of anything other than professional interest as he escorted his bruised groom from the chateau and along the narrow, winding path that would take them to the paddock. As they went, he spoke of the tasks that Jack could do on his imminent return to duty, things that couldn't be neglected any longer, and that certainly couldn't be left in Bryn's hands, since he had his own horses to care for. To any idle spectator there was nothing that might be worth hearing, yet to Apollo, who galloped at full tilt across the grass at the very sound of his friend's return, Jack was clearly a very welcome sight indeed.

The horse waited at the fence, head high, ears alert, his tail swishing as he gave a long and happy whinny as soon as Jack came into view.

Jack gave the horse a whistle, a bright *whoosh* of sound that he had trained Apollo to respond to. He hopped over the fence with a slight wince and embraced the horse.

"My poor old mate—I missed you!"

"Didn't I tell you that he was coming back?" Thorne scrubbed Apollo's mane with his gloved hand. "And your pa's never wrong!"

"Your dad has drawn a very beautiful portrait of you, Apollo. He's a very talented chap." Jack dropped his voice to a whisper, though there was no one about to hear. "And I love him."

"And your—" Thorne laughed. "Well, your *other* pa, has a poem for you, but he's stuck for a word or two."

"Perhaps you can inspire me, Apollo. I shall stay out here all night with you, until you tell me what the last line should be."

Jack's smile alighted on Thorne. He was thinking of their first night together in the stable, and from the look on Thorne's face, he appeared to be remembering the same thing.

"And I shall stay with you both, because there's nowhere else I'd want to be." Thorne shrugged, blushing.

"I want nothing more than to hug you, Captain Thorne, but you won't give me permission because anyone coming round that corner will see. Shall we take Apollo along by the stream, where the trees are?"

"Will you ride?"

"Bareback?"

"Are you suggesting, Trooper"—Thorne narrowed his eyes, his voice growing hard as granite—"that your captain lug a saddle down here for you like a damned groom?"

"Perish the thought, Captain!" Jack pouted at him, enjoying Thorne's switch into the persona of the stern officer once more. "Bareback it is. But you might have to help me up…"

"It'll be a pleasure."

Jack climbed onto the fence and whistled and clicked for Apollo to come to him. Once he was sure that the horse was content, he swung one long leg over Apollo's back and with agile grace was mounted. He grinned down at Thorne, whispering, "You can hop on once we're behind the trees."

"What a generous sort you are." Thorne laughed and began to walk down toward the stream. "I might even take my swim tonight, since I'm not required at the sickbed of my gentleman friend."

"Would you mind your gentleman friend coming in with you?"

"Permission granted, Trooper."

They crossed the paddock toward the far gate and the promise of the woods beyond. With Jack settled into the rhythm of his mount's gait, Thorne opened the gate for them and secured it as they passed through. Once Apollo was screened from view by the tree-lined stream, Jack turned and patted Apollo's back.

"Come on — ride first, swim after? You might work up a sweat."

Thorne hauled himself up onto Apollo's back without any trouble and took his place behind Jack. He slipped one arm around his waist while the other settled on Jack's thigh.

Jack leaned back against Thorne, and as Apollo made his quiet away along the bank of the stream, farther into the woods, Jack curled first one arm then the other up behind him, crossing them behind his lover's neck, his head cushioned on Thorne's strong shoulder.

"My lovely captain," Jack murmured.

"We'll ride like this in Shropshire one day, you and I." Thorne kissed Jack's cheek. "And remember our fairytale castle…"

"Yes, we shall, we most definitely shall. I'll hold you to that—as a promise."

On they rode, the shadows lengthening in the dying late summer sun, with only the birdsong and the soft sounds of the stream to accompany the gentle beat of Apollo's hooves. The captain occasionally shifted to caress Jack, his lips brushing his lover's cheek now and again as the horse carried them farther and farther into the woods.

Jack crossed his arms more tightly behind Thorne's neck, holding him closer.

"Unbutton me," he sighed. "I want nothing more than to feel your touch."

The captain removed his gloves and tucked them into Jack's pocket. Then his fingers moved with sure confidence over the buttons of Jack's shirt, unfastening them until he could slide his hands over Jack's chest, caressing the now-fading bruises. As he did, he murmured softly of his love, humming their song.

Jack moaned at Thorne's touch. The same hands that had nursed him now tenderly passed over his skin, and even the lightest touch made Jack tremble.

"I love you, Robert. No matter what happens, I always will."

"Wherever we may be, I shall never love another but you." Thorne's voice trembled, just a little but enough for Jack to sense the trepidation in him. "And I never have until I saw you."

Jack pressed his lips to Thorne's neck.

"I loved you from the moment you first smiled at me."

"And I smiled at you because I loved you." He kissed Jack's earlobe.

Jack turned to Thorne as best he could and claimed his mouth, his arms still linked behind Thorne's neck.

Apollo was carrying them through a small clearing, the branches reaching overhead to form a thick canopy of leaves. Underfoot the ground was mossy and soft, the air rich with the earthy scent of the woodland.

"I think," Thorne whispered, "that Apollo might be ready for a rest."

Jack reluctantly let go of Thorne. His lover's warm, soft lips brushed for a moment against the top of his spine. Then in one elegant movement, Thorne dismounted. Jack began to maneuver himself to climb down but Thorne was beside him, like Lancelot ready to hand down Guinevere.

He gladly submitted to his captain's gentlemanly attentions and allowed himself to be helped delicately to the ground. Thorne greeted him with a tender kiss and told him, "I believe we have found our fairytale glade, darling."

"The honorable captain...or whatever way round it is. Sir Robert de Thorne! But can I be something a little more elegant than Jack and the Beanstalk, please?"

"If you're looking for a title, my fair Guinevere, I shall have to introduce you to my older brother." Thorne kissed him again. "But I warn you, he's terribly, terribly dull. And he doesn't even own a whip."

"Trooper Guinevere will have to do!" Jack gripped the belt over Thorne's tunic and unbuckled it with what had become practiced speed. "How the hell can you be related to someone who's boring?"

"Are you undressing me, Guin?"

"I most certainly am, my noble knight."

"I shall enjoy that." He scooped his cap from his head and placed it on Jack's. "Consider yourself promoted."

Jack kissed his captain as he skimmed off the officer's tunic, unfastened his tie and hurried off his shirt. He pulled Thorne to him so that their bared torsos could touch while he guided Thorne's hands to his trousers, his own attention on denuding Thorne of his breeches. They scarcely broke their kisses for air, bodies pressed tight together once both were naked, yet still the captain was gentle, mindful of those bruises that faintly stained Jack's skin.

"Lay me down on my mossy bed, Sir Robert."

Thorne drew them both down to settle on the soft ground. The air smelled clean and fresh, alive with the scent of the woodland at dusk. The chill of the moss against Jack's skin was bewitching after the heat of the summer's day. As they caressed and kissed, the only sounds were of the distant splash of the stream, and of Apollo as he cropped at the lush grass.

"I should probably admit that I don't own a Palladian mansion." Thorne's voice was a playful whisper. "I do hope my Guinevere won't object."

Jack tangled his fingers in Thorne's hair. "You've never told me where you live, but then, I've never asked. I just imagine there's a barracks bedroom somewhere, exceptionally neat and tidy, save for a framed photograph of Apollo on the windowsill. And sometimes you put on your silk dressing gown and retire to a folly in the woods."

"I don't really have anywhere other than the barracks bedroom," Thorne admitted. "The ma and pa have places but...I've always been a solitary sort, snippy, some would say. Just me and a long line of horses."

"My wandering knight errant." Jack kissed him slowly, but excitement broke him from the kiss. "When we get back to England... Oh, come and live on the farm! Or you could take lodgings in the village. If, that is…you decide you've had enough of your barracks room."

It was better to think that there would be a time when they would both return to England than to spare any consideration for the mere idea that there might not be.

"Would you really want a snippy old soldier under your feet?" The captain met his gaze and Jack saw a spark dancing there, a flare of hope, tempered by the fear that this might just be a joke, or something said in the heat of a kiss.

"Of course I bloody do!" Jack's caresses became more urgent, his words punctuated by kisses. "Under my feet, and in my bed and riding a horse through my fields."

"Winter night in front of a roaring fire, snuggled up with brandy and kisses?" Thorne lay back in the grass, bringing Jack into his arms. "Hot summer evenings swimming in the stream as the sun sets?"

"Yes! Oh, don't you think it would be lovely? We'll have the most marvelous time."

"If—" Thorne ran his hands through Jack's hair, cradling his face gently. "This war, darling. If I don't make it home, if we can't have all those dreams… Promise me that you'll find someone? Don't be alone like I have been, Jack, promise me?"

Jack attempted a brave smile but his lip wobbled. Tears rose in his eyes, threatening to spill over.

"P-Please don't…don't, Robert. Please don't say that. I can't imagine the world without you in it. You will get home, I know it. And how would I ever find another man to match you? I would always think back, and — I would rather be alone for the rest of my life, Robert, remembering what we had—what we *have*—than endure some pale imitation of love."

"Whatever happens, I promise you that you'll see home again." Thorne kissed him with a fierce intensity. "I swear it, Jack."

"But *this* is home. This. When your arms are around me. It's the only home I want." Jack, who had once asked the captain to make love to him, now made love to his captain. As Thorne lay on his back, Jack kissed him across his shoulders, nibbling each nipple. Down that strong chest, to the muscled stomach, sliding over the hips to the firm insides of Thorne's thighs. Stroking softly with his tongue, he licked the length of Thorne's erection. Holding Thorne steady at his hips, with tender fierceness he took him in his mouth as far as he possibly could.

Thorne caught his hands gently in Jack's hair and surrendered to his ministrations. Soft gasps escaped his parted lips, deep moans catching in his throat as he lay there in the grass. His hips rose but Jack's hands stayed him, as firm as his touch was delicate.

Jack lifted his head, his eyes fixed on the sparkling depths of Thorne's gaze. Between them stood Thorne's erection, glistening with Jack's saliva.

"Keep still," Jack whispered.

There had been many intimate moments between them since that first night in Thorne's bed. But Jack, as was his way, always submitted with joy, his captain above him, beside him. Never below him, until now. He knelt over Thorne, his hands planted on his lover's waist, and slowly he lowered his hips.

He only stopped once the entire length of his lover was inside him, and there he waited, his eyes still locked onto Thorne's, his whole body tensing as he readied himself to pleasure the man who had so skillfully, passionately, pleasured him.

And his captain obeyed, his whole body held still other than his taut, muscled chest, which rose and fell with each hoarse, heated breath. He held Jack's gaze with his own just as surely as his hands now rested on Jack's thighs, his lips parting very slightly to allow him to murmur, "I love you so bloody much."

"I know you do…"

Never losing eye contact, Jack let his hips lead. He felt only intense sensation, alive to the movement of Thorne's body. As Jack's thrusts grew more powerful, Thorne's hips rose up to meet his, their contact all the deeper. Thorne's strong hand caught Jack's erection, his wrist moving in just the way that Jack needed. The look in his eyes told Jack so, a reminder of what Thorne had breathed against Jack's neck, on the night they had spent in the summerhouse. '*I know your body, I know its secrets, I know each and every one of your desires*.'

Together they approached the pinnacle of pleasure, moving as one, and Thorne seized Jack's hand, entwining their fingers together.

Jack's fringe had tumbled into his face, the long strands sticking to his skin. But his eyes never left his captain's until the moment that his bliss claimed him, and he tipped back his head and moaned his pleasure into the tall branches of the trees, into the stars and the nighttime. And as he did, his lover bucked one final time below him, his own cry of pleasure blending perfectly with Jack's.

Chapter Nineteen

The Army chaplain was very young. Barely a curate. Straight out of theological college and into a theater of war. He had blond hair and a kind face, but a certain twitch in his hands gave him away as a man who had been to the front. His black shirt and dog-collar peered out from his khaki.

Why would a man choose to become a preacher, Queenie wondered, *especially a man who was far from ugly?* It seemed such a waste, all that piety and false modesty, when one could be having fun. When one could be singing.

He stood now in front of the grooms and the officers and staff of Chateau de Desgravier, his hands folded neatly in the ecclesiastical way. He bowed his head, his eyes closed, his mouth moving silently. Then he looked up.

"As you will no doubt have heard, there is intense fighting not far from here, outside Ypres. Several battalions of our regiment are there and yesterday our regiment suffered severe losses."

He swallowed, looking across at all the eyes that met his, looking more intently still at the ones that looked away. Queenie met his gaze, smiling that serene, choirboy smile of his, thinking only of his packed belongings and the car that would be there soon to take him to Daddy.

"Some of you will have known these men. Some of you will have been their friends. Your general wants you to take comfort in the knowledge that they all died as heroes. Each and every one of them, dying or wounded in the service of King and Country."

There was something hollow in his voice as he relayed the general's sentiments. But he went on.

"Blessed are they that mourn, for they shall be comforted."

His hands twitched and he took a deep breath.

"Greater love hath no man than this, that a man lay down his life for his friends."

Someone coughed. A horse whinnied in the paddock. As the chaplain told them a sermon, a light rain began to fall. The sun cast its rays through the drops and a pale rainbow appeared for a moment over the chateau.

Lay down his life for his friends. Queenie sniffed and rolled his eyes heavenward. *The man who lays down his life for* anything *is a fool. You lay down your friends for your own life first.*

The chaplain smiled gently at his congregation. "I am told that there is a poet among you. A reluctant chap. He wouldn't come up in front of you to read, so Captain Thorne...if you would."

Oh, it would be.

As Captain Thorne, still the most handsome chap at the big house, stepped up to take his place beside the preacher, Queenie did his best to catch Jack's eye, but little Jacky wasn't playing. He had eyes only for his hero, the captain who had saved him from Queenie's blade.

And Queenie knew *exactly* who the poet was as soon as Thorne began to speak, each word perfectly enunciated, his diction clear as Daddy's crystal. The poetry seemed to settle in the yard like a snowfall, resting gently on each man who stood there, but not on Quentin Charles. He listened, of course, but he didn't really see what good sweet words were to those crawling belly-deep through the inferno. What could words do when the artillery came raining down, when shards of shrapnel went flying?

What good was poetry to the likes of Wilf –

Queenie swallowed and returned his gaze to the captain, wondering when *he* would be in the inferno. The day was coming, the day when Queenie would wake up in Daddy's bed and hear that Captain R. B. Thorne and Trooper Jack Woodvine had fallen to the guns or gas.

And when that day came, he would throw his head back and laugh.

"Thank you, Captain Thorne."

Thorne acknowledged with a nod and took his place beside Marsh, who had looked at nothing but Queenie all day. All day, every day, in fact, since the news of his new detail had been announced.

Pathetic old bugger.

"And now… I would like to close on a hymn. It is my pleasure to tell you that we will be led by one of your number who is a choirmaster at home. Trooper Pritchard will sing the first verse and then the rest of us shall join in."

Bryn, blushing slightly, came to the front. He folded his hands neatly behind his back, his feet planted just so, and began to sing, his voice filling the stable yard.

"Guide me, O thou great redeemer…."

Oh God, for a gas attack right now. Queenie sighed a theatrical sigh. *Take out the bloody Welsh Caruso before he hits the high notes.*

He drifted his gaze to Marsh and blessed him with a smile in anticipation of whatever going-away gift his pathetic not-quite-lover had bought for his Queenie. It was worth suffering through this caterwaul for that.

At the beginning of the second verse everyone in the stable yard, except for Queenie, joined in. Even the ones who didn't know the words made a game attempt at singing, picking up the tune even if the lyrics were utterly alien to them. It started to sound very much like a chant from the stands at a sports match, and the chaplain caught the glance of one of the officers and started to laugh, conducting the rabble in their song. His laughter was infectious, and soon even Bryn, the only person in the yard to know all the words, was smiling.

"Thank you, Trooper Pritchard." The chaplain gave Bryn a pat on the shoulder and the groom rejoined the ranks.

"Well, that brings our service of remembrance to a close, but should any of you ever feel the need to pray with…"

The chaplain's words were lost as the stable yard was filled with conversation, laughs and shouts, the man in the dog-collar too nice to bellow at them for silence.

"Fall in, you bloody shower! Show the man some respect!" Captain Thorne cracked his whip against his boot and the hubbub in the yard fell instantly silent as discipline descended once more. He nodded his approval, tucking his whip beneath his arm as he waited for absolute order. Only then did Thorne address the chaplain. "Thank you for taking the time to visit us."

He turned back to the ranks and bellowed, "Company, attention!"

Every man snapped into line and the captain dismissed the chaplain with a nod that Queenie thought was *almost* friendly. Perhaps some of Jacky's disgusting, cloying sentiment was rubbing off on him.

The chaplain's hands twitched again before they were still.

"If any of you feel the need to speak to someone…about…about…" The chaplain's hands wafted ineffectually at the air. "All this…then, you know where I am. Thank you, chaps."

He turned on his heel, his shoulders sagging as he walked away.

"Dismissed!"

As soon as the word left Thorne's lips, Queenie was moving on light feet toward Marsh, smiling his most pretty smile. In less than an hour he would be gone, off to see the lie of the land, to see how many other pretty boys must be deposed on his way to the throne, but for now he had his goodbyes to say.

"Captain Marsh, sir, I just wanted to say thank you." Queenie gave a dismissive salute. "And *au revoir*, sir!"

Marsh returned the salute, a sharpness in his manner.

"Thank *you*, Trooper Charles. For making my time at Chateau de Desgravier…most memorable. Off to the general, what?"

Lowering his voice, his face damp with perspiration, he remarked, "How clever you are, my little Queenie, eh? Won't get sent to the front now, will you? No mud in your trousers, what? Don't suppose you'd put in a good word for your old Uncle Edmund, would you?"

Queenie settled his face into its most cherubic expression and nodded understandingly, letting one pale palm come to rest on Marsh's forearm as he whispered his reply. "I wouldn't let you fuck me, so I'm not about to save your worthless bacon, sweetie."

Marsh's face turned gray, the same color that men of a certain age and paunch turn as their heart switches off in the middle of a family party and they collapse helpless into the blancmange. But then he rallied. Marsh put his wet mouth close to Queenie's ear.

"You do know what they say about old Bowes-Fitzgerald, don't you, boy? He's *riddled*. So I'm actually bloody glad I never fucked you, for I shouldn't have wanted to go back to Blighty with twenty-seven different strains of the clap."

"I hear you're marked for Ypres, love, so you probably won't be going back to Blighty at all." Queenie's rage didn't show in his measured, merry tone, or when he pressed his fingers to his lips and blew Marsh a faint kiss. He turned and wandered through the yard one last time, blowing kisses this way and that to his former comrades, to men and boys who would be dead by Christmas, to the flea-bitten horses and the so-called stallions and—

One last goodbye to say.

Past the stables he strolled, around the mud at the pump and down the lane between the trees. Toward the fence and the paddock where even now he could hear that ludicrous gray of Thorne's making all manner of fuss at his approach.

"Fairy horse!" Queenie stooped to pick up a fallen branch just as he had on that fateful evening with Jack, then he climbed over the fence and stopped, bowing low to Apollo. The horse's eyes rolled. It pawed its hoof against the earth and flared its nostrils. Slowly Queenie approached, wondering why the horse wasn't taking fright as he usually did, but glad for it. In fact, Apollo stood there, pawing and snorting, watching his approach. Watching until he was close enough to reach out and touch that snow-white coat should he wish.

"I'm going, horse." He bowed again. "You shall never see me again and I shall never see you, unless I'm feeding you to my gentleman's hounds. The trenches await you, Apollo Thorne, and I shall give you something to remember me by before I go on to a bigger and better castle."

With a smile, Queenie drew back the branch and slashed it against Apollo's rump. The sound of the impact split the air wide open and a moment later Apollo planted his forelegs firmly on the ground and bucked his rear hooves up hard, kicking Quentin Charles in the face with all his might. The impact sent Queenie's body flying into the fence, where he slid down the rough wood into the nettles, his neck twisted like a broken doll's and the grass around him growing dark with blood.

Chapter Twenty

Two days later Jack was in the paddock, brushing Apollo while trying not to acknowledge the bloodied grass. Someone had been out, after the dead boy had been taken away, showering the grass with a watering can to dislodge the clots and what one groom had helpfully pointed out to be brain matter. It hadn't worked.

Perhaps Jack should have felt pity on seeing Queenie's fate, but try as he might, it wouldn't come. Here, too, in the paddock, Jack had endured a savage attack. And here, too, had Apollo — again and again.

Nothing had been said. A terrible accident. Marsh had taken himself to bed with a headache. He'd certainly had once he'd finished all the Scotch in the chateau. It happened with horses, of course. And no one — no one — had pointed the finger of blame. There were six horses in the paddock that day. Perhaps all that singing had unsettled them. Bryn had said that, laughing. And Jack had nodded, not wanting to believe that his friend Apollo was a murderer.

How ridiculous.

But what about Sherlock Holmes and 'The Adventure of Silver Blaze'? A horse had been a murderer then. If Queenie had goaded Apollo, then Apollo was a killer.

Not one person had wept for Queenie. No special service of remembrance in the stable yard for him.

"Come along, Apollo!"

Jack didn't want to see the waste of blood anymore. A horrible end for a rotten boy. He made a soft clicking noise in his throat and Apollo, without reins, followed Jack as loyally as if he were his dog.

While Apollo drank from the stream, Jack sat with his back against a tree, sunlight falling on his upturned face. It was peaceful now. And nothing in his heart rebuked him for it. The rot at Chateau de Desgravier had gone.

Almost.

"You've got some bloody nerve, boy, haven't you? Sitting here having a picnic in your comrade's blood?" Marsh was picking his way down toward the stream. His uniform was unkempt, his cheeks red with drink and his eyes swimming with sleepless desperation. "Did you train Thorne's old nag to do it, did you? Point him at little Queenie and say, *have at it*?"

Jack got to his feet. He eyed Apollo, whose ears were warily flattened at Marsh's approach.

"Captain Marsh, sir. Good morning, sir." He saluted as if nothing were out of the ordinary.

"Oh, don't worry about all that silly old protocol, we're all chums here." Marsh approached, drawing closer. "What do you think about our Queenie then, missing him? Bloody rotten luck, what?"

Jack looked ahead, standing to attention, his voice a monotone. "It's a terrible shame, sir."

"It does mean, however, that a vacancy has opened for the prettiest lad in the palace." He smiled, showing yellowing, tobacco-stained teeth. "And that lad is you, young sir."

Jack remembered the discarded glove in the stable. That horrible, stinking leather *thing*. The proof that Queenie had no scruples at all. How on earth could that compare with what Jack and his captain had? With *love*?

Ignorance seemed the best policy.

"I don't know what you mean, sir."

"There are some ladies in the village who will do *anything*, you know, but I've a wife!" He finally stopped walking just a few feet from Jack. "And I could hardly look to another lady when I have one of my own at home, but a chap must take his comfort somewhere, mustn't he? What about you, girl, where do you take yours?"

"Excuse me, sir, but I am not a girl." Jack began to move away. He knew Marsh wouldn't come near Apollo, so he stepped subtly toward the horse. "And I take my comfort in my duties."

"I'm not a girl either. You'll find I won't disappoint, lass." Marsh reached out and caught Jack's hand in his own sweaty palm. He dragged Jack toward him and held his captured hand against his own groin, nodding as though he were offering the finest prize in France. "What do you say to that, eh? And I'm a generous sort of uncle too. I won't see my girl struggling for her smokes and brandy."

For a moment Jack was no longer in the paddock at Chateau de Desgravier. He was standing at a urinal in a public convenience, the sharp smell of disinfectant in his nostrils. A white-haired man with lonely eyes was touching his pale hand to Jack's elbow. *Looking for something?* And Jack had said no, and the man had nodded and walked away.

"No." Now all Jack could smell was stale sweat and tobacco and the reek of booze. He said "No" again, but Marsh did not relinquish his hand.

"Let my hand go, Captain Marsh, or you'll be sorry for it."

"I've seen you making eyes at old Thorney. He doesn't with *anybody*, girl or boy, lass. You'd be better off fucking the bloody horse." He thrust his hips toward Jack's hand. "Or your Uncle Edmund."

Jack's mouth was awash with bile. He turned to spit it onto the ground. Marsh was distracted by it, as if he found it alluring. Then Jack remembered something. A game the bullies used to play at school when a fellow's voice was breaking.

Putting all his energy into his fist, Jack gripped Edmund Marsh's balls so tightly that he was fairly sure one of them had shot back up into his abdomen.

"Like it, do you?" The veins stood out on Jack's neck as he gripped tighter and gave a quick, sharp twist. "That what you want is it, you disgusting old pervert? Have to offer bribes, don't you, because you're too repulsive to come near unless you pay!"

Marsh's eyes grew so wide that they looked ready to bulge out of his skull. His free hand clamped down atop their linked fingers, trying to claw himself free, but Jack wasn't about to be so easily dislodged. Sweat beaded on Marsh's forehead and he gave a strangled shriek, his face growing as deep red as the grass where Queenie had died.

"You're a bully! And you lay down with a bully!" Jack twisted again. "And if I ever hear that you've been after any of the other boys in that stable yard" — Jack found a reserve of strength and gripped even tighter — "I will come after you." He twisted once more. "And I will pull your balls off and serve them to you on a silver fucking platter!"

The expletive took not only Marsh by surprise but Jack too. It seemed as if Marsh's feet had lifted clean off the ground, and Jack pivoted on his toes and shoved the red-faced boozing officer and his stack-heeled boots off the bank of the stream and into the cold, fresh water.

There was a resounding splash and a yelp — Marsh helplessly beating his hands against the water.

"Oh, laddie — m' boy! I can't swim!"

Jack grimaced, tensing his fist as he watched the entitled buffoon wash downstream toward the chateau. Where, unfortunately, he would be easily fished out by the NCOs.

"What a shame, sir. What a terrible, bloody shame."

Chapter Twenty-One

And the days rolled on.

Summer became autumn and the sun-dappled evenings grew darker as the Western Front crept closer to the chateau, inch by inch, foot by foot, yard by yard. It was as though all who lived there in the shelter of that fairytale castle could sense what lay just beyond the next horizon, because the chatter grew lighter than ever, the determination to stay chipper outweighing the inevitable truth that all had to face. This was a lottery. Some would go, some would stay and some would never see home again.

Yet Jack and his captain still clung fast to each other as the nights drew in. The day was work for both, with the general at the chateau more than ever and Thorne's desk no longer a place where they might snatch a few minutes of passion. Now it held maps and telegrams, papers and battle plans so sensitive that no man was permitted access, no matter how much Captain Thorne adored him. Yet still they had that rococo bedroom where they made love deep into the darkest nights, where Jack would shelter in his lover's arms, the piano shawl about his shoulders, his kisses keeping Thorne from the worries that clouded his handsome face all too often nowadays. Still they had the summerhouse or the woods and still, as autumn deepened, Captain Thorne took his evening swim and there on the bank would be Jack, his paper and pencil at the ready should inspiration strike.

This evening though, there had been no swim, and instead they walked along the bank of the stream hand in hand, strolling as though it were a particularly bucolic stretch of the Thames. Thorne was all good humor and still trying to summon the words that might make Jack's ode to Apollo complete, yet his lover knew him well enough to know that something was amiss.

"It's a lovely evening, isn't it?" Jack breathed in the soft scent of the oncoming night. He wanted a comforting thought to cling to. "Almost as if we were back in England."

"How I wish we were." Thorne's smile was rueful and he squeezed Jack's hand. "How lucky you are, to know that your farm is still waiting to welcome you home."

"And you as —"

Jack froze to the spot. There, in the stream…the water billowed with blood. It was red, so red, sanguine and bright. Onwards it rolled toward them, rubies in the flood.

He heaved for breath, shuddering, even as he realized that all he had seen was a fall of red autumn leaves as they cascaded through the water.

"Hold me, Robert — I'm afraid."

"You have nothing to fear." Thorne drew him into his arms, kissing Jack's forehead. "I swore I'd keep you safe, didn't I?"

"Yes. And you will be safe as well, won't you?" But even as Jack spoke, he read the look in Thorne's dark eyes.

"You're going home, darling. Pa doesn't have *much* influence, but— You're a young man, a farmer. You should never have been sent out here in the first place." He managed a smile, but Jack could see the struggle between relief and utter despair. "Three days from now, you'll be safely on your way."

"Back to Shropshire? Back to the farm? But...no...I can't just go. I can't leave you. I can't!"

"We need every man we can get. HQ's closing down." Thorne took a deep breath, his voice firm. "The rest of us are moving up."

"The chateau—? But...*everyone?*" Jack couldn't bear to form his question, because he knew what the answer would be. "Including...you?"

"A few chaps will stay behind with you to tidy the place up before joining us. I've managed to get your Welsh chum on that but—" Thorne nodded. "We leave at first light."

"But *you're* staying too, aren't you?" Jack was cold, as cold as if he had fallen into the stream with the blood-red leaves. "You are, you are! Please say you are! Please say you're not going!"

"Buck up, Trooper Woodvine." Thorne mustered a little of the captain he was, his gaze fixed on Jack's eyes. "It's not my first trip to the trenches, and young Pritchard will be here to keep you company."

He pressed his palm to Jack's shoulder, resting it there softly. "I need you to be strong, to be the chap who nearly tore Captain Marsh's balls clean off. Can you do that?"

It had been funny when Jack had first told Thorne about the furious, red-faced man drifting helplessly downriver. But it wasn't now. It was just another incident of violence in an unending stream of pain and blood.

But what choice did Jack have?

"Yes…yes, all right. I'll be strong. I promise you. I'll write to you from the farm. I'll write to you every day. You'll get so annoyed with all my letters, you'll laugh! And I'll be waiting for you, at the farm. I'll stand at the top of the lane every day and I'll wait for you to come."

"Jack, please— I'm sorry we never found the ending to your poem." Thorne shook his head and reached into his pocket. From it he withdrew a folded piece of paper, which he pressed into Jack's palm. "I want you to take this, and then— Whatever promises were made— Go home, find someone. Love and be loved."

Find someone. So this was the end? All through those nights he had spent at Thorne's side, their bodies becoming as one, divided only by the morning light. He had thought that only death could tear them apart. But he had been wrong.

With a rage he hardly dared acknowledge, he saw that he had been dismissed. Thorne may as well have raised his hand rigid in a sharp, unfeeling salute.

Dismissed. He had promised Thorne his love, unchanging and constant, eternal and abiding. He was a fool to have ever given this man his heart, to have believed his loving words, only to be thrown aside.

Angry tears fell heavily on the paper. Jack knew it was a drawing, but he couldn't bear to look at it.

"Is it that easy for you? Is it? Just give me a bloody drawing and send me off? You love me, you told me — again and again, you did! And now — you're just sending me away. Like a parlormaid you grew tired of because she kept breaking your posh vases. Just a wave of the honorable captain's wrist and I'm gone!"

"Your poem" — Thorne pressed his hand to his breast pocket — "has been kept next to my heart since the day you gave it to me. It always will be."

"You're a liar — you'll only hurl it into a ditch, just as you have my heart!"

Jack wadded the drawing into his fist.

"Did you ever even love me at all? Was I just a convenient distraction for a bored officer? Because I love you — and maybe I shouldn't. Maybe I can stop as easily as you."

"A wave of my *honorable* damned wrist has sent you home —" He blinked quickly and withdrew his hand from Jack's shoulder. "I'm about to tell a gang of decent young lads that they should be honored to lay down their lives for a few feet of mud and a war that was never ours to start with, so perhaps you're right, maybe you shouldn't love a man who can do that."

Jack started to turn away. He looked back for a moment, his anger blown out like a sudden storm, feeling somehow older than he had been only minutes before.

"I would have died for you. I would have gone into battle at your side and laid down my life for you." He shoved the ball of paper into his pocket. "And I would have been *proud.*"

"And I would rather face hell itself than ask you to spend a second at the Western Front." Thorne heaved in a deep, hoarse breath. "So I'm sending you home."

"I saw it in your palm—I knew we'd be severed. You said you make your own fate, but…I have to go, I can't bear to look at you anymore."

Jack tried to hide the love in his heart as he looked back for what might be the last time in this world at his captain. *Lone in the field*, just as Jack had once written. He wanted to hate him, but he couldn't.

"Goodbye, Captain Thorne… And good luck."

"Goodbye, Trooper Woodvine. My very best wishes go with you, and Apollo's too."

Jack couldn't speak—if he had opened his mouth he would have cried, would have run back and embraced Robert Thorne and told him that he loved him and that he hadn't meant what he'd said in anger.

But he couldn't.

The severing had come.

Chapter Twenty-Two

That night, Jack wasn't the only person to lie awake, restless. He heard the other grooms sigh and turn in their beds, the occasional grunt and expletive rending the stuffy air. At each sound from one of the grooms, Jack felt guilt afresh. That he was going home, and some of them never would. And that it was the love of his captain that had saved him.

Thorne loved him. How stupid Jack had been, to shout at him, to screw up the drawing, to part — maybe forever — under such a cloud. When he'd headed back to quarters, he had tried to flatten out the paper. He had seen then that it was the drawing of Jack and Apollo in the paddock. But because he was surrounded by the other grooms, Jack had forced himself not to cry.

Alone in the long night, Jack got half-dressed, just as he had on the night of the storm, when he had gone down to the stable. It had been a lifetime ago. There was one goodbye that he still had to make, and that was to Apollo.

The horse was resting, neat under the blanket that Jack had covered him with earlier. Apollo whinnied in greeting and Jack put his arms around the stallion's strong neck.

"Evening, soldier." Jack pressed his lips to the horse's mane. "Now, you be a good boy at the front, eh? Don't kick anyone, don't get your coat muddy, and whatever you do—" Jack swallowed down his tears. "Whatever you do, look after your dad. There's good pasture in Shropshire, my lad, and it's yours for the taking if you bring him home safely to me. Is that understood, soldier?"

A rumble in Apollo's throat told Jack that his orders had been received. The horse lowered its mighty head and butted against Jack's gently, snorting his goodbye.

And for a time they rested, face to face, Jack and Apollo, the fiercest horse in the company, the stallion that no groom had ever tamed until Trooper Woodvine came to the castle.

Chapter Twenty-Three

Each soldier stood to attention at the foot of his bed. The walls were bare now of magazine cuttings — no more ladies of the stage displaying their legs, no more postcards from home. It was Captain Marsh who came bellowing into the quarters. Even showering the grooms with spittle as he shouted, it was plain to Jack that the man was terrified.

If Thorne came too, then Jack would apologize. Somehow. Would try to make it better, even though Jack had made it all the worse. Jack waited as Marsh screamed his orders, but still Thorne didn't come.

The soldiers who were off to the front filed out of the attic, kitbags on their backs, caps not always on straight. They shook hands with the few who had been given a short reprieve. The attic steps creaked under their footsteps for the last time, leaving Trooper Woodvine, Trooper Pritchard and the other almost-lucky few alone.

Bryn patted Jack's shoulder.

"Better start getting tidied up then."

"I'll…give it a going-over up here, if you chaps want to go down. See if there's anything left in the bathrooms."

There was a strange selection of items — loose bristles from shaving brushes stuck to the sinks, ends of soap, a snapped comb, a well-chewed toothbrush abandoned on a windowsill.

The noises from outside grew louder — horses' hooves in the stable yard, the shouts of officers. Jack heard the unmistakable bark of Captain Thorne and his heart leaped. Perhaps he would come back to the attic, just once more, then Jack could say goodbye and hold him, even for a moment, and tell him that he hadn't meant what he'd said.

Bryn knocked on the bathroom door.

"They're ready for the off, I thought you'd like to know. We can get a good view at the window at the end."

The attic overlooked the driveway as it followed up from the ancient stone archway. Jack and Bryn, side by side, watched the field of khaki below. Orders to march, orders to load up. Thorne was about to pull his whip from his boot at the infraction of some soldier — instead, he placed his hand on the boy's shoulder and gave him a careful smile.

For a moment, Thorne turned his head. He looked up at the attic, the windows that were still grimy no matter how hard they had been scrubbed.

He can't see me watching him. He can't.

Jack placed his palm against the cold glass, as if it were a caress. He mouthed the words.

I love you.

Then the khaki was gone, the horses, the staff cars, the wagons, the boxes.

The soldiers had gone to the front.

Later that day, Jack and Bryn were sweeping the yard. Bryn had spent the day singing to himself. Snatches of hymns, lines from folk songs, sometimes in English and sometimes in Welsh. Sometimes with the original lyrics and sometimes with his own, usually involving feats of swearing that were quite remarkable for a chapel choirmaster.

He began to sing a song that Jack had heard at Mrs. Byatt's knee. Jack joined in. To block his crowding thoughts, he kept his mind on home, and on the farm and on his father and Mrs. Byatt's splendid pies. He had been spared by his captain.

Nor father nor mother shall make me false prove,
I'll 'list for a soldier and follow my love.

Jack stopped singing, his heart leaping in his chest even as Bryn carried on, the song of a girl who disguised herself to go into battle to find her sweetheart.

In a few days' time he'd be on a ship crossing the Channel. He'd be put on a train. He'd cross over two hundred miles of England, then he would be home. While Thorne and Bryn and Trooper Burney and every other one of them would be in a trench. Or in a makeshift grave.

Jack's life was no more important than anyone else's. *Follow my love.*

Then and there, Trooper Woodvine decided — he would go to the front.

Chapter Twenty-Four

Two days passed.

Two days in the trench.

Two days beneath the bombardment, the guns falling silent as the long night drew on, the last night that many would ever see.

Thorne was no novice to this, of course. He had been here before, or somewhere very like it, and he had survived each time. He had done his stint, had his time behind the lines, come back to the front and so the cycle went on. This time was different, though. Here, deep beneath the earth, picking through mud, lodging with rats, sharing the air with gunpowder, it already felt as though the world had come to an end.

By the light of a low trench lantern he stood before a tiny hand mirror and ran a tortoiseshell comb through his pomaded hair. With a *tut*, Thorne plucked out a silver strand and discarded it, smiling at his own ridiculous vanity, at the man who would comb his hair as he prepared to meet his maker. His smile faded as quickly as it had appeared when he thought of Bryn and his friends, the men who would arrive here at nine only to be told that the order had come in from the powers that be.

We go over the top at eleven hundred hours.

Over the top.

Over the top and into the guns, to the barrage that would cut them apart, would scythe through them before they had a chance to draw breath, and he would be at the head of the column, leading out his brave boys. Thorne swallowed and plucked his cigarette up from the ashtray. He put it between his lips and turned away from the mirror.

Captain Robert Brereton Thorne, youngest son of Lord Brereton, cavalry officer, was not a man who admitted defeat easily, and he might just as easily be back here tomorrow. God willing, he might be farther up the line in a new trench, one where a man just like him currently stood smoking a cigarette and thinking of all the things he should have said, a man who happened to have been born in Germany rather than England. Or he might be dead in no man's land, hanging like a scarecrow on the barbed wire, caught in the makeshift gibbet as a warning to those who followed.

But Jack was safe, and if sending him home to the farm, to a life, meant that Robert Thorne was hated then so be it. Better to have the man you love curse your name than die at your side.

He pressed his hand to the poem in his pocket and closed his eyes, tears welling again at the thought of Jack, the warmth of him in his arms. From the gramophone his mother's voice sang of the raggle-taggle gypsy and on the bed lay the letter received from his father that morning. Lord Brereton had worked the miracle that had saved Jack Forrester Woodvine but despite his best efforts there was to be no like miracle for Apollo. The white stallion who had grown from a little gray foal with hurt and anger in his eyes, who had overcome his birth lameness, would be with his pa to the end, whatever the end might be.

Only now did Thorne allow his tears to fall. Tears for the love he had destroyed, for the gypsy who had won his heart, for the horse who stood even now brave and firm in his stable, blanketed against the cutting winds. If Apollo Thorne fell tomorrow, he would fall a hero, safe in the eternal care of the man who had raised him.

Thorne dabbed at his eyes with his handkerchief, cursing the tears, cursing the reports of ships being lost at sea, cursing the fact that he might never even know if Jack had made it safely across that treacherous water. He cursed love, cursed the memory of Jack's chestnut hair against his shoulder, his soft, full lips against his skin, and more than any of it, he cursed himself for not being as strong as he wished he could be. He couldn't afford any hint of this tomorrow, no suggestion of fear for the lads and, most of important of all, no suggestion of fear for Apollo. As far as his boy was concerned, this was nothing more worrying than a gallop across the summer pastures at home in England.

That was enough to pull Thorne up sharp. He dried his tears, smoked the cigarette down and wound the gramophone once more. Then, standing there beneath the same lamp that had lit the stable where he'd slept in Jack's arms, he closed his eyes and listened to their song play.

Somewhere along the trenches he could hear someone take up the melody, plaintive and tuneful, then another voice joined and another until a ghostly choir rose up into the silent, smoky night, singing of the gypsy and his lover, forever roaming, forever in each other's arms. And silent among the singing, his eyes closed and his hands clasped tight behind his back, Captain Robert Thorne waited for dawn to come.

"What's all this fucking racket?"

"Marsh." Thorne opened his eyes and blinked in the dim light. "It's my old ma, Edmund, so watch your language in front of her."

Marsh slurred in his drunkenness. "Oh...yesh, Antonia What's-her-face, the one with the splendid legs. And" — he extended a hand in the vague direction of the gramophone — "and a spectacular pair of...lungs."

Thorne sighed, unable even to work up the energy to be offended by this sad character anymore. What a woman Mrs. Marsh must be. She was either very patient, very stupid or very often absent.

"I'm just about to turn in," Thorne lied, the image of Jack snuggled beneath the sumptuous covers at the chateau jarring him. Or Jack slumbering in the summerhouse, his head pillowed on Thorne's chest, their hands linked. "What can I do for you on this fine evening?"

Marsh propped himself up against the makeshift wall.

"You don't want this any more than I do, eh, Thorne. This — this going over the top business."

"No man here would ask for it, but each must do his bit, eh?" He sounded like his father, Thorne realized, or like his father *used* to sound. His letters didn't have quite that tone anymore, not now his own boy was one of the *lads*.

Captain Edmund Marsh pulled his service revolver from its holster, weighing it on his palm. Its metal was dull gray in the lantern light.

"Do a fellow a favor, eh, and I'll do one for you. Have a drink, old boy, and you'll barely feel a thing."

For a moment, *more* than a moment, Thorne looked at Marsh, not entirely sure he understood. Only when he had stared at the revolver and turned the words over in his head did he say, "Don't be a fool, man."

"A fool? I'm offering you a Blighty One, you abject halfwit! A ticket home! Shoot me in the toe and I'll shoot you in yours, and the two of us hold hands in the ambulance all the way to Boulogne."

"I'll pretend that you didn't just say that, Marsh, for the sake of the men out there."

"They've done it too!" Marsh's face turned redder, drool gathering at the side of his wet mouth. "They bloody well have. When I was last out here, three of the little sods did it in the space of a week, and they all went home to their mummies. It's not my fault if it hasn't occurred to that bovine lot out there — maybe they *want* to die in the morning? But I *don't*."

Thorne crossed the dugout in three paces and seized Marsh by his lapels, thundering him back into the earthen wall.

"What the bloody — " And Edmund Marsh, pathetic, desperate, terrified, was the focus of all the sadness and fear that Robert Thorne now carried on his shoulders. The gentle man who had cradled Jack was gone and in his place was the furious captain, the soldier whose withering bark could stop a man in his tracks at forty paces.

"Nobody wants to die, Marsh, but every one of those lads has more courage in his little toe that you do in your bloody body. Give yourself a bullet, Edmund, and remember their faces when you look in your mirror each morning. You're a damned coward, man!"

Marsh was choking on his own spittle, his eyes bulging.

"But cowards get to live."

"I don't even care enough to pity you." Thorne released him and stepped back. "You're pathetic."

"*I* am? I'm not the one who'll die a virgin."

Marsh, his eyes crossing from drink, raised his foot and put it on a stool. The revolver slipped in his clammy hands as he tried to grip the handle. A muscle tightened in Thorne's jaw at the sound of Marsh releasing the safety catch.

The drunk officer looked up at Thorne, and a thin, weedy song about *dear old Blighty* slid from his lips.

The dugout rocked as a shell landed nearby, the lantern swung above their heads and shouts came from outside. The report of a service revolver rang out and Captain Edmund Marsh collapsed screaming to the floor.

Chapter Twenty-Five

It wasn't yet light as they lined up in the stable yard. The last few lads from the company HQ at Chateau de Desgravier, kitbags primed, yawned in the cold autumn air. There was a hint of ice on the breeze.

Bryn's voice was low. "You're a bloody idiot, you are."

"Possibly — but at least I'm not a coward."

"You didn't believe all that tosh, did you? '*Greater love hath no man*' and all that. It was never meant to be about all this — it was never meant to be about war. You can still go home, Jack. Go on!"

"Keep it down at the back there!"

The NCO, who proudly bore the nickname 'Walrus' on account of his enormous mustache, bellowed across the yard. He stamped his feet from the cold, examining a letter under torchlight. Then he turned the torch onto the sparse rabble before him.

He counted their heads, nodding with each number. He counted three times. He yawned, looked at his watch, counted again.

"Is one of you lads playing silly buggers? I've got one more in this stable yard than there is on my list!"

Bryn's voice was low and urgent. "Piss off out of here, Woodvine!"

Walrus had his back to them, pacing back and forth. Jack caught Bryn's glance and shook his head, his finger to his lips.

"For the love of God…" Bryn fell back into line, pinching his nose as if he was trying not to cry.

"Right, chaps!" Walrus bellowed, "Time we were off! The charabanc's arrived!"

Bleary-eyed, they climbed on board. Walrus sat at the front, unable to hear the grooms who had spotted the cuckoo in the nest.

"Thought you was going home, Woodvine? Why the hell are you going to Wipers?"

The cuckoo met their curious stares, holding his gaze steady. Jack was here because he always did the right thing.

"Because you're my mates, and I'm coming with you."

The charabanc bounced along the chateau's driveway, resounding with the soldiers' cheers.

As it drove past the gatehouse, the enchantment broke, and the fairytale castle was lost to them all forever.

Chapter Twenty-Six

With the dawn came the barrage, wave after wave of artillery slamming into the earth as though God himself were hurling down his wrath upon them.

Through it all, however, Robert Thorne was serene. He listened to their song time and again and, when he went to where Apollo waited, whistled the melody to his only remaining friend on this godforsaken earth.

By now his beautiful Jack would be on his way to the coast and by lunchtime he would be safe on British soil. He could ask for nothing more than that.

Once again before his mirror, Thorne shaved his jaw and pomaded his hair, combing it just so amid the shaking earth. He could do nothing about the sleepless rings around his eyes or the pallor of his skin, let alone the way the grime settled into the faint lines around his eyes, highlighting the years he had seemingly gained in the last seventy-two hours.

The last shave, the last comb of the hair, the last listen to the song…

The severed line in his palm had told a tale — he had just been too bullish to hear it.

He wondered about Edmund Marsh, whose Blighty had gone awry and taken half his kneecap with it, leaving the man writhing in agony here in the dugout where Thorne now straightened his tie and checked his kit once more.

Let him die out here, die with a gun in his hand and Jack's name on his lips, Apollo's reins firm in his hand. They would die together if they would die at all and when the end came, both would go without fear, in the sure knowledge that, in a fairytale castle, they had been blessed.

Because, once upon a time, the snippy captain and his bad-tempered steed had known the kindness of Jack Woodvine.

Thorne held his hand to his heart, to the poem that sprang to his lips now as easily as a breath. He checked his watch, set his cap on his head and whispered, "Go safe, my gypsy. I love you."

A sharp knock at the door announced a soldier, tin hat dented, oilskin over his shoulders to defend him from the thin, persistent rain. This was no place for embroidered shawls on the bare skin of a lover.

"Captain Thorne, sir — the charabanc's arrived with the last of the lads from company HQ."

"Good man." Thorne gave him the shadow of a smile. The lads from the castle, the lads bound for no man's land. "I'll be along in a minute or so."

The soldier lingered a moment.

"One of them has a message, Captain, that he particularly wanted to give you. In person, sir."

Thorne pinched the bridge of his nose and was about to tell the NCO that there was no time for such things, that officers weren't at the beck and call of troopers. Then he thought of Jack, that this was someone's son, one of the chaps from the stables, that the message might be from his gypsy —

Has he forgiven me for shattering his heart?
Don't be absurd.

"Very well." He nodded. "Send him in."

There was a shout farther along the trench, a bark of, "Slow down, Trooper! No running!"

Boots clattered along the duckboards, the hurrying trooper not dissuaded. Closer and closer the footsteps came, and the soldier in the doorway stood aside.

For Trooper Jack Woodvine.

Framed by the rough wood of the doorway, his cap at an angle on his chestnut hair, mud already spattered on his smiling face, his sea-green eyes glowing with the only ember of hope that Thorne had seen since leaving the chateau.

"Captain Thorne, sir!"

He executed a perfect salute and stood to attention before his officer.

Was he dead already? Had the bombardment brought the dugout down and given him this last hope in hell, this last moment between this world and the next, forever trapped with the ghost of what might have been? Was heaven a trench containing the vision of Jack Woodvine?

"What—" Thorne saluted, his mouth dry. Then he looked to the NCO and told him, "Dismissed!"

Jack closed the door. They were alone now.

His eyes gleamed softly, like glass washed smooth by the ocean. He cast a glance at the gramophone — it was still playing their song. He rushed at Thorne to embrace him, to reach up to his mouth to kiss him.

"Please forgive me for what I said, my dear darling—I didn't mean it. I love you, Robert, and I know you love me. I can't live without my heart—and you have it, there, in your hand!"

"What in the name of God—" Thorne stepped back, staring at him. "I sent you home! I cashed in every favor I— My father—"

"But...but I had to see you again." Jack tried to approach but, as Thorne took another step away from him, the trooper came no farther. The light was dying in his eyes. "I couldn't...I couldn't bear it, that you thought I didn't love you. I've driven myself mad, my words repeat and repeat in my mind—I had to tell you that I love you. That I never stopped loving you and I never will!"

"Then you're a fool." Thorne knitted his gloved hands behind his back, just to stop himself from reaching for Jack and drawing him into his arms. If he allowed himself to do that, he knew, he would never dare to let go.

Jack being safe was all that had kept him standing firm in hell and now... Now it all meant nothing, now they would all die here anyway and that love, that great blossoming love, would bleed into the mud of no man's land.

"You were right with what you said, I'm a rich brat. How many troopers do you think I've declared undying love to? How many do you think I send home when they get too attached?" He set his jaw, hating himself with every false, cruel word. "You were just a nice way to pass a boring summer."

Jack recoiled as if he had been slapped. He bunched his fists and kept them at his sides, his body heaving as sobs tried to shudder through him. When the tears

The Captain and the Cavalry Trooper

began to fall, they washed tracks through the patina of mud on his face.

"Don't say that! Because it isn't true! You loved me—you did! You still do, because I can see it in your eyes! I *know* you—better than anyone else on earth."

The gramophone had stopped playing, the needle bumping through static. Jack pressed a fist up to his mouth, but it didn't quite suffocate the cry in his throat. The dugout was filled with his hopeless whimper.

"Why should you wish to wound me so, Robert?"

"I'm your captain, soldier. Anything else was a silly game. How was I to know you were stupid enough to believe in it?"

And he would die, he knew. If there was a God, He would reach down from the heavens and throw Robert Thorne against the wire, leaving him there to bleed.

And I deserve it.

"You're going straight from here to the ship, Trooper, and from there back to England." He drew in a sharp breath. "And think yourself bloody lucky that you're not in serious trouble."

"You're a bloody liar! You were listening to our song—I could hear it all the way down the trench, and I ran to it as though you had called to me!"

Jack strode to the gramophone and kicked it over. The brittle record flew free and smashed to useless pieces on the floor.

"Soldier!" Thorne bellowed to the NCO who had brought Jack to the dugout. He seized Jack roughly by one arm and hissed, "I don't fall in love, Woodvine."

"I bloody well wish I never had!"

Jack's free hand shot out and slapped Thorne across his perfect, square jaw.

The NCO shoved open the door.

"Do you want me to fetch the military police, sir?" Grabbing the young man from Captain Thorne, he bellowed, *"What's all this, Trooper?"*

"Trooper Woodvine has papers to sail for home, he's discharged." Thorne looked at a spot over Jack's head, no trace of a flinch at the sound of distant artillery. "See that the MPs get him safely out to sea, however much he complains."

Jack had to be almost carried. He hung against the NCO like a puppet with cut strings. He blinked at Thorne, then squeezed his eyes tight shut.

They sprang open again at the sound of a voice shouting along the trench.

"It's Apollo!" Bryn yelled. "He's kicked down the stable door and he's out in no man's land!"

"Wha—" Thorne could hardly process this new horror, his feet suddenly rooted to the spot.

Before anyone could stop him, Jack had wriggled free of the NCO and leaped onto the nearest ladder. He glanced from one side to the other, and as Thorne lunged for Jack's legs, the trooper was over the top.

No whistle had been blown.

Over the racket of the continued bombardment, the distressed whinnies and thundering hooves of Apollo could be heard. Thorne could hear Jack's voice too, but the sounds were becoming more distant as each second passed.

"Sir?"

Bryn, his hand resting on the rung of the ladder as if he was about to follow his friend, stared at Captain Thorne. There was steel in his tawny eyes as he was waited for an order.

"I didn't mean it," was all Thorne could say, his voice weak. Then he pulled Bryn clear of the ladder and threw himself up and over the top. He dropped down onto one knee, looking out into the wasteland for his lover and that snow-white steed, but there was only thick smoke, slowly clearing.

"Hey, handsome boy! Hey!"

Jack's voice, his fingers clicking. And Apollo—a whinny, the sound of hooves thumping against the soil, as if he had reared up and returned to four feet.

"That's it…come along… Let's get you back to your stable, nice and safe—that's it, there, I've got your bridle now. Aren't you good, my handsome fellow? Home safe in time for elevenses—that's it, that's—"

A huge explosion ripped the air. Jack never finished his sentence. Apollo uttered a high-pitched whinny and shrapnel thudded across the mud.

"Jack!" Thorne gave a cry of pain as hot shrapnel seared into his calf, embedding itself in his boot and the flesh beneath it. "Jack!"

A low moan of pain sighed on the smoky air, and a cough, as of someone struggling to breathe, their lungs giving up.

"Sorry…so sorry."

What a thing for a lad to say as he lay injured, in a war he had never asked to join.

"Robert…hold me… I'm scared."

"Keep talking." He dropped down to the ground, his leg dragging. "I'll find you!"

"I dreamed of you last night…" Jack coughed and another pained sigh escaped him. "I tried to reach you…but I couldn't."

"This time, you're going home." Thorne finally made his way through the smoke, mud slicking his entire body from chest to toe, and he pitched headfirst into the shell hole where they were.

Now he could take Jack's hand, holding it tight. Apollo stood over him, frozen, a smear of blood on his white shoulder. "Both of you."

The heat in his leg was growing, though, and so was the pain, but this was more important than him. This was Jack, this was Apollo—they were the only things worth a damn out here. They wouldn't breathe their last in this hellish place.

"I was never good enough to deserve either of you," he whispered.

Jack's voice was a slow rasp. "What…do you mean? You are a good—a great—man…honorable Cap…Captain…Th-Thorne…"

Thorne tried to stand, but he realized that his leg wouldn't take his weight, even the touch of his foot on the ground sending pain lancing up his body. Instead he stayed on his stomach and, with a monumental effort, managed to drag Jack onto his back. He took Apollo's reins and looped them around his shoulder then, letting out a gasp of pain, pushed himself up to all fours.

And so, his injured leg dragging uselessly, the weight of Jack against his spine and the unsteady horse walking alongside, the usually immaculate Honorable Captain Robert Brereton Thorne crawled through the filth and blood of no man's land. Around them the world shook and the shrapnel flew but still he struggled on, a foot at a time, toward the trenches.

Jack shivered and gasped in his agony. Thorne could feel the blood from Jack's wound seeping onto his body, garlanding him like wet flowers. Each breath was labored, each more of a struggle than the last.

Then, with no effort at all, his voice light, Jack said, "I can hear my mother calling me. It's cold…so cold… Am I going home?"

"Only…as far…as Shropshire." Thorne stopped, sinking down a little, the insistent flame in his leg burning afresh. Yet Apollo did not stop but continued forward, leaving him with no choice but to go too, tethered as he was to the animal's reins. He could hear voices shouting now, but he couldn't tell where they were, or what they were saying. He could only keep on moving, a creature of dirt and blood that had risen from the earth itself, creeping agonizingly closer to safety.

"In my pocket… Look in my pocket, promise me, Robert."

Delirium. Nonsense. But he felt Jack's hand sweep for a moment against his hair.

"It's in my pocket. Then you'll know that I…"

Trooper Jack Woodvine fell silent.

"No! Jack, no!" Thorne heard his own frantic voice and moved with a renewed determination. He crawled on, gently singing their song, lost now on that smashed record, as though that alone might keep Jack alive. The world was swimming, smoke stinging his eyes and the noise of the bombardment deafening, with sanctuary somehow growing farther and farther away with each passing moment.

Then a hand rose up out of the earth, and his first instinct was to recoil from this creature of the pit, this open grave, but the hand was too quick, its grip too firm. Only as he was dragged over the edge and eased down into the dugout did Thorne realize that the hand belonged to Bryn and there, staring in horror and wonder, was a cluster of familiar faces. They went to catch the reins from his shoulder and Apollo slid and slipped down into the trench with them but Captain Thorne was already emerging. He heard his own voice, sure despite the hoarseness, telling Bryn, "Get him right back as far as you can, he's got a shrapnel wound. If anybody tries to take him, tell them I'll have them cashiered!"

"Yes, sir." In haste, Bryn dispensed with a salute and shoved his way past the men from the chateau, Apollo's reins tight in his hands.

The stretcher bearers arrived almost at once.

With fingers to Jack's neck, they pronounced him to be still alive and lifted him carefully onto the stretcher. Jack stirred with the movement. He half-opened one eye and fixed it on Thorne. His mouth shaped some words that could not be heard and the bearers carried him away.

"You next, sir!"

"It's a scratch. My soldier comes first." As if to prove it, Thorne rose to his feet once more. Pain blazed up from his leg but he gave no indication of the agony, merely snatched up a rag and wiped the mud from his eyes before he bellowed, "Fetch me Marsh's horse, now!"

Then he was heading for the stables, sheer nervous exhaustion driving him on, cutting through the pain and keeping that foot rising and falling despite the injury to his calf. Apollo was the fastest horse in the regiment, of course, but Tsarina wasn't far behind, and with Captain Edmund Marsh currently languishing in hospital with his leg hanging off at the knee, he wouldn't be calling for his horse anytime soon.

Thorne unfastened his tie and pulled it tight around his boot in a makeshift tourniquet for the wound that still seared in his shin. This time he wasn't too proud to use a mounting block, and in truth doubted he could take his swing up into the saddle without one. Yet here there was no block to be had and it took the helpful hand of a trooper to hoist his captain's foot up so that he might take his place atop the midnight-black mare. Thorne didn't even know the man's name but he barked a command of, "Help Pritchard with Apollo. Keep him calm, keep him safe!"

Then he kicked Tsarina with a gentle force, urging her on after the ambulance.

Thorne arrived at the Dressing Station just in time to see a figure on a stretcher being loaded into the back of a motor ambulance. The soldier was half-mummified in bandages, but his chestnut hair, slightly too long by regulation standards, made it all too obvious that it was Jack.

Thorne called his name just as the doors slammed shut and the engine growled into life. The ambulance accelerated through the mud, its large-spoked wheels churning over the mire.

They were taking him to the Clearing Station.

The ambulance had a head start and a two-horsepower engine. But Captain the Honorable Robert Brereton Thorne had the second-fastest horse in the regiment and a soul that burned with fire.

Through woods, through copses the ambulance drove, through the burned-out husks of hamlets, where people somehow still lived. Flat farmland passed by on either side, Tsarina foaming at the mouth but still carrying her rider onward.

At last, the Clearing Station came into view. It had once been a farmhouse, its barns and stables now converted into wards, the field behind full of row upon row of hastily built huts. A train rattled by, its desolate whistle echoing over the fields.

The ambulance drove beneath a stone archway and into the yard with its outrider just moments behind. Tsarina's hooves clattered and echoed and Thorne pulled her up sharp amid the medics who hurried here and there, the walking wounded who looked on dazed from the sidelines and the nurses, brisk and focused as they crossed the cobbles.

Thorne remembered his injured leg too late as he threw himself from the saddle. As soon as his foot hit the ground his leg buckled beneath him and he caught Tsarina's reins, somehow forcing himself to stay upright. He felt a warm cushion of liquid beneath his sole, his boot soaked with his own blood and, within the limb itself, the insistent stab of shrapnel. He knew that he looked like a madman, a mud-caked, bleeding figure with wild eyes, but he could see only the ambulance containing the man whose heart he had broken, and he cared for nobody but his gypsy.

But the damned leg…

And Jack's last request— *'Look in my pocket.'*

No, not his last request. Thorne blindly handed the reins to a nurse, stumbling again but still keeping his balance somehow.

"Easy now…" The doors of the ambulance were opened, Jack on his stretcher lifted out. A thin groan of pain escaped his parted lips, his eyes rolling under his struggling eyelids.

"Excuse me, sir." A nurse had her hand on Thorne's elbow. "This way, sir—how did you get here on horseback with that wound?"

"It's nothing—" He tried to pull free, but she tightened her grip and somehow, somewhere along the ride, Captain Thorne's strength seemed to have bled out. Yet still he dragged his useless leg toward the ambulance, taking the nurse stumbling with him.

"Jack!" Thorne called his name desperately. "I'm with you, Jack!"

The figure on the stretcher reached one arm toward Thorne, fingers clasping at empty air as he was carried toward the entrance.

With an effort, Jack moaned, "Don't leave me — I'm scared!"

"Sir, there's another ambulance on its way." The nurse's grip hadn't faltered. A cold breeze whipped her white headdress against Thorne's cheek. "You can't stand about here, and we need to take a look at that wound."

"Robert!"

Jack disappeared into the building, his voice left on the icy wind.

"You don't understand." Thorne looked at the nurse, aware only now of the smell of no man's land that he carried with him, of smoke and gunpowder and filth. "That's my boy."

This time he managed to yank his arm free of her grip. He followed Jack and his stretcher bearers into the hospital, pausing on the threshold as he looked this way and that for any sign of where they might have gone. At the realization that the hallway was as briskly busy as the yard and Jack had disappeared, panic began to well in Thorne's gut.

"Jack!" He seized a passing medic by the shoulder, leaving a filthy handprint on the man's tidy uniform. "Where did they take my boy?"

The tall man's gentle blue eyes met his.

"Jack, you say? There's a lot of boys here called Jack."

"He just — It's his shoulder, they have to be careful —
He broke —" Thorne swallowed hard, fighting against
the tears that welled in his eyes. "He wanted me to
check his pockets."

A hand alighted on the small of Thorne's back,
guiding him along the corridor.

"They brought in a young man with a lump of
shrapnel in his shoulder only moments ago — you must
be strong — he's lost a lot of blood. I'm about to scrub
up to operate." The surgeon raised an eyebrow as he
looked down at the handprint on his sleeve. "The
nurses are preparing him for theater. If you have any
information on his medical history — a break, you
say? — then we need you to tell us. Just go up to the
third door on the left. That's where he is. And you must
see a medic about that leg, young man."

Thorne could only nod in the face of this gentle calm.
Then he made his slow, agonizing way along the
hallway and through the door that the doctor had
indicated.

Jack was a shivering figure on a wooden trolley, a
gown half-covering him like a shroud. The nurses had
snipped off the bandages from the Dressing Station, the
brutal damage to his shoulder revealed, his pale skin
torn where once Thorne's kisses had traveled. His
filthy, bloodied uniform had been cut into tatters to free
him, the useless rags flung onto a chair. Jack murmured
under his breath, hiccups of pain and fear escaping his
soft mouth as the nurses bustled around him.

Thorne began to push his way through the figures
who were crowding around Jack. Yet he seemed to
suddenly be dragging lead weights in his boots, to be
caught in quicksand. Again and again he gasped Jack's

name, the shrapnel in his leg somehow having transferred itself like a red-hot lance into his heart.

"Who is this man?" The imperious matron turned on Thorne. "We're preparing the patient for surgery — you need to leave at once!"

But Jack was reaching for him.

"My pocket…"

"Now shush with all this nonsense about your pocket, young man!" She sounded as if she was quelling a cantankerous child. Then she rounded on Thorne.

"Do you know the patient?" It was an accusation more than a question. Thorne ignored it, reaching for Jack's hand, but the matron grabbed him by the pips on his arm and marched him out of the room. "I really don't care if you're a captain or a brigadier, you're not bringing all that mud into my prep room!"

"He broke his shoulder before— He needs me with him!"

"Broke it?" Her fierceness seemed to ebb. "And it's the same one that's injured? Do you know how long ago?"

"1916." That much he could say with certainty. "It wouldn't heal, it still gets weak— Let me see him!"

The matron placed her palm on Thorne's chest.

"Captain, I must ask you not to come any further. We can't have you and your mud around him, he needs to be clean for surgery. I'm not a dragon, sir — I only have the patient's best interests in mind."

Thorne looked down at her hand, clean and pale against his filthy uniform. It seemed to draw the fight out of him and he stumbled, only the impact of his shoulder on the wall keeping him from falling altogether.

"In his pocket—" It sounded weak, pathetic. "He said I had to look in his pocket—"

"Wait here, please, Captain…" She rustled into the room, and Thorne heard her make a curt announcement about Jack's old fracture. When she returned, she was carrying a bundle.

She passed it into Thorne's arms.

"Now take his uniform. He has twittered on and on about his pocket—I shall be very disappointed if all that's in there is a bag of barley sugar!"

One of the nurses came out into the corridor. "He's unconscious, Matron."

In a bark that would not have been out of place on a parade ground, the formidable woman ordered, "Get him to theater—on the double!"

The nurses hurried the trolley out of the room. Jack lay upon it as still and as pale as a knight carved on a tomb. He was dashed along the corridor and vanished out of sight.

"You bloody look after him," Thorne told her, clutching the humble bundle tight to his chest. "Please, please look after him."

"I wish more officers were as caring as you, sir. Now—would you like me to look at your leg?"

"No—" He dropped his face to rest against the bundle. "It's nothing—"

The matron looked him squarely in the eye, then gave a smile of recognition.

"It's Viscount Brereton's boy under all that mud, isn't it? I once knew your uncle. Now come along and let me look at this leg of yours."

"Everyone knows my uncle," he whispered, his face somehow managing to conjure a very faint smile. It was only then that Thorne realized, to his horror, that a tear was threading its way down his mud-caked face. With a quick movement he dashed his hand over his eyes and straightened. "My leg, yes. Took a bit of shrapnel, me and my horse—"

And that almost undid him again, the thought that he had brought Apollo out here, had betrayed the trust the horse had placed in him.

"I tried to tourniquet it—"

"Lean on me, Captain—arm about my shoulder, that's it... Hobble just down here to my office. We'll soon have you fixed up, don't mind about that. The three of you were all injured at the same time, then?"

"Apollo got out, he was terrified. Jack, he could always keep him calm, nobody else—" The captain drew in a deep breath and leaned heavily on her. "We got caught in no man's land, they were shelling us."

The matron tutted as if she had just found a footman making eyes at her daughter. She opened the door to her office, a sparse, plain room.

"On the chair, Captain Thorne. Boot off." She produced a pair of long-bladed scissors from a drawer. "Don't look so worried, I'm only going to cut up the seams of your joddies!"

Thorne managed to remove the boot with his shaking hands. Freed from the makeshift tourniquet and the tight leather, a fresh jolt of pain jabbed at him, this one stronger than any other. He couldn't help but give a gasp at the sheer agony of it and his hand on the bundle grew tighter, his knuckles showing white through the dirt. He vaguely tried to apologize for making such a show, but the words wouldn't come through his gritted teeth.

Matron was unfazed. She brought a jar down from a cupboard. "A morphine lozenge for you, I think. Open wide, Captain."

"I won't take it," he told her firmly, shaking his head. If he could feel pain, he knew he was still alive, still here. He couldn't be numb.

"If you insist on suffering through, that's up to you."

"I do."

She brought his foot onto her knee and knelt in front of him, wiping away the blood and filth to see the wound more clearly.

"Ah, there it is!"

She reached for tweezers from a ceramic kidney dish.

"Be a brave soldier for matron—I'll have this little bastard out in a jiffy."

Thorne nodded tightly, clenching his hands into fists as he waited.

With a sure, swift move, matron held aloft the lump of lead.

"There we are! Troublesome little sods, aren't they?"

She carefully palpated his calf and announced, "That's it. No more in there. You might need a stitch or two, but a bandage should see you right. Just as well you have such...such well-developed muscles." A delicate flush came to matron's face. "You might limp for a while, and I can't see you going back into a trench any time soon. Bite your lip, Captain—time for the iodine!"

Chapter Twenty-Seven

On a bench outside the hospital, soldiers with bandages and crutches shared their smokes and tall tales. Silent among them was Captain Thorne. He could hear the arrival of the ambulances — the lads from the chateau had gone over the top.

'Look in my pocket, promise me.'

So Thorne did exactly as Jack had asked of him. Such a simple act, for a boy who might even now — So much blood, the fabric in tatters. In the pockets, Thorne found ends of string from the stables and small, shiny pebbles from the stream. Was this what Jack had wanted him to see, reminders of the happy time they had shared?

Thorne went on with his search. Then, in an inside pocket of Jack's tunic, just below the holes left by the shrapnel, he found a neatly quartered sheet of vellum, dark with Jack's blood.

Thorne's heart thudded in his chest, a pulse leaping under the bandage on his leg.

The dried blood cracked as he opened it.

For R.B.T.
He walks in beauty, like the night
Under distant, unknown skies.
I saw a gleam; eternal light,
Twined with the darkness in his eyes.
Though no more before my sight,
My heart to his forever cries.
For what was said, in rage and fear,
Can time undo, draw back the flood?
And now that night again draws near,
I hear his voice sing through my blood.
Held in arms no longer there,
A ghost, a memory: I once was loved.

Then the tears came flooding from his eyes, coursing down over his face in hot, agonizing streams.

Once loved…

Still loved, forever loved.

How could I have done this to my gypsy?

There was a hand on his shoulder. The rustling of the starched uniform could only signal the presence of matron.

"Captain Thorne, am I to understand from this burst of emotion that you should like one of my morphine lozenges after all? It will pain you now, but wounds do heal. Even though this one'll leave a scar. Anyway, I came to find you because the surgeon wanted you to know that Trooper Woodvine is out of theater. He's very weak, and there's a long road ahead of him until he'll be back on his feet, and you must be prepared for — But I hope that with time and with care…"

And love.

"I don't care about my —" He folded the paper and placed it in his muddied breast pocket. "Can I see him?"

Matron prefaced her reply with a long sniff.

"It is somewhat unusual. And we are rather busy. However—I'm willing to make an exception. I like to see an officer care about his boys."

She patted his arm and strode away. A tired-looking nurse approached her, pointing toward the yard where the ambulances were arriving. Matron turned for a moment, indicating the captain on the bench, then she was walking toward the ambulances, parting the hubbub of orderlies and stretcher-bearers, nurses and medics like the prow of a ship cutting through the waves. The nurse pulled her cloak around her against the cold wind. She glanced at Captain Thorne, hiding a yawn behind her hand, and headed to the wards.

Thorne had no hope of looking his usual pristine self, covered in mud, one boot torn, his tie missing, but it didn't matter. None of it did because Jack was alive and they would be together, just the two of them and Apollo, on the farm.

The nurse returned. Her sleepless eyes were ringed with dark circles as she met Thorne's gaze.

"I'm very sorry, sir… I spoke to the patient on the ward, the one brought from your trench. He…he's very cantankerous. He refuses to see you. He wanted me to tell you, exactly, his sentiments. He said— '*Send the bastard away.*' I explained you had waited, but he would have none of it. I'm sorry, sir, I apologize—I must get on."

Her cloak huddled ever more tightly around her, she hurried away to meet the ambulances.

"Thank you," Thorne called, because politeness dictated that he should. Then he turned from the bench, from the patients and the hospital, and went to collect Tsarina.

Perhaps they might still let him go over the top. His heart had stopped already, after all.

Chapter Twenty-Eight

"How long have I been here?"

The young nurse brushed Jack's long fringe out of his eyes.

"Two days."

"Have I been asleep?"

"On and off."

"Did — did anyone come to see me?"

She put the thermometer under his tongue.

"No. Were you expecting some boys from your company?"

Jack couldn't speak with the thermometer in his mouth. He shook his head.

The nurse guided him to lean forward against her arm so that she could beat his pillows. Her hand near the site of his wound and he winced. She let him lie back and he closed his eyes.

Maybe it was better to be asleep.

But what had passed while he was awake and asleep had merged into a foggy morass. He had memories, but whether they had happened in reality or only in his mind he didn't know. He saw the trench again, heard the song about the gypsy, saw Robert. The music stopped and a great sensation of pain overwhelmed him. There had been an explosion, and there was Apollo, moving through the smoke. And there was Robert—but he must have imagined that, because what he remembered could not have been real.

Robert, carrying him on his back while he crawled through the mud. And Jack's mother, calling to him, *Come home, Jack, it's nearly dusk*. The song playing again then, or at least a version of it. Reaching for what was already lost. Reaching for his lover.

In the ward, Jack had heard voices he recognized, other lads from the chateau who had gone over the top that day. Captain Thorne's name was mentioned. Captain Thorne had been injured. But he wasn't at the hospital—Jack had asked the nurse. And that could only mean one thing.

Captain Robert Brereton Thorne, the honorable, the noble, was dead.

Because if he had been alive, he would have been here. He would have sat by Jack's bed, just as he had at the chateau, and nursed him and cared for him.

And—how perverse—it was better to think that Thorne was dead than that he no longer loved him.

Chapter Twenty-Nine

England
1918

The shadows were long when Jack awoke. It must've been late afternoon. The train had slowed down to take the last curve before the station. He always woke up here if he nodded off. *Not long now. Home soon.*

Jack had been given a spare, ill-fitting uniform at the base hospital, once he was recovered enough to get on his feet. He'd asked what had become of the original, but he was told that someone had mislaid it at the Clearing Station.

"Venbrook Halt!"

Jack dropped the window and stuck his head out of the carriage, waving his cap as the train pulled in. There were few people on the platform, and he was watching for his father. But he was nowhere to be seen.

Jack hopped off, dragging his luggage after him. In the few months since...since that terrible day, his wound had almost healed, but he couldn't swing his bags up onto his damaged shoulder. There was one lump of shrapnel that they hadn't been able to remove.

"Hello there, Jack Woodvine!" The station master came up to him, his watch chain shiny across his waistcoat. "We read about you in the newspaper. What a brave lad we have!"

"Oh, thank you, but I'm not brave, I'm really not. Is— is my father here?"

The station master scratched his head.

"Nope, that he's not, but Morris is out the front with the wagon."

Jack walked through the station to greet his old friend.

"Mr. Jack!"

Morris, smelling of whisky and the cowshed, creaked off the wagon to greet him.

"Look at you, what a fine boy you are, eh?"

On their way from the station, winding through the spring lanes, Morris told Jack about the comings and goings of the countryside. Names and faces Jack had almost forgotten, so alien had they been to the life he had lived in the year since he had last seen home, returned to his mind. Not very much had changed.

But he had. He must have been kidnapped by fairies and lived a year in only an afternoon.

"And Dad—where's Dad? I thought he'd collect me from the station?"

"He's busy, Mr. Jack."

That was all Morris would say.

The first stars were showing in the sky as the wagon finally rolled into the yard. The old stone farmhouse was like a familiar, friendly face, and Jack dashed away a tear.

'You and me and Apollo could live on the farm.'

Well, he wouldn't want Jack now, would he? An invalid with a piece of lead near his heart.

Because Jack had discovered that Captain Thorne wasn't dead after all. Not long after arriving at the base hospital, another lad from their company had been there and told him some heroic tale about Thorne's long horse ride with his leg ripped apart.

Jack had nearly written a letter then. Had begged ink and paper and pen from an orderly. Had sat outside, despite the cold day, but couldn't write the first word.

And everything had come back to him, and he had cried so hard, and had been so incapable of describing to anyone what hurt him so, that a doctor had knocked him out with the contents of a large metal syringe. The doctor must have thought it was something he'd seen in the trenches, like all the others.

Jack dropped his bags in the kitchen. He could smell eucalyptus and cloves. He went into the parlor, the large old room with its beams and its chimney with the arms of some old Woodvine in the plaster, and there he saw his father.

Jack fell at his feet and pressed his face into his lap. Each breath was a struggle, and the prematurely old man touched Jack's hair as if he wasn't sure he was real.

"It's me, Dad, I'm home now… I came home."

"I waited," John whispered. "I knew my lad would get home."

They sat very still for some moments, the fire in the large grate falling in on its glowing heart.

"Dad…why didn't you tell me you were ill again?"

"And give you something else to fret over, son?" He stroked Jack's hair as he had when he was a little boy. "I had Mrs. Byatt to look out for me, I've done all right."

"Dad—if I'd known... How have you managed with the farm?"

I would've come home when Captain Thorne sent me. I would've come gladly and...

What was done was done.

"Me and Morris and the boys, we've been doing this since you was a nipper." His father gave a gentle smile. "We're not falling apart just yet!"

"You're ill. You shouldn't be wearing yourself out. Let me take over the running of the farm. Please—I need to."

"You've just come home, son," John whispered. "Let's not worry about that now. You get yourself settled and I'll get the tea brewing."

"If you're sure you can manage? I wouldn't—"

There was no telling his father otherwise once he had an idea in his head.

Jack collected his bags and went to his room. Up the old wooden stairs, along the corridor, to his large bedroom at the end of the house. Even though it was late, there was still enough light when he opened the curtains to see the view along the valley. It was peaceful and still.

He tipped the contents of his bags out on the bed. A notebook of poems, a pencil stub in a metal holder, an assortment of clothes that didn't really seem to be his. From the notebook he took out a piece of paper that he had almost got the creases out of—a drawing given to him, he knew now, as a tribute to their love. A love he had scorned and destroyed.

He sat on the bed and gazed at the valley. For a moment he imagined what he would do if, just around that corner, there was a figure on a horse. His captain, his lover, come to claim him.

He looked through his records. At the top of the pile was Antonia Sheridan's rendition of *The Raggle-Taggle Gypsy*. It wouldn't hurt, would it, just once more?

He cranked the gramophone into life and there she was, the woman he had daydreamed about, the woman he had once hoped would be his mother. He curled up on his bed, the embroidered shawl from Chateau de Desgravier wrapped around his shoulders. It still carried with it the scent of his lover, a smudge of his pomade on the rich cloth.

Chapter Thirty

What use was a soldier without a war?
What use was a man without a profession?
Captain Robert Thorne didn't feel much like a captain anymore. He didn't feel much like anything at all, just a shell, empty and hollow with a void where his heart had once resided. He had sat down to write to Jack so many times, yet each time the words wouldn't come, each time he thought of Jack's words at the hospital, of the despair in his eyes when they parted.
'Send the bastard away.'
And he had been sent away, far away, home to England to a desk job that didn't exist, a desk job that seemed to consist of doing nothing at all. He no longer had a purpose — he was a leftover from a war that was nearing its end and no one in Whitehall had any use for him now. Of course they applauded him. Medals that rained down for valor and gallantry, for courage under fire, and they said, *'You've done your bit, you've earned some time in Blighty.'*

Then, this morning, had come the telegram. It was a telegram that some men dreamed of, offering him his freedom, should he wish it. A position at Sandhurst was his too, but the decision was his to make. The army and a life that was regimented, training other young lads to go to hell, or life on civvy street, a hero of the war who would never need to scream at a soldier again. What a wonder it would be to take the latter choice, not alone but with Jack Woodvine safe in his arms, wrapped in that soft shawl, their kisses mingling for the rest of their lives.

'Send the bastard away.'

And he had gone away, gone back to the trench and found himself sent back to the hospital. Back and forth, bewildered, lost and heartbroken.

It might have been yesterday, every evening bringing that dream of his beautiful gypsy, the kisses, the long, loving nights and the last, terrible day when Jack had looked at him as though he were a monster.

Here in the sun-dappled grounds of a Sussex mansion where Viscount and Lady Brereton spent their carefree weekends, Thorne settled to sit on the grass. Beside him Apollo grazed, the wound in his shoulder long since knitted. The great horse hardly moved as his master leaned against his leg and tore open the letter that had arrived that morning. He barely blinked as he read the contents with a sense of disbelief and, somewhere in his soul, hope.

My dear old Thorne,
How goes it all in your pomaded life, lad?
Well. Though it gives me no pleasure to admit, you were proven quite right. My Blighty one turned out to be a very big one indeed, and they took my bally leg for my sins. Mrs.

Catherine Curzon & Eleanor Harkstead

Marsh believes that the best cure for a lost leg is a trip to take the coastal air, and though one remains unconvinced that the Welsh air is likely to regrow a limb, one knows better than to upset Mrs. M.

And this brings me to my true reason for writing.

You and I were not close, my boy, but I didn't do right by you when they put me in the old hospital. You had the grace to visit and I told them to send you away, which was no way to treat a chap who I've since discovered knows HRH.

So I do apologize for that. And finally, I have a little favor to ask of you, you fine fellow. Tsarina has never settled since she returned home and I seem to remember that your young friend had a knack for the tricky ones. I've no doubt that you and your chum (he was in my hospital ward – quite the coincidence!) are still firm friends and if you would like to take Tsarina and see if she might be happier with your old nag, I'd be happy to let her go for a good price.

Do give your lordly pals a nod from me, and let them know that I do look quite the chap in ermine.

Your good friend,
Cap Edmund Marsh (Rt)

"*Meu querido!*"

Thorne was too busy reading Edmund Marsh's letter to hear his mother for a moment, and when he did he folded the paper, reeling from what it contained. Only then did he offer a brief wave as Apollo lifted his head to watch Antonia Thorne approach.

She switched easily from Portuguese to English. "Darling, don't sit on the lawn like that. You'll get a chill."

"I survived the war, Ma, I don't think a little bit of dew is going to finish me off." What had become of that captain he had once been, he wondered? The fearsome bark and the cracking whip, now reduced to hiding from the world in his mother and father's stately bolthole.

"That's what your Uncle Afonso said, and he ended up with terrible piles."

She pressed her lips to the top of his head.

"Don't fuss." He smiled, though, because for the first time, Edmund Marsh had given him something to smile about. Maybe.

But so much time had passed, and he had broken Jack's heart, and he loved Jack as much now as he ever had. It was a love, a regret, an agony, that would torture him to his grave.

"How would you feel about having a major for a son?" Thorne tested the sound of it in his head. *The Honorable Major Robert Brereton Thorne*. It sounded old, fusty, like the men who smoked pipes in his father's club and reminisced about the days in the east. "They've offered me a position at Sandhurst."

He leaned back, palms flat on the grass, and peered up at his mother. She looked down at him through dark eyes, along her aquiline nose, and blinked.

"Or I can chance myself in the real world, whatever that is. Though I'm not sure I'd do all that well out there."

Yet perhaps he had inherited some of her talent for the stage, because he was doing a damn good job of playing the part of a man whose heart hadn't been dashed in a dugout somewhere on the Western Front.

"I will be proud of you whatever you do, my *Roberto,* but you must ensure that it makes you happy." She leaned over her son, her arms about his shoulders. Her long chiffon scarf slipped from her neck and she laughed as it draped over him. "My poor boy…you have been so sad since you came back, but…who is that letter from? You're smiling. In your eyes, my son, if not your lips."

The bangles on her wrist clicked and jangled as she reached for his letter. He snatched it away and she laughed again.

"Do you have a *querida* after all... So secretive over the years, my handsome boy will have a wife? Is she beautiful—say she is."

"I knew a very beautiful someone once. A gypsy." He swallowed hard, trying not to meet her gaze, but it was impossible. It always had been. "And I thought my beautiful gypsy had come to hate me and I've just found out that I was wrong. And it's too late, Ma. I'll go the rest of my life never knowing—"

"My darling *Roberto!* If your gypsy does not hate you, then...do they love you? It is never too late."

She took her son's chin in her hand.

"And do not fear any scandal. The viscount's son and the gypsy... I nearly lost your father, you know... He came to me backstage with his flowers and his love, and I pushed him away—because I loved him too much for him to risk the approbation of his class. But he was determined... Love does that to the Thornes. Apart from your brother, but then..." Antonia winked, laughter trilling from her scarlet-painted mouth. "He *is* a crashing bore!"

"I'm never going to have a wife, Ma." That was true, no matter what happened. "Although that old reprobate Marsh has asked if I'll buy his bloody horse *and* get him a title too! The horse— Well, that part goes without saying."

Antonia drifted to the grass to sit beside her son, her sharp chin resting on his shoulder.

"A horse? You will need your own stables!" She mused for a moment, staring out across the lawn to the hill that had been moved from left to right across the vista by Capability Brown.

"But...the gypsy. I want to know. Was this in France? You can tell your mother. What color were their eyes, their hair—so that I can picture them. Did you kiss them, *Roberto?* Was it a grand *affaire*?"

"Don't, Ma, please." He heart skipped a beat, the familiar stone of regret in his gut once more. "Apollo and I are better alone—" Thorne looked down at the letter he still held and told the horse, "But you won't be, will you? Because you'll have Miss Tsarina Marsh to contend with, boy!"

Apollo lifted his head and blinked as though considering that. He turned his head to look at Thorne then went back to chewing the grass, as gentle now as he once had been unpredictable.

"They say gypsies have a magic way with horses—is that who it was, *Roberto,* who calmed Apollo?"

"A magical sort." He nodded, patting Apollo's leg gently. "And my gypsy thought you were the most splendid woman ever to tread the boards."

"This magical gypsy of yours has excellent taste." Antonia tickled the tassel on the end of her scarf against her son's nose. "You have love in your voice, *Roberto*— I can hear it."

"*Amor*, Ma?" Could he, though? Could he at least say *I'm sorry*? "Should I slope off to Shropshire and throw myself down at the feet of the gypsy who used to love me? I couldn't bear to see the hurt—"

Antonia dragged her long scarf about her son's neck and pulled him down to lie in her lap as he had when he was a boy. She passed her long fingers through his pomaded hair and looked down at him with eyes that flashed as darkly as his own.

"Throw yourself down before your gypsy! If they are hurt and if they hate you, then you come away having lived and learned. And if they still love you...*meu querido!* How can you bear to stay another minute here, and not know?"

"Because I'm frightened, Ma. I'm more frightened of that than I was of any trench, any bloody bullet." Thorne closed his eyes, assailed by the memories once more. "I'm frightened to stay, frightened to go— More than anything, I'm frightened of waking up in fifty years and wondering, *what if?*"

Because what if is the worst thing.

And what if is all I've got left.

Chapter Thirty-One

Summer began in Venbrook with a wedding. Although war still raged, it was somewhere else, on the other side of the rolling hills. The village square was decked with blooms, and the locals perched along the churchyard wall to sneak a view of the blushing bride and her even more blushing beau.

Jack had pomaded his hair, had bought a new suit and a hat. He'd found his grandfather's walking cane under the stairs and polished it to a shine. Beside him in the church his father looked radiant, and as Mrs. Byatt began to walk up the aisle, her arms full of flowers, Jack had to dash a tear from his eye.

His father was doing the right thing, marrying the woman he loved. *At bloody last.*

The newlyweds were gone by the afternoon, off for a week in Llandudno. Woodvine senior had spent the past month moving his belongings, bit by bit, the two miles to Mrs. Byatt's cottage. Day by day, familiar objects vanished from the farmhouse. But as each object went, Jack replaced it with something of his own.

He had put Thorne's drawing in a frame and hung it over the desk in the study. Almost all the creases had come out. Those that remained reminded Jack that, whatever should happen in the years ahead, he should never let anger overrule his heart.

Jack had moved the gramophone into the study. He liked to sit there on warmer days, the window open, serenading the sheep and the donkey and the farm cat that stretched along the wall, with a song that took him back to a fairy-tale chateau. To a time before the enchantment had snapped.

But he didn't want to play it this evening.

Seeing the newlyweds hand in hand, seeing them so happy, Jack had inevitably thought of Robert. Would it really be so ridiculous to write to him? Just as a friend. He had letters from Bryn, who had a managed to get a desk job away from the front line. He had letters from Wilfred, who had been invalided out after the loss of an eye.

I look bloody amazing in an eye patch, mate – the girls love it!

But what could Jack possibly say to Robert Thorne, the viscount's son?

He could always ask about Apollo.

Jack primed his pen. He took out his letter paper. He cut some blotting paper to size. He rummaged for an envelope. Wondered where he'd put the stamps.

He was prevaricating.

Time, then, to make a pot of tea.

Jack saw his reflection in the kettle as he waited for the water to boil. He'd keep the suit on a bit longer, the rose in his buttonhole. He'd lounge about and drink brandy, like a grown-up. Maybe assume a manly habit and take up an evening cigarette. He was now the owner of Woodvine Farm, his father officially retiring on his marriage. He would do well to look smart at market. *'A good, firm hand at the market and you'll never have your prices beaten down,'* his father always said. And now he would find out.

He hummed to himself as he carried the tea tray along the flagstone corridor. He suddenly felt very lonely.

But then, as if attempting to write the letter had somehow summoned Thorne into being, like a specter at a séance, Jack had the distinct impression that he was not, in truth, alone. He could feel the presence of the man he had dreamed of and lost. Some tautness to the air, and the very scent of him — so out of place in the humble stone corridor with its worn scarlet runner on the floor.

And that song.

Jack's heart had melted away like snow.

No. No, it must be the wine Jack had drunk earlier. Thorne wasn't here. He couldn't be. Unless — was he still out there somewhere? In some trench, had Thorne at that moment passed over? And was this his final goodbye?

Jack left the tea tray on windowsill. The very thought that Captain Thorne was no longer in this world left him weak. He held his breath as he went back to the study, slowly nudging the door open, not knowing what he would find.

"Somehow, and I have no idea *how*, I have managed to acquire Captain Marsh's mare."

The Honorable Captain Robert Brereton Thorne made his announcement as though it was the most natural greeting on earth for former lovers meeting after what seemed like a lifetime apart. He was perched on the edge of the desk, a faint tan on his skin made all the more noticeable by the bright white cricket sweater and flannels that he wore. The tip of one shoe rested on the chair and he reached up to run a hand over his carefully pomaded hair, as though such care was *ever* necessary.

"And I thought, perhaps, you might like to join me for a canter through the Shropshire Hills. If you've nothing else planned, of course."

"I-I've just made a pot of tea." Jack fidgeted with his tie, his heart leaping in his chest. "Are…are you real? Or have I well and truly lost my mind?"

"I'm real, Jack, and I—" Thorne shook his head, his dark eyes glittering with a thousand stars. His voice, initially light and confident, faltered. "I'm so very sorry for what I said to you. And I never for one moment stopped loving you, but I would've said anything to make you go home."

Jack's hand involuntarily moved to his shoulder. He dropped his arm to his side.

"That wasn't much of a salute, was it, Captain Thorne? Sorry. I was a bloody terrible soldier!"

"Your hair was too long, your boots were never polished but you kept the horses immaculate." Thorne smiled, a spring sun dawning over a frost-shrouded world. Then he slipped down from the table and snapped a perfect salute for his soldier. "You were the finest bloody fellow ever to serve, Trooper Woodvine."

"You never found it, then. In…in my pocket? I hoped you'd understand. I regretted it so much—you only wanted to keep me safe. I know that now. I had such a silly idea that love could exist among all that blood and thunder—and then I nearly killed the pair of us for some boy's idea of romance. I wish to goodness I'd gone home when you told me to, but then... I sometimes wonder if that wasn't what kept us both alive. Because you didn't go over the top."

"*He walks in beauty.*" Thorne drew in a deep breath and nodded. "I found it that day and I knew then that we— I asked to see you in the hospital but a nurse told me in no uncertain terms that you didn't want to see me ever again."

"But no one asked me! If they had told me you were waiting for me, I would've smashed down the door myself to let you in!"

"I found out *this* bloody week that she managed to ask the wrong fellow." Thorne reached into his pocket for a folded letter, which he held out. Jack realized then that the captain's hand was trembling, just a little. "She asked Captain Marsh if he'd see me, rather than Trooper Woodvine."

Jack laughed, because it was the only possible reaction to have.

He came a step nearer to Thorne, his fingers twitching.

"I'm not a vain chap, but I find myself wondering how on earth anyone could muddle up me with that repellant old twit!"

"You look so well, Jack." The captain withdrew the letter and placed it on the desk. Was that a smile that twitched those full lips? A light sparking in those dark eyes that shone once again with undisguised affection? "So full of life."

"Unlike the last time you saw me."

Jack wasn't going to hold back anymore. He strode straight up to Robert Thorne and put his arms around him, resting his forehead against his cheek.

"I thought I'd dreamt it, that you carried me on your back, on all fours, through no man's land, with shrapnel in your leg. And then I came home and it had been in the newspapers!"

Thorne laughed softly and admitted, "It gave me a new appreciation for what life must be like for Apollo!"

"You didn't even have a saddle." Jack took Thorne's face in his hands. "I bloody well love you, Captain Thorne. Every handsome, stern, adoring inch of you. Now…whenever are you going to kiss me?"

"Before I do, I have to tell you something." He blinked, fixing Jack with a mischievous look. "I'm not a captain anymore. I'm afraid I'm just a plain old *Honorable* these days."

Then he pressed his lips to Jack's for a kiss that pushed away all the months apart, the tears and the longing, his strong arms encircling Jack's waist so tightly that he might never let go. "And I love you, Mr. Woodvine, with all that I am."

Jack trembled in Thorne's arms, touching his fingertips to his face.

"Tell me that you forgive me." Thorne searched Jack's gaze. "I felt as though my heart had been torn out. Every day, every hour, I could think only of you. If they had told me to walk out into no man's land on the promise of one more night with you, I would have gone gladly. Please, Jack, say you forgive me."

"I forgave you in no man's land, when you called my name."

Jack took the rose out of his buttonhole and touched its petals to Thorne's face.

"I never hated you. I knew, deep down I knew, you only did it to save me. To push me away, push me home where I'd be safe. And how did I thank you?

With a slap across the face, and a broken record on the floor. Do you have any idea how I lay there in hospital, playing it through in my mind again and again – hating not you, but myself."

"But you survived, we're here." Thorne let his forehead rest against Jack's and clenched his fist tight over the lines in his palm. "We made our own fate, Jack. That's why the poem was never finished, because *our* poem goes on."

"I love you, Captain… I mean, Mr. – "

"As of midnight, plain old mister." There was another kiss and another, every tear, every moment of lonely despair ebbing like the ride. "But always *Robert* to you."

Jack swept his hands across Robert's broad back. The strong, protecting presence of him, that wonderful scent, exotic and masculine – it was as if they had never been parted.

Desire hitched in Jack's voice.

"So there's still a few hours left then – you're still my captain?"

"I'll always be your captain." With his arms around Jack, Thorne sidestepped as neatly as though he were squiring a blushing deb at a village dance. In one elegant movement he dropped down to sit in the desk chair and pulled Jack into his lap, whispering, "Always."

Passion surged through Jack's veins and he kissed Thorne with all the power that was left to his damaged body. He twined their fingers together and brought them to rest over his heart.

"Can you feel it? Can you feel how hard it beats for you? And it never stopped, not once."

"I'm yours, Jack, if you'll have me." They kissed again, the answer already told. "Say you will, gypsy, please."

"Do you even need to ask?"

"My Jack, my beautiful gypsy—" And he had no more words, lost in their kisses.

Jack delighted in ruffling Thorne's perfect hair, knowing that it was he who had peeled away the stern captain, knowing that it was he who had made him smile. Right from the very first time that their paths had crossed in this world.

"Will you stay here? Will you live with me on the farm? Just as I promised you... It was just a dream then, but now I've got you back, I'm not going to lose you again."

"Apollo is in the paddock already, I don't think he wants to move again." Thorne smiled tenderly into the kiss. "And Tsarina is but a day away. Am I home, Jack?"

"You've brought my friend Apollo? Well, you do know how to please a chap! And Tsarina's coming too? Yes—you're home—both of you—we all are home."

"Come and see your boy?"

"*Our* boy."

Jack let Thorne lead the way, back along the corridor, past the forgotten pot of tea.

"You've settled in fast, Robert."

"Getting Apollo and my bags here was a bloody nightmare, darling. We're here to stay."

"I should bloody well hope so! Oh, now wait...there's some cake left over from the wedding breakfast—yes, my dad married Mrs. Byatt, and they'll be in Llandudno by now. I'll get the cake...and some bread and butter. Shall I bring it out on a tray, and we can have a sort of picnic? I bet you're starving. And — "

Thorne saw it at once, as soon as they were through the low door into the kitchen. The shawl from the chateau, draped haphazardly over the back of a chair by the stove.

"You have my drawing, I have your poems." Thorne scoped up the shawl. "*We* have *our* shawl."

Jack kissed Thorne's cheek as he went past him into the pantry. He clattered about, loading a tray, regaling Thorne about the wedding. And Thorne sat in the large wooden chair and smiled as Jack told him about the flowers, Mrs. Byatt's new hat, the granddaughter of one of the farmhands who had been flower girl.

"There's elderflower wine here, as well," Jack announced.

"Don't even begin to imagine I'm going to let you lug that tray." Thorne stood in the doorway, the shawl slung over one shoulder. "That's my job."

"Captain Thorne, ever the consummate gent." Jack winked at him, and they went out into the sunshine.

There in the paddock, as though he had always lived in a peaceful corner of Shropshire, Apollo grazed. At the sound of his approaching masters he raised his head, and let out a joyful snort at the sight of Thorne. Apollo's dark gaze moved over the captain and settled on Jack then, with a whinny of sheer delighted welcome, he cantered across the pasture toward the couple. With the tray held safe in his hands, Thorne told his horse, "Here's your other pa, boy, he's missed you!"

Jack rubbed his cheek against Apollo's, whispering to the horse who he had nearly died to save.

"We're all safe now, Apollo — we're all home!"

In reply, Apollo snorted softly, his face snuggled close to Jack, and Thorne told his steed, "And the answer is yes, Master Thorne, you can bring your lady friend to stay."

"But no hanky-panky, Apollo—I'm far too young to be a granddad."

Jack's hair was defeating his pomade. His fringe caught in his eyes as he grinned across to his lover.

"How do you get your hair to stay so neat, Robert?"

"I shouted it into submission." He laughed. "You're perfect as you are!"

"I propose a toast." Jack poured the elderflower wine into teacups. "To us, and to home...and to peace."

Thorne went down on one knee to place the tray on the grass, no doubt so he could join Jack in the toast. Yet he didn't stand, didn't take the cup, didn't do anything but simply meet his gaze. Then he slipped his hand into the pocket of his trousers and withdrew it, something cupped in his palm.

"Jack, my beautiful gypsy." Jack saw him swallow, his lips caught in a hopeful smile. Then he opened his palm and the sun glinted off the gold band that he held, the same gleam shining in the darkest depths of Robert Thorne's eyes. "Although we can't have the ceremony your father and the new Mrs. Woodvine did, would you do me the honor of being my husband or wife or whatever you would rather call yourself, as witnessed by the fine Mr. Apollo Thorne? Soon to be Apollo Woodvine-Thorne, I hope."

Jack gazed down at the viscount's son, seeing before him the man he loved. The man he adored. Jack dropped the teacups and clutched his hands to his chest. Whether it was what one did or not at a proposal, he sank to his knees and embraced his husband.

"Yes — yes, yes!"

His lips met Thorne's. The kiss went on and on. They had a good many to make up for, after all.

Until a soft, whiskery muzzle decided to nudge against them.

"You'll always be trouble, won't you, Apollo?" Jack rubbed the horse's nose, receiving a friendly snort in return. Yet Thorne had more weighty matters on his mind and took up Jack's hand, gently sliding the gold band onto his finger.

"This was my grandfather's wedding ring. The late Viscount Thorne was a bit of a hellraiser." Thorne kissed Jack on the tip of his nose. "And I think, in true British style, it's beginning to drizzle."

Jack collected the scattered teacups and Thorne picked up the tray.

"To the kitchen?" But Jack saw the corner of Thorne's mouth quirk up. He was looking in the direction of the stables.

There was an echo of the wide-eyed groom in Jack's voice. "I promise, Captain Thorne, those stables are immaculate."

"Trooper Woodvine, shall we inspect Apollo's quarters?" He rose to his feet. "Lead the way, soldier."

Off they went toward the yard, leaving the paddock behind them. Apollo threw his head up into the rain then took off at a happy canter, his mane flowing in the soft summer breeze.

"This one, I think." Jack unbolted the split door and showed Thorne in. "Spacious but cozy. And a fashionable address to boot!"

Thorne stepped into the cool interior and set the tray down on a bale of hay. He filled the teacups with another helping of wine then put his hands on his hips and looked around, his face set in a serious, stern line.

"Not bad, Trooper Woodvine, not bad at all." He turned to Jack and opened his arms wide. "Now come here!"

Jack rushed into his arms and kissed him.

"My husband dear, my captain. Now let's have our picnic and shelter from the rain."

Thorne's arms encircled Jack and lifted him clear off his feet for a few seconds. "Does that make you my wife? I love you, Jack, so bloody much."

"I'm your darling, that's who I am."

The drizzle fizzed against the yard, and Jack watched it for a moment through the half-open door, his head resting on Thorne's shoulder.

"Do you remember — the night we spent in that stable?"

He could see from the smolder in Thorne's gaze that he certainly had not forgotten. His captain pressed a gentle kiss to Jack's hair and whispered, "I told you that I didn't fraternize. What a fool I almost was."

Thorne drew back just a little and with one hand draped the shawl over Jack's shoulder. His smiled, his face utterly serene when he asked, "Might I tempt my darling to a wedding night roll in the hay? For old time's sake?"

"Our honeymoon in the stable...why not? And every anniversary to follow!"

Jack kicked off his new brogues, careless as to how they landed. His eyes on Thorne, he started to unbutton his jacket. Urgency building within him, he pressed his mouth to his husband's ear.

"Help me out of this ridiculous suit, for god's sake!"

It was a delightful jumble of eager hands and gentle laughter, loving kisses and irresistible embraces but eventually, somehow, Jack and his captain found themselves naked in their impromptu marriage bed of straw. Now, for the first time, Jack knew that they had all the time in the world, and the evening sun and the trilling birdsong and nothing but this waiting on the horizon. They lay wrapped around each other, legs entwined, bodies pressed together, kisses and soft words ringing on the evening breeze. How many times could Jack hear the words 'I love you' and not tire of it? How many times could he be caressed, by the same hand, over the same few inches of skin, and at each stroke only feel the intensity of that love and the strong unyielding bond all the more? How many times could their bodies — scarred and beautiful, lost and found — reconnect and recombine?

For Jack and his captain had passed through a furnace. And love had survived, and so had they. They had wandered into hell and emerged in their earthly paradise, where there was shelter enough, and where there was peace. Jack had heard the earth shake under battle, but he now heard it sigh with the rain.

There was nothing else Jack needed to say and Robert fell silent too. Instead Robert Thorne — not captain, not Honorable, just Robert — devoted himself to kissing Jack's throat, his lips, his shoulder. Jack held the man who was his whole life as they made love. His hips barely moved yet the faintest thrust was enough to send thrills of pleasure coursing through him. Jack felt as though they were two halves of one, joined by an invisible thread even when a whole world stood between them.

And still he whispered, *I love you*.

Jack loved as he was loved, sure that loneliness would be banished for all the days yet to come. The seasons would change, the moon rise and the sun shine but here in their sanctuary he and his captain would be undiminished, safe beneath the unbroken blue of a summer sky. This was a refuge they would enjoy together, forged from artillery and fear and the love that had come so close, horribly so, to being forever lost.

All that was lost is found, all that had been severed has been mended, every wound has healed.

Jack let his captain love him, tenderly, absolutely. Their bodies twined together, completing, adoring.

And the captain was there with him, no longer a dream, no longer a thought of what might have been, but forever his, safe in this place where nobody would find them. His captain, his Robert, whose every muscle seemed to be tensing, whose skin was hot, whose body was hard and whose kisses were so soft when their lips met again in the moments before they left the world behind completely.

They soared up into a bright, white space, brighter than any phosphorus flare. Into a place where there would be no more partings, no more pain.

And on it went until Robert's head sank to rest on Jack's shoulder. He gasped for breath and repeated again and again those declarations of love that had seemed lost. There was something else too, the sensation of warm tears rolling over Jack's scarred skin as they fell from the captain's eyes. When he lifted his head again to meet his lover's gaze there was no sadness, only the bright light of joy.

The rain outside had stopped and the air was alive with the scent of a summer evening and the sound of

Apollo's happy whinnies from the neighboring paddock. Jack and Thorne lay there in the straw, gazing at each other in, satisfied contentment until Jack smiled brightly at the disarray of his usually so pristine lover.

"That straw in your hair definitely suits you." Jack went to brush it free but Thorne stilled his hand.

"Leave it." Thorne smiled and snuggled against Jack, holding him in a tender embrace. "I think I'm going to enjoy being a farmer."

Jack leaned toward his husband, waiting for his kiss. Robert took Jack's face in his hands and pressed his lips gently to Jack's but this time there was no sadness, no thought that this was the last, but the sure and safe knowledge that they were just beginning. It was a kiss that said *forever*, and it went on and on and on.

Want to see more from these authors? Here's a taster for you to enjoy!

Captivating Captains:
The Captain and the Cricketer
Catherine Curzon & Eleanor Harkstead

Excerpt

What on earth are they feeding these babies?

Another ruddy-cheeked mother passed her enormous child to Henry. He balanced it on his hip, smiling politely as he jiggled it up and down.

"What a lovely boy!"

Puppies, kittens, foals, lambs, calves and piglets were more Henry Fitzwalter's style, the daily business of a countryside vet. He was at ease around them. But not human babies—they were strange and alien beasts indeed. The infant reached out its pudgy hand and tugged Henry on the nose, yanked Henry's neatly trimmed sideburn then grabbed a length of his hair and pulled.

Henry winced. "Certainly a strong 'un!"

"Daniel, you bad boy!" His mother at least had the grace to be contrite regarding her infant's outrageous thuggery, and wrestled the unfeasibly large child from Longley Parva's vet.

Nestled in the South Downs, Longley Parva had been the home of Henry's family for generations. And today, on this sunny Sunday afternoon, Longley Parva was closed for a street party to raise funds for the roof of the village hall.

Daniel was swapped for another child, who came accompanied by the odor of milk. Henry bounced the baby and it cooed at him. It appeared to be a little girl, judging by how frilly its outfit was, and although it was almost entirely bald, it was wearing a sequined Alice band.

A car tooted, an engine revved. A nearby shout of, "The road's closed for the party — what's the bloody matter with people?"

Women's Institute stalwart Mrs. Fortescue tutted. "Mind your language in front of the babies!"

Henry, ignoring the baby's grip on his knitted tie, stared from his vantage point at the top of the village's High Street toward the other end, where barriers and stalls were being shifted as a car approached.

A classic car in British racing green nosed its way toward him. He knew it, because it had been tootling around the village for Henry's whole life and for decades before that too. Everyone in England knew it, because this was the soft-top Jaguar of Captain George Standish-Brookes. This was the soft-top Jaguar that had transported its driver and his popular histories straight into the nation's hearts.

Henry clenched his jaw. *That bloody man.*

Cries of "It's Captain George!" filled the street, the Longley Parvans nudging one another and grinning, some even waving as the car wound its way along the crowded road. The final of the Bonny Baby Competition was forgotten.

George drove into the center of the village like the returning hero he was, classic Wayfarers hiding his eyes, the car horn blaring merrily and a crowd following as though the Red Sea had just parted.

George — Henry's childhood friend through thick and thin, until the day the Longley Parva Cup disappeared. George — the television historian with the knowing wink and dazzling smile. George, who sailed through life without a care in the world, waving now at the locals as he drove toward the podium with one hand on the steering wheel.

The handsome bastard.

Of course the road closure didn't apply to George, even though the vicar on his bicycle had been turned away and told to come back on foot. Rules *never* applied to Captain George Standish-Brookes. Not at school, not in his Bohemian home, and now, not at the village fête.

George made his own rules.

Unable to raise a hand in polite though grudging welcome without dropping the baby, Henry gave George a terse nod.

"Fitz!" George turned off the ignition and the car, somehow, came to rest at just the right angle for a classic car shoot. He pushed open the door and hopped out onto the green, a vision of easy, casual confidence in cricket sweater and chinos, his dark hair tousled just so, the sun glinting from the face of his watch.

Who still wears a watch these days, anyway?

Captain George did, because then he could wear a regimental watch strap too.

"What a welcome." George laughed, pushing the Wayfarers up into his hair. He looked around at the bunting and sausage rolls, the orange squash and bonny babies. "Have I crashed a party?"

Henry clenched his jaw. "I suppose those sunglasses prevented you from being able to read the sign at the top of the road, Captain George? '*Street party – strictly no entrance*'. You nearly mowed down half the village, you fool!"

He had forgotten that he was standing in front of a microphone. After a blast of feedback, his sarcastic reprimand echoed down the bustling street.

"Shut up, vet'n'ry!" someone shouted from the crowd.

"Yeah, you shut up! It's Captain George!" someone else chimed in. Within moments, the street was full of jeers aimed at Henry. Even the baby joined in, yanking Henry's tie so hard he nearly headbutted the microphone. George stepped up, his hands held in front of him in a call for calm. Naturally, *he* knew how to use a microphone, there was no wail of aggressive feedback to deafen *him*.

"Hello, Longley Parvans!" A chorus of greeting went up. "Sorry for nearly mowing you down – blame my enthusiasm to see this marvelous village once more. Some things, I notice" – he cast a long, comical look at Henry – "never change!"

Henry glared at the car and glared at George. "No, they don't, do they?"

The baby started to grizzle, its face turning tomato red. Henry bounced it more energetically on his hip, just as a hiccupping noise started up in its throat. He looked over his shoulder, wondering where its mother had got to. A reporter from the local paper had slipped in between the locals and had clambered onto the podium. "Give us a smile, Captain George! Can we get a few words for *The Bugle*?"

"I've just been around the world for my *Secret History of Magellan*, which you can watch this Christmas on the

Beeb!" He winked, a twinkle in his eye that made at least one of the girls from the riding school fan her face. "And I *still* haven't found anywhere as beautiful as good old Longley Parva!"

Applause rippled through the crowd, along with enthusiastic nods. And—*for heaven's sake, was it really necessary?*—a cheer began.

"Hip-hip-hooray! Hip-hip-hooray! Hip-hip-hooray for Captain George!"

Mrs. Fortescue's shoes banged loudly across the podium as she approached their returning hero. "Captain, could I possibly ask you to assist with the Bonny Baby Competition?"

"The divine Mrs. F.!" George kissed her on both cheeks. "It would be a pleasure!"

Henry knew better than to cross Mrs. Fortescue. She took the frilly child from his arms and deposited it in George's embrace. Laughter echoed through the crowd, and the child's mother now appeared, beaming up at George. Henry could do nothing more than stand there as George bounced the baby more and more, the hiccupping noise now a rumble.

The baby opened its little mouth and ejected a vast stream of curdled milk.

All over the shoulder of Henry's tweed jacket.

"Brilliant!" The photographer tipped his head back, laughing. "What a great photo!"

"You can't print that!" Henry stared in horror from the mess on his shoulder into the hungry lens of the camera. He dug in his pocket to retrieve a handkerchief and began to mop at the sour-smelling deposit. If it wasn't enough that Longley Parva's animal population voided their bodily fluids over him on a near-daily basis, now the human residents had joined in as well.

"You're a poppet, aren't you?" George bounced the now empty baby, who gurgled happily at him. Then the mother, who was even more thrilled by the celebrity in their midst, slipped her arm through George's and grinned for the photographer.

"Would you mind just sort of utching up a bit?" The photographer gestured Henry to step to his right. "I need you out of frame, mate!"

Henry closed his lips in a tight line and nodded. "Of course. The local vet isn't as exciting as a *bona fide* TV historian, after all."

"And war hero," the photographer reminded him saucily.

Henry manfully resisted the urge to roll his eyes. Still dabbing at his jacket, he walked past Mrs. Fortescue, only delivering a tight smile of acknowledgment, and hopped down from the podium. Henry was supposed to be judging the jam-making competition in fifteen minutes, but he wondered if he would be ousted from that gig too.

At least jam couldn't vomit on your shoulder, though, there was that.

"God," the stable girl told her equally flushed friend as Henry passed, "he's even *more* gorgeous in the flesh than on the telly!"

Then she glanced at the sick-stained vet and touched her hair self-consciously. With a grimace, she murmured, "You missed some puke, Mr. Fitzwalter."

Henry indicated over his shoulder with a jab of his thumb. "Will you tell Miss Watson on the jam stall that I'm going home? I can't judge jam like this." Once more, he pressed his lips into a thin, disapproving line. "But I'm certain that our resident celebrity will *relish* doing the honors."

Somewhat proud of his pun, Henry went on his way. Longley Parva Manor was but a short walk from the main road and Henry would go home, sit in the bath with a whiskey and hope George left again soon.

"Fitz!" George's voice again, full of laughter and carefree bonhomie, *smooth and easy as hot chocolate*, as one of his adoring Sunday newspaper critics once said. "I say, Fitz!"

Henry skidded to a halt on the gravel at the bottom of his driveway and turned to watch George approach. Behind him trailed a long line of smiling faces, the ladies who adored him and children who wanted to be him and men who wanted to buy him a pint. George the handsome, tan Pied Piper leading his faithful.

"What do *you*, of all people, want with *me?*"

"Mrs. F. tells me you're on jam duty." He slapped his hand down against Henry's clean shoulder. "When I was stung by a ray, did I let it put me off finishing my secret shipwrecks filming? No. When I broke my wrist wielding a war hammer, did I give up my location work for *Secrets of the Vikings*? I did not! Come on, Fitz, are you going to let a bit of baby sick defeat you?"

"Defeat me? I smell of vomit, Captain bloody George. I can't taste the jam with the tang of baby sick in my nostrils!"

"It's a jacket, Fitz." George laughed, a long, loud bray. "Take it off, man!"

"That's altogether too casual for a man of my position." Somehow, Henry had managed to speak though he had barely moved his lips. But his hand had already drifted to the top button of his jacket, as if George had him mesmerized by the sheer force of his personality. "Very well, then."

Henry unfastened first the top button, then the second, his eyes never leaving George's.

Oh, come to your senses, you idiot.

Henry broke his gaze and focused on his remaining buttons. George turned back to his adoring fans and, caving in to the clamoring of some of the children in the crowd, took a pen from one of the blushing mothers and began happily signing autographs. Cameras clicked, children laughed and right there, all smiles in the summer sunshine, George Standish-Brookes no doubt sold a dozen or more books on that magnetic personality alone.

Jacket draped over his arm, Henry cleared his throat, trying to make his way through the crowd, back to his jam-judging duties. If only he was on television and had recklessly driven a classic sports car through a group of pedestrians, it would've been much easier.

He took his pocket watch from his waistcoat and checked the time.

"Excuse me—please—would you—mind your back, sorry, coming through."

"Jam-judging vet incoming!" George clapped his hands and the crowd parted ahead of Henry. "Thank you, my fellow Parvans!"

Henry looked back at George. As he raised his hand in a quick, small gesture of thanks, a smile edged onto his face. And that would never do.

He strode into the stripy gazebo, where there were trestle tables loaded with jars of jam. The jam makers' looks of pride exceeded those of the parents in the Bonny Baby Competition.

"Where have you been? Teaspoons at the ready, Mr. Fitzwalter!"

Mrs. Fortescue pressed a metal spoon into Henry's hand. He looked at his face upside down in its curved surface. Was there any point in him even beginning this, when George would surely arrive at any moment and charm everyone into submission? The jam was in neat, unlabeled pots, laid out side by side, just waiting to send him to an over-sweetened, sugary grave. And on the edge of his vision was George, still signing and posing, kissing cheeks and throwing babies aloft and ruffling the hair of adoring little children.

He probably makes bloody jam too.

"Greengage? Very good. Excellent." The fruit had just the right sharpness, just the right sweetness. It was the best jam Henry had tried. But he should've guessed who'd made it before he locked eyes on Steph, who was grinning at him from outside the tent, her bobbed hair shining in the sunlight like an advert for shampoo.

And if she was here, then Ed wasn't far away.

George *and* Ed — the most popular boy in school and the scourge of the common room together once more.

Can today could get any worse?

When Henry tried the next, sugarless, jam, he realized that he was wrong.

He couldn't spit it delicately into his handkerchief, which was now wet with baby curds. He couldn't see a paper napkin anywhere nearby. Henry would have to swallow it and nod politely, as he did with everything in his life.

Don't make a fuss.

Except, wasn't that just what he had done by rushing off from the Bonny Baby Competition?

"Now, Mr. Fitzwalter, is there a winner?"

Henry glanced toward Steph. She had, without doubt, made the best jam. But she couldn't win. Because for several years, more off than on, they had had what one might call a dalliance. An understanding. And she had finally broken it off and married Ed. Ed, who had made his millions in the City and had returned to Longley Parva to live in the world's most garish new-build faux-Georgian pile. The village gossips would have a field day if Henry awarded Steph the prize.

"I think it has to be the...the raspberry. This one." Henry held up the jar, which should've been awarded a highly commended second place.

Steph's grin faded and she wandered away.

Outside he heard George's voice on the microphone once more, something about letting children have their photos taken with the Jaguar, *television's most famous motor*. None of those children would be sick, Henry knew that already. Life just didn't work that way. There was always sugar in George's jam—the heavens were just aligned like that.

Henry shoved his hands into his pockets, his soiled jacket draped over his arm. He left the jam tent and paused, watching George. His erstwhile friend posed against his car, mugging for the cameras, arms around the shoulders of grinning children. It was so easy for him, the grin, the sparkling glance—he had never been any different. The most charming boy in the South Downs. And for some reason, George had been Henry's best friend. It seemed impossible now. Henry was boring and George glittered.

"Fitz!" George waved his hand as though Henry might not be able to see him. "Come and get a snap with your old chum!"

No escape route presented itself. Henry crunched across the road, his brogues carrying him inexorably onward to the man who had once been his friend. Until that very public spat. Until Henry's accusation. And everyone in the village knew. Perhaps, for appearance's sake, it was best to pretend that everything had been smoothed over. Even though it hadn't been and never would be.

"Captain George, old bean! Righty-ho, then."

Henry wondered who on earth would bother taking a photo of him, but Steph emerged from the crowd, her phone angled for a landscape shot.

"That's it, the invincible boys! Smile!"

Henry flinched as George's arm came around his shoulder in a matey gesture, but he pasted on a grin nonetheless.

"Guess what, Fitz?" George squeezed Henry's shoulders. "I'm here *all* summer. Isn't that marvelous?"

Henry fidgeted his hands in his pockets.

"Erm…yes, that's marvelous. Any particular reason why you're gracing us with your presence for so long?"

"I'm mugging up on the ancestors *and* delving into the mystery of the Longley Parva Cup!"

Henry was still smiling because now other residents of the village had decided, for reasons best known only to themselves, to photograph their local vet with their local television celebrity. But there was no smile in his voice.

"The mystery is why you've never owned up to stealing the damned thing."

"I didn't steal it." George's fingers tightened on his shoulder and he whispered through his grin, his tone as cold as his smile was warm, "You've got me all wrong."

"Don't be daft, of course it was you. But go on then—" There was a challenge in Henry's voice, the same tone he had used as a boy. *Bet you can't climb that tree, bet you can't hit this ball for six, bet you can't swim underwater all the way to the boathouse.* "Prove me wrong—I'd love to see you try."

"I shall! And I might even turn it into a program." George held up one hand as though writing in the air. "*The Secret History of Longley Parva!*"

Henry threw back his head and laughed. "You don't change, do you?"

"Neither do you, despite being covered in baby sick!" George looked at Henry, who was determined not to return his gaze. He wouldn't, he told himself, because if he did, George would wink and laugh and try to win him over. "Bit whiffy in this hot sun, Fitz."

"I'm a vet, I have a strong stomach. When did *you* last put your arm up a cow's backside?"

"Last year!" George released him to take a baby from a young mother, his face a photo-perfect smile as he struck a pose. "For *Comic Relief Does Farming*? Didn't you pledge a few pounds, old pal?"

"Only after you skidded over in a cowpat. Best laugh I'd had in ages."

George laughed and turned away to sign another autograph. He always laughed at himself, and it was one of his more annoying traits. The fellow was mostly impossible to rile. Not totally, but mostly.

"Righty-ho, I'll be off then." Henry was sure that George was too engrossed in his fan club to hear him. He could make his escape from the damn man unnoticed. But the devil had stolen his tongue and spoke for him. "You know where to find me."

"Fitzwalter!" Ed Belcher's bellow shattered the gentle sounds of the summer gathering. Its owner was striding across the crowded green toward Henry, incongruous in a pinstriped suit, his red tie caught over one shoulder and his slicked-down hair glistening in the sunlight.

Henry tried a polite smile but could only manage a grimace. "Ed, what can I do for you?"

"What's this business with Stephy? Broke her back over the Aga churning out that jam!" He stopped a couple of feet from Henry. "Come on, let's talk turkey. What was the deal?"

"The raspberry pipped the greengage to the post, I'm afraid." It was a weak pun, but Henry went with it, and smiled at his adversary.

"That's balls, Fitzwalter," Ed barked. "Raspberry balls!"

"Easy, old thing." George glanced back at them. "Women and children present!"

Henry took a step toward Ed and lowered his voice. "I could've given my ex-girlfriend first prize — and then all the gossips in Longley Parva *and* Magna would've done their worst. You need to remind yourself how village life works, Ed, because you'll find yourself in a jam if you don't."

Henry grinned at his own joke, but Ed only glowered.

"You always were a little squirt, Fitzwalter, and you still are. If I were Alan Sugar, you'd make sure my wife won that ribbon and we both know it!" He attempted a smile, showing sharp, white teeth. "And I'm not far behind him nowadays, you know!"

Henry the judger of jam was silent, but Henry Fitzwalter the vet didn't rest. He was fond of his patients, even if he wasn't always fond of their owners. "How's that pregnant mare of yours?"

"About to drop another winner for Epsom, I bloody hope!" He laughed, as though there was something hilarious about that statement. "Deal with many racehorses, do you? I thought you were a cow's arse sort of chap!"

"Women and children!" George reminded him, earning another scowl from Ed.

"Mine is the nearest veterinary practice for miles, so…up to you, isn't it?" Henry extended his hand to shake. Ed took it, gripping tightly enough to prove that he wasn't *only* manly, he was the *most* manly in the village. It was a stock exchange sort of grip, a grip that said, *I've made my millions, don't get in my way.*

"And you, Georgie-boy, you should be making a series about me! One of your things for the BBC — *Ed Belcher, Millionaire!*"

George's reply was a disinterested smile and Ed looked back at Henry, still pumping his hand. Henry began to wince. He had only meant to shake hands as a gesture of farewell, not a fight to the death.

"Righty-ho, Ed — time I was gone, they're announcing Guess How Many Sweets in the Jar in five minutes. Wouldn't want to miss that!"

Henry turned away from Ed and rubbed at his hand, trying to revive his circulation. He bit back his retort. *Stephy shouldn't enter competitions if she can't cope with losing.* He wandered toward George's car again, drawn there as if by a magnet. Its immaculate paintwork gleamed in the early summer sun.

Imagine going for a spin in it, roof down, wind in your hair, threading through the leafy Sussex lanes. Imagine how perfect that would be. Then imagine George sitting beside you.

Henry felt George's eye on him.

"I mean it, Fitz," George called in a mirthful tone. "I am not and never was the Longley Parva Bandit!"

"An elaborate double-bluff, Standish-Brookes!" Henry laughed. "What's your plan, then, to unmask the Bandit? If — *supposing* — it's not you? Because I never got to have the trophy, even though I won it, and I don't like to sound like a man who bears grudges, but — "

"Tonight!" George stooped to address the little boy whose T-shirt he had just signed and told him, "Spread the word, my young friend, George Standish-Brookes will be revealing his next big project at seven in the pub and the whole village is invited. Drinks are on me!"

The boy blinked up at him and asked, "Can we be on the telly?"

"If your mum says yes!" George scrubbed the child's hair. "Now go forth, spread the word!"

Henry took his fob watch out again. "What *are* you planning, Captain George?"

But Henry didn't wait for an answer and began to make his way to the tea tent. He couldn't face the evening without a stomach full of scones.

"Seven o'clock, Fitz," he heard George call cheerily. "I'll even buy you a drink, though I bet you won't accept it!"

Henry skidded to a halt. He turned back to face George and pushed a lock of his unruly hair from his forehead. "Mine's a pint of our local ale — if you can remember what it is!"

"Since I'm the face of Longley Spitfire, I have no trouble recalling it," the newcomer laughed. "You might even see my mug gracing the pumps by Christmas!"

And I'll take a marker pen and add comedy mustaches to them all.

"I'm sure I will!" Henry raised a hand in farewell and trudged toward the tea tent.

PUBLISHING

Sign up for our newsletter and find out about all our romance book releases, eBook sales and promotions, sneak peeks and FREE romance books!

About the Authors

Catherine Curzon

Catherine Curzon is a royal historian who writes on all matters of 18th century. Her work has been featured on many platforms and Catherine has also spoken at various venues including the Royal Pavilion, Brighton, and Dr Johnson's House.

Catherine holds a Master's degree in Film and when not dodging the furies of the guillotine, writes fiction set deep in the underbelly of Georgian London.

She lives in Yorkshire atop a ludicrously steep hill.

Eleanor Harkstead

Eleanor Harkstead often dashes about in nineteenth-century costume, in bonnet or cravat as the mood takes her. She can occasionally be found wandering old graveyards, and is especially fond of the ones in Edinburgh. Eleanor is very fond of chocolate, wine, tweed waistcoats and nice pens. She has a large collection of vintage hats, and once played guitar in a band. Originally from the south-east, Eleanor now lives somewhere in the Midlands with a large ginger cat who resembles a Viking.

Catherine and Eleanor love to hear from readers. You can find their contact information, website and author biographies at https://www.pride-publishing.com.